The
BOOK

a novel

of
HANNAH

A Tragicomedy
in Three Trimesters

D0813940

Ellen Gelerman

ISBN: 978-1-7338973-5-8
Library of Congress Control Number: 2019909974

Gelerman. Ellen
The Book of Hannah

Edited by: Uma Hayes

Published by Warren Publishing
Charlotte, NC
www.warrenpublishing.net
Printed in the United States

For Dad

THE BOOK OF HANNAH:
A TRAGICOMEDY IN THREE TRIMESTERS

TRIMESTER 1

HANNAH 1:1

As always, the lights were too bright; the room, too cold. The baby-blue paper dressing gown Hannah wore and the white paper liner she sat on rustled in tandem like dead leaves as she perched restlessly on the edge of the examination table.

The last thing she wanted was to be alone with her thoughts. For the hundredth time, she wished she'd brought her knitting with her or, barring that, a magazine from the waiting room—a three-month-old *People* maybe, something shiny and mindless. For a moment she considered retrieving her phone from her purse but discarded the idea. A game would be distracting, but the temptation to start yet another internet search of her symptoms once her phone was in hand would be too great. And somehow, she didn't want Dr. A to catch her engaged in such a frivolous activity after her urgent phone call.

So she stared instead at the old poster, cheaply framed in peeling gold metal, hanging on the wall. The details of the poster (a cross-section of what her body contained within, in once-lurid, unnatural colors now faded with age, labeled with straightforward medical terminology in an old-fashioned black serif font) she had committed to memory long ago, down to the "Copyright © 1984 AnnaTomMichael Products Inc." in the lower right-hand corner.

"AnnaTomMichael."

In the excess of time Hannah had available while waiting in this room over the years, she had often occupied herself pondering whether the company's founders had been blessed with three fortuitously named children, or whether the children of the founders had been named with an insider's sense of humor. Or even whether the names belonged to the founders themselves. Most likely it was none of the above and was merely a joke, a way to set themselves apart in a humorless industry. In any event, Hannah doubted anyone else had invested as much time in such pointless speculation as she had.

The only other decoration in the exam room, an equally unattractive poster of the developmental stages of a fetus printed by the same company, she chose to ignore as she had very effectively for a couple of decades.

Still, Hannah supposed with a sigh, it was better than waiting in Dr. A's office, where the knotty pine-paneled walls were wreathed with a series of bulletin-board collages: smiling babies, sleeping babies; twins, triplets; newborn photos and posed holiday greetings—happy families, all who owed their existence in part to the skills of Dr. A. Over time, the collages had grown and spread to surround the room, displaying the fruits of the womb like a wildly colorful, fecund flowering vine. On good days, the chubby cherubim seemed to gaze fondly down at Hannah with hope shining in their eyes. On bad days, it was with pity.

And there were so many bad days. So much bad news.

In the first two years that she and Ryan had been married, Hannah had tentatively shared her concerns with Dr. A that maybe something was wrong. The doctor had first counseled patience, and then tests. Endless tests. First, of course, Ryan went to see a urologist. His semen sample, though, had shown a normal sperm count—"healthy little swimmers," as the urologist had put it—and Ryan walked away relieved of any responsibility for their situation ... and just plain relieved. Hannah's turn would be much more extensive and invasive. Under anesthesia, she had submitted to a scope through her navel that had searched for abnormalities in her reproductive system. No abnormalities had been found. Then came the colposcopy, an examination of her cervix. Despite the visible absence of anything suspect, biopsies were done, and no abnormalities had been found. Finally, the hysterosalpingogram, an injection of dye intended to show whether her fallopian tubes were blocked. No blockages, no abnormalities.

Nothing abnormal. And yet, the perfectly normal eluded them.

After the tests, inconclusive as they were, came the interventions: half a year of artificial insemination. Every month, when Hannah was deemed most fertile, she'd call Ryan to come home from work to provide a "donation." Instructed to keep the sample warm, Hannah—aware of the irony—had stuck the vial between her thighs for the drive to the specialist's office. She reclined, patiently, on the table for the insertion of her husband's sperm, six months in a row. When that proved ineffective, Dr. A had suggested a last-ditch effort.

"A sperm donor?" Ryan had been offended. "There's nothing wrong with my sperm. We've established that. I don't understand why we need to be paying good money to a donor for something I'm able to provide myself."

Between Hannah's incessant tears and a roaring argument lasting three days, Ryan had reluctantly agreed, on the off chance that his sperm was somehow incompatible with Hannah's body. They had even been able to find some humor in the situation as they shopped for a donor with similar physical characteristics.

"I never knew there was a catalogue for these things," Hannah had said, genuinely surprised. She winked at Ryan. "Maybe I'll find someone better."

"Nah, they only look better on paper," Ryan had fired back with a grin.

Several months of attempts at insemination later, Hannah and Ryan gave up. They were exhausted, and so were their finances. While insurance covered most of the fertility testing, the Murrows had been on their own when it came to the artificial insemination. In the final accounting, Ryan estimated that they had spent nearly $100,000 on their ultimately unsuccessful undertaking. Giving it up as a lost cause, they decided to adopt, and a daughter named Natty was the result.

And this, now ... *this* was her body's final insult: a quarter-century later, there were symptoms of something terribly wrong, something that Hannah couldn't identify. Hours spent on WebMD and Wikipedia only served to frighten and perplex her. Some of her symptoms were consistent with devastating prognoses like ovarian cancer; others pointed to conditions that were entirely benign and common to women in their midfifties. Telling the difference, though, that was the trick, which was what necessitated a call to Dr. A.

Samantha, the apple-cheeked nurse who had delivered Hannah and her urine sample to the exam room, now knocked briskly and peremptorily on the door, popping her head in. "Hi, Mrs. Murrow," she said in a deliberately cheerful manner that immediately put Hannah on edge. "The doctor will be right in." And three minutes later, there she was.

Like her examination room, Dr. A hadn't changed much over the years. The long, thick braid she wore twined down her back was now heavily threaded with silver and her glasses were several degrees thicker, exaggerating her already large brown eyes, but somehow her body, face, and energy level had scarcely declined. She was tiny, barely 4'11", if Hannah had to guess, about the same size Natty had been when she was in middle school, before her growth spurt.

Dr. A was actually Dr. Lakshmi Anandanarayan, but most of her patients had long ago given up trying to do justice to her husband's mouthful of a name, and she was more than happy to answer to "Dr. A." When Hannah had first become a patient, the two shared a good laugh over the linguistic delight that would have ensued had Hannah married Anandanarayan Parthasarathy instead of Ryan Murrow.

Laughs between the two of them had become far fewer over time.

"I'm always glad to see you, Hannah, but you're not due for another annual exam until February," Dr. A said, getting right to the point as she scrubbed her hands at the sink. She pulled on purple nitrile gloves. "You said it was important. So what is troubling you?"

Hannah struggled to put her fears into words.

"I'm, um, not really feeling like myself. I guess the biggest thing is the nausea. I've been queasy a lot, especially when I first get up. Getting breakfast down is a problem. Keeping it down is a problem. Even something simple and bland like scrambled eggs in the morning ... I can't look at them." Hannah shuddered. "And I've thrown up more than once." She didn't tell Dr. A that the delicious spicy scent of curry her clothes always carried, redolent of cumin and turmeric— which usually made Hannah hungry for sambhar masala from her favorite Indian restaurant—today turned her stomach. It was only her deep respect for Dr. A that stopped her from wrinkling her nose or shifting her face away.

"And for all that, I'm not losing weight. In fact, I seem to be *gaining* weight. I'm all bloated; my clothes don't fit me anymore. I can barely close my jeans." This was despite the regular regimen of step and cycle classes that Hannah felt had kept her naturally bottom-heavy figure from turning into a full-blown pear. "I mean, I don't expect to be built like I was in high school, but this is getting ridiculous. I've been adding more cardio to my workout and I've even started skipping dessert, which is one thing I never, ever turn down, as you know." Dr. A did know it, and nodded. "I'm not about to buy myself a whole new wardrobe; Ryan would have a fit."

"I see. Well, lie back, please, Hannah."

Hannah complied, putting her feet into the stirrups and sliding her bottom down to the edge of the table.

Her brow furrowing, Dr. A started the pelvic exam, gently probing and prodding with a tender, almost maternal touch.

A rapid-fire series of questions, asked without any indication of their level of importance, ensued. Did Hannah have any discharge? Pain during sex? Unusually frequent urination or pain during urination? Night sweats? Mood swings? Fatigue? Difficulty sleeping?

Finally: "My last period?" Hannah thought about it. "Ehh, sometime in June? Or July, maybe?"

Unlike most women her age with a long-time gynecologist, Hannah still had to field the question about when her last period had been, as she had been a late bloomer, always irregular, and still continued to menstruate on and off long after what she jokingly referred to as her "expiration date." But she no longer paid much attention to it. In her younger years, she had seen her period as a big, red "F" on her reproductive report card, concrete evidence of her failure, month after month, to conceive. Now, getting it was merely something mildly inconvenient that happened to her for a few days from time to time, without any discernible pattern.

"You know, Hannah," Dr. A said in a reassuringly even tone, "at least some of what you're telling me could be consistent with the onset of menopause. And you're really past due."

That would be good news, of course. The diagnosis she was hoping for. But there were a couple of things that didn't fit that narrative.

Dr. A gave her an opening. "Anything else I should be aware of?"

"Um, breast sensitivity?" Hannah was definitely experiencing some soreness in her breasts and it had become an issue, since Ryan's idea of foreplay consisted mostly of using them as some kind of human stress balls, squeezing with gusto one, then the other. It was the furthest thing from erotic and did nothing at all for Hannah sexually, but she had good-humoredly endured it throughout the entire course of their courtship and marriage because she didn't want to dampen his mood. Lately, though, the squeezing had grown too painful to ignore, and she had to tell Ryan she didn't want to feel as if she were having a mammogram every time they made love.

"Oh? All right."

"And then there's Sadie," Hannah said.

"Your dog, Sadie?"

Hannah might have been reluctant to share this piece of information with anyone else, but no one, not even Ryan, knew her as intimately as Dr. A. Sadie, the Murrows' Australian shepherd, had started acting peculiarly around her. She was six years old and smarter than a fifth grader (or so Hannah liked to say), the kind of dog everyone dreamed of owning until they realized they had to keep her constantly engaged to prevent her from tearing up the carpeting or chewing on the living room furniture out of boredom and frustration.

Sadie and Hannah enjoyed cuddling in front of the TV at night, Hannah's fingers running through Sadie's thick merle coat and scratching behind the flopped-over ears. Lately, though, the dog had been poking her snout obsessively into Hannah's belly. This type of behavior, Hannah had read somewhere online, had frequently identified a tumor before the patient had even received a diagnosis.

While she didn't discount this piece of information outright, Dr. A simply nodded. "Anything else?"

More than anything, Hannah just didn't *feel* right, or rather, she didn't feel the same. She had awakened one morning, looked at herself in the mirror and known that something was different. "The only way I can explain it," she told Dr. A, "is it's like someone had flipped a switch inside me—like a light—and whatever had been *off* is now most definitely *on*." She likened it to the feeling that presaged the onset of a cold, that little twinge in the throat, and wondered if there was a moment a scientist could identify when a tumor became malignant or maybe when an illness had first taken root, a little *ping* that completely changed the direction and quality and length of your life.

Dr. A was well versed in Hannah's medical history, and knew that her Aunt Connie's death from ovarian cancer at thirty-six had traumatized the whole family. Hannah had only been a teenager at the time, but she vividly recalled her usually unemotional mother sobbing, coatless, in the summer rain at her younger sister's grave, and the fear of losing someone in so cruel a manner, at so early an age, had made her unusually alert to any symptoms. That Mom was still alive and well at eighty-two was some comfort, but Hannah was aware her familial relationship to Aunt Connie was close enough to warrant concern.

Her research into her symptoms, such as it was, had done nothing to ease Hannah's anxiety and in fact had made her hair stand on end, so she had finally swallowed the worst of her fears and made the first available appointment.

Hannah scrutinized Dr. A's face during the course of the exam, trying to intuit if she should be considering a major panic attack. Not yet, it seemed: rather than concern, Dr. A's face reflected confusion.

After a moment, Dr. A rose from her stool, tossed her used gloves into the bin, and washed her hands at the sink. Pulling on a new pair of gloves, she turned to the countertop where Hannah's urine sample squatted in its little plastic cup. Her back to Hannah, she rustled around in a drawer. There was the crinkling sound of something being unwrapped.

"Hannah," Dr. A began, her South Indian accent still musical but with the edges worn smooth over the decades like a rock polished by a stream. She stopped abruptly. Then, sniffing in a breath, she turned back to face her patient and tried again. "Hannah, how is your relationship with Ryan?"

Well, this was unexpected. "Um. What?"

"How are you two getting on these days? Are you still intimate?" The doctor paused, then asked delicately, though her gaze was still direct, "Or is there perhaps someone else in your life now? A younger man?"

Hannah was struck speechless and had to resort to sputtering, "No! I mean, yes, yes, *we* are. Ryan and I, that is. Having sex and all. Not particularly frequently, of course, but it is what it is. And there's no one else; hasn't been since the day we got married." She had no secrets from this doctor, so her question was oddly awkward. "You know that."

And of course, she and Ryan were still intimate, although boredom and bickering had taken their toll on their sex life. On the infrequent occasions when they did make love, he still did it with a teenager's enthusiasm and finesse (or lack of it), if no longer with quite the stamina or duration. Would she like more romance, more variety? Sure, but her requests, once subtle yet growing increasingly direct over the years, had borne little fruit, and she had long ago stopped trying to improve him.

An affair was out of the question. She would never betray him, as she was hard-wired in both personality and religious training to recoil from that kind of behavior. Besides, in every other area Ryan was what she expected a husband to be:

smart, loyal, funny in his own way, hard-working. In fact, what had attracted Hannah to Ryan in the first place was his solid reliability, his practicality, his lack of guile, after two far more interesting and passionate relationships shortly after college (*Oh, Andy! Oh, Sergio!*) had ended disastrously. Ryan was older, focused, more serious than the boys she'd been dating. He was already a dentist; established, settled. If he was somewhat self-centered, if he was often less than thoughtful, if he was maybe more than a tiny bit dull ... well, she excused his minor shortcomings because he was, after all was said and done, a good person. Dependable. Honest.

Realistically, Hannah knew it was no grand passion they shared, not of the "soulmate" variety claimed by some of her starry-eyed friends, but she loved him in her way. Though their relationship had hit many rocky patches over the years, particularly during their futile attempts to start a family, she was hardly going to start over at almost fifty-five, for heaven's sake. Hannah thought Dr. A should know her better by now.

Seeing her bewilderment, Dr. A laughed a little and patted Hannah on the shoulder. "I'm sorry to be so blunt, Hannah, but there is good reason for me to ask. It's important for me to know if something has changed in your sex life, particularly if you have a new partner."

"Nothing's changed, Dr. A. I think I've been pretty clear that nothing ever changes."

"I see." Long after the brightness of her early romance with Ryan had faded like that damned poster, in a moment of candor brought on by decades of frustration, Hannah had broached the subject of their plain vanilla love life with Dr. A. At every exam since then, Dr. A had just to lift her eyebrows and Hannah would respond, "Same old, same old." It was their little joke.

"So," Hannah said, trying to sound casual, as if her life didn't depend on what Dr. A would say next. Despite her efforts, her voice trembled a little. "So, what are we looking at here?"

Dr. A's eyes darted toward the countertop and back and she pursed her lips. "I'd like to do an ultrasound, Hannah, to rule out some of the more unlikely issues," she said. "I'm going to go make sure the technician is available. Do try to relax for a few minutes."

Relax, she said. As if.

Once again left with nothing else to occupy her, Hannah stared down at her hands, wondering where the age spots and bulging veins had come from. When had she turned into her mother ... no, her grandmother, whose hands had been topographical maps, their rivers prominent even before the rills and gullies of her skin had deepened?

Samantha returned with a thin, blue cotton-wrap robe and instructions for Hannah to follow her down the hall to another exam room, which she did, treading lightly in her stocking feet. There she met the young sonographer, Daphne—tall and thin with a long face and stick-straight, light-brown hair, an entirely vertical woman in horizontal-striped medical scrubs. Despite the passage of time since her last experience, Hannah was a veteran of ultrasounds. Lying down on the table, she braced herself for the chill of the gel.

Daphne, however, explained that since Hannah had come to Dr. A's office today without a full bladder, she would be performing a transvaginal ultrasound, using an inserted wand instead of an external transducer. Although she had heard of this procedure, Hannah had never had one before, and was unhappy with the intrusive nature of it. Still, she supposed it was better than waiting days or even weeks for another appointment when she might be able to come in with her bladder uncomfortably full.

After Daphne had showed her the wand, sheathed it, and described how it would be used, Hannah lay back and stared up at the ceiling. She was grateful she couldn't see the screen. Though logically she knew otherwise, she had already grown used to the idea of her uterus as a lifeless, shriveled husk, sometimes picturing it as a dead spider crumpled on the windowsill, fallopian tubes curled into themselves like desiccated legs, useless.

The sonographer inserted the wand and began to rotate it, simultaneously rolling the trackball on the control panel. At first she was blessedly impassive. But then she stopped abruptly, leaned toward the screen, blinked, and shook her head. Moved the wand again. Stopped.

After making a few clicks on the the control panel, Daphne withdrew the wand and stood up. "Will you excuse me for just a moment?" she said, her eyes not quite making contact with Hannah's, and left the room in a hurry.

Hannah was alarmed, her heart pounding. Daphne had seen something awful, Hannah was sure of it. She wouldn't have bolted out of the room like that had there been nothing of concern on the screen. Hannah's greatest fears were coming true, and it was only through sheer force of will that she didn't begin to hyperventilate.

When Daphne returned, it was with Dr. A directly behind her. Daphne resumed her seat, Dr. A peering over her shoulder, and pointed at the saved image on the screen.

"Right there, Dr. A," Daphne said. "See that? I mean, there's no way ..." The doctor silenced her with a firm squeeze to her shoulder.

Hannah shivered.

"Thank you, Daphne, I'll take it from here." Without so much as a nod to Hannah, Daphne got up from her rolling chair and withdrew. The door clicked quietly behind her.

Her mouth trembling, Hannah stared at the ceiling again, blinking rapidly to avoid crying.

"Hannah," Dr. A said earnestly, leaving her spot beside the ultrasound machine and sitting down next to her patient. "Hannah, look at me."

Reluctantly, Hannah turned her head to face the doctor, the stress of the moment finally overwhelming her. Tears spilled from her eyes, one rolling into her ear.

Taking Hannah's cold hand in both of her warm ones, Dr. A said, "I think you need to prepare yourself for some very shocking news."

Hannah could hardly bear to hear the diagnosis but was grateful it would come from someone as dedicated and trusted as Dr. A. She would be comforting, of course; she would help Hannah find the best treatment options, she ...

"You're pregnant."

"What?" Certain she must have misheard, Hannah asked again, "What? Who's pregnant?"

"You are, dear."

At first Hannah frowned, then she barked out a humorless laugh. Was this some kind of a joke, meant to soften the blow of a serious, maybe even fatal, diagnosis? If so, it was a particularly cruel one, considering. How could someone as gentle, as empathetic, as Dr. A even say such a thing? The tears that trickled down Hannah's cheeks were now driven by anger just as much as by fear, and she pulled away from the doctor's grasp to swipe at them with the back of her hand. When a tissue materialized in Dr. A's hand, Hannah snatched it away and pinched it over her eyes.

"That's impossible and you know it," she said, her voice muffled behind the tissue.

"I beg to differ." Dr. A moved back to the ultrasound machine and turned it toward Hannah. "A geriatric pregnancy is highly unusual, I'll grant you," she said. "In fact, at your age it is extraordinarily rare. Yet it happens, apparently even to someone with your medical history. You can see the evidence right … there." She gently pried Hannah's hand away from her face and pointed at a small, bean-shaped object on the screen.

"That's your baby, Hannah. I'd say you're about ten weeks along. Congratulations."

As Hannah gaped at the screen, her mind struggled to grasp what she was being told.

Pregnant. Pregnancy. Geriatric pregnancy.

Was it possible, could it be possible, that she, who for some twenty-five years had shown herself incapable of the regular variety, had somehow managed to stumble into the world's most unusual kind? Hannah hurriedly swiped the tissue once more across her eyes. Her throat constricted; she was almost unable to ask the question. It came out as a croak. "Am I really pregnant?"

Dr. A smiled. "Yes. Yes, you are."

At that moment, Hannah finally understood the expression "a world turned upside down." She felt dizzy, disoriented, as if she had been physically flipped over, the blood rushing to her head. Or was it draining out? The pressure in her ears changed, giving her the feeling of being underwater.

"Hannah?" Dr. A's voice seemed to come from light-years away.

"Oh, my God!"

Hannah's eyes again filled and spilled over, though this time she wept tears of wonder and relief. As she gawked at the light and shadows that made up her baby, she pressed one hand over her mouth and for good measure covered it with the other, as if she were afraid of what might issue from it: Vomit? Screams? Singing? Hallelujah, prayers of praise and thanksgiving?

"Do you have any questions?" Dr. A asked in a low voice, concern in every line of her beloved face.

Of course Hannah had questions! But at first she couldn't speak. She took a few moments to compose herself, then asked the only question she could manage to articulate.

"How? How is this possible?"

"And that is the only question for which I cannot provide an answer," Dr. A said with a smile. "The universe is filled with wonders, Hannah. Sometimes science can explain them, sometimes it can't. In this situation, I am at a loss.

"But what a marvelous place in which to be lost, wouldn't you agree?"

Nodding vigorously, Hannah returned her smile. After a moment, though, when her shock faded sufficiently, she cleared her throat and asked, "I ... look, I need to know ... can I even do this? I mean, is a woman my age even physically able to give birth to a healthy child?"

There was a short pause. Then Dr. A said, "I do want you to celebrate this pregnancy, Hannah; you certainly deserve to. But I am not going to sugarcoat the situation. There is still a chance that you'll miscarry or that a host of other things will go wrong. A pregnancy with as many challenges as this one ..." She paused again. "You're going to want to talk to Ryan and do some serious thinking about the future. In the meantime, I would be remiss if we didn't discuss your options."

My options.

HANNAH 1:2

I f she could only stop her hands from shaking, she could pick up her damn latte—decaf from now on!—before it got cold. Hannah stared resolutely at the table, breathing deeply, and managed to still her hands long enough to raise the cup to her lips and take a few sweet sips.

Half-laughing, half-crying in what her mother would have, disapprovingly, called "a state," she had fled the doctor's office without making a follow-up appointment, without paying her copay, without saying goodbye to a very confused Maya at the front desk. Hannah had headed to the nearest Starbucks because she needed to sit down in a "normal" environment, surround herself with (mostly) "normal" people, and think "normal" thoughts.

The morning rush had long since passed; there were only a handful of other people in the place. A prematurely bald thirty-something man, dressed in nice khakis and a subtle checkered shirt, had what appeared to be his entire office set up at a corner table: his laptop open, a small stack of files to the left, a note pad and pen to his right, his cell phone pressed to his ear. It looked as if he had been there a while already and had settled in for the day, a large glass of something iced and frothy at the ready. A young couple on opposite sides of another table ignored each other as they typed on their laptops. They seemed to be playing a duet, their stops and starts in rhythm, and Hannah had the absurd idea they were speaking to each other through a messaging program instead of carrying on a conversation face-to-face. Or maybe it wasn't so absurd: after a minute they both stopped abruptly, looked up and smiled at one another, and then continued on.

And directly across from Hannah there was a woman with a baby, a child of about six months old with enormous blue eyes and wisps of brown hair tied atop her head in a pink bow, seated in a wooden high chair. *That's the best age*, Hannah thought wistfully. *When they're sitting up on their own and developing their own personalities.* As the woman leisurely sipped from a venti cup and scrolled through her iPhone, the baby banged a set of colorful plastic keys on the table, her feet waving in soft white socks with crocheted pink trim, relishing the noise. Suddenly she turned toward Hannah with an angelic smile and blew an enormous spit bubble, jumping in surprise when it popped. A squeal of delight followed. Hannah smiled with the full force of her long-repressed maternal impulses and newly discovered hormones and breathed a sigh of pure happiness.

My options.

Hannah had frowned at Dr. A then. "What do you mean, 'options'?"

"We must be realistic. A pregnancy at your age holds risks for both you and the fetus. There's a great deal that could go wrong: serious genetic abnormalities and the like. You're not very far along, as I've said, about ten weeks."

She had stopped abruptly, pressing her lips together, clearly reluctant but obligated to continue. "You could choose to terminate, Hannah."

"Terminate. You mean, an abortion."

Dr. A's voice had been calm; even. "Yes, that's what I mean."

Despite Hannah's Catholic upbringing, she had always considered herself a feminist, a pragmatist, a progressive. She was solidly pro-choice and had donated to Planned Parenthood regularly to prove her *bona fides*, particularly to herself. Of course, she had also gone to church after every negative test result and had prayed to St. Anne, the Virgin's mother, and St. Jude, who heard prayers of desperation and lost causes. For good measure and at her mother's suggestion, she had also said a novena to St. Philomena, the patron saint of infants and babies.

So now, sitting fully dressed in the same office where she had sat in disappointment amid piles of damp tissues so often during what she had assumed had been her fertile years, every nerve in her body firing joyous messages of her impending motherhood, the idea of terminating this particular pregnancy had seemed an affront to no less than God and the universe.

"I know, perhaps better than almost anyone, how badly you've wanted a baby, Hannah, and for how long," Dr. A had continued. "But take some time and think about it, will you? Talk to Ryan. There could be some very rough times ahead for both of you should you choose to continue. Your eggs are exceptionally old. And there is a reason menopause happens when it usually does. Our bodies are not really equipped to handle childbirth at this late date."

The conflicting messages—the good news (the *very* good news), the bad news—had driven Hannah's hasty and emotional departure from the office. She'd have to call Maya later and apologize.

When she realized she had been staring at the baby in Starbucks a little too long and perhaps a little too hungrily for the comfort of the mother, Hannah quickly looked down at her phone. It was 10:30 a.m.. Her appointment had been only an hour ago, yet in that hour her whole life had changed. And she had no idea what to do with herself now.

She yearned to call Ryan, but they had an understanding that she wouldn't call him at the practice unless it was an emergency. Besides, it wasn't exactly a conversation she intended to have with him on the phone when he was between patients. If he was half as thrown by the news as she was, he would be completely useless for the rest of the day.

Hannah ran her hands down her face. She wanted to tell *someone*. Yet whom should she call? She could talk to any one of the girlfriends she had made in recent years, Donna or Denise or Linda, but they had never suffered as she had; none of them could relate to what she had been through, imagine how she felt now, help her process her emotions. They had all enjoyed normal pregnancies and healthy births, their children all in college or working in health care, law, accounting, education.

"The Three Witches," though ... they *would surely understand.*

Hannah was still close to two women who had been part of an infertility group with her. They'd bonded almost immediately, labeling themselves after Macbeth's Three Witches because their lives often felt like a Shakespearean tragedy. At first they had met several times a month, for hours at a time, leaning on each other—sometimes physically—for support. Then, as both family demands and their adopted children grew, they saw each other less frequently. But while phone calls still bounced back and forth among the trio and were still eagerly anticipated, ultimately Hannah decided it was improper for anyone to hear this news before Ryan did.

At some point, of course, she'd also have to tell Natty. But at the moment her daughter was angry with Hannah—which was not unusual—and hadn't called in almost a week. Near as Hannah could tell, this time it was over the nickname itself.

"Oh, for heaven's sake! You never used to mind it," Hannah had said defensively. "Do I have to remind you that you're the one who chose it in the first place?"

"I was three at the time! What did I know? You don't respect my heritage," Natty had shot back, redirecting her liquid dark hair, like a stream of spilled ink, to flow behind her ears. *Her heritage?* As if she hadn't been whisked out of Russia before she could even talk and adopted at twenty-nine months. From her single, nightmarish visit, Hannah still remembered that orphanage, although Natty certainly couldn't. It was a sterile, regimented place of stained, worn-thin blankets and paint-peeled steel bars where the children were toilet trained as soon as they could stand on their own but would never know the comfort of a loving lap and a lullaby. No surprise, then, that Natty had been late to speak; she hadn't been read to or sung to and barely spoken to.

And when she did begin to speak, Natty's words had often been filled with anger and rebellion. Her childhood was a trial; her high school years, a nightmare. It was only as she matured into young adulthood that the anger began to dissipate. The rebellion, the need to assert herself, however, remained. Hannah was still convinced Natty had gotten her nose pierced just to annoy her.

Under the cover of draining her latte, Hannah watched the young mother strap her baby into her stroller. It looked like one of those expensive European models that some of Hannah's more well-to-do friends were currently investing in for their grandchildren. Donna had bought one for her son and daughter-in-law's first child, and Hannah had nearly gasped out loud at the price, restraining herself only in fear of seeming ungenerous or out of touch. *Could get a used one, I suppose*, she mused. But she was getting ahead of herself. So much could go wrong ....

She walked out into the brilliant October sunshine and the world still seemed surreal, or perhaps hyper-real, as if she had just discovered high-def after years of watching static-filled TV with rabbit-ear antennae. Colors were brighter; edges, sharper. The leaves—still on the trees, tricked out in their bright oranges and yellows and reds—flapped in unison in the breeze like an audience full of people applauding Hannah's new status of mother-to-be.

Hannah took a deep breath, then exhaled. As she walked back to her car, she ticked off what she had planned to do for the day: supermarket, dry cleaner, library ... none of which now seemed the least bit important. How could she go on with her life as if nothing had changed?

Instead, Hannah headed straight for St. Agnes, the church where for the past fifteen years or so she had attended only Midnight Mass on Christmas Eve and Easter Sunday worship. Hannah had wrestled with her faith mightily during her failed efforts to conceive, and had ultimately tapped out of the match. All the prayers, the candles, the novenas had come to nothing, and she'd had no more energy to spare for religion or what she had come to believe were fruitless expressions of faith.

Father Aloysius, old then and ancient now, had been patient and kind through it all, even when she had not. When she had first come to him with her troubles, he had told her the story of the Old Testament Hannah, a barren wife who cried unto the Lord and was blessed with a son, Samuel. At first she'd latched onto the story with her whole being; it gave her hope. If Hannah demonstrated her own faith, surely God would hear her, too.

But ultimately she had grown angry. According to Father Aloysius, Hannah's faith now demanded that she accept her infertility as God's will. She couldn't grasp it: How could it be God's will that she, of all people, not be a mother? She, who at the age of three had called her little brother Jason "*my baby*" and insisted on holding him and giving him his bottle, to the amused delight of her parents. She, who had played with baby dolls until long past the time when other girls had moved on to the more fashionable Barbies. She, who had started to babysit for neighborhood children the minute she'd turned thirteen and had continued on well into her teenage years, even while her friends were going out on dates.

She, who had married a man from a large, affectionate family with dreams of big Christmases and noisy Thanksgivings ... the same man who had, early on, joked that she had "perfect child-bearing hips."

When Natty's adoption had come through, the priest had pointed to it as evidence that this was the path God had chosen for Hannah: not to bear a child herself but to provide love, security, and a home for an orphan who had none of those. Father Aloysius had termed it "a very high calling." But Hannah's joy at knowing that Natty was joining her and Ryan in their two-bedroom townhouse (they had not yet moved into the neat, four-bedroom colonial that had once been Ryan's parents' home and was now their own) was tempered by the disappointment that her child would already be two-and-a-half years old by the time she arrived. There would be no layette, no nursery. No sweet-smelling, fresh-from-the-bath babbling. No chubby cheeks and baby-fat belly to blow raspberries on. And no nurturing and nourishing of her own blood with her own milk. Instead, she'd welcomed a sullen, unsmiling little girl smack in the middle of the "terrible twos" that were made worse by the damage done by an impoverished, possibly drug- or alcohol-addicted birth mother and a cold, unstimulating environment from birth until her arrival in the US. It was, God forgive her, hardly what Hannah had spent her whole life dreaming about.

The church was quiet and nearly empty, not unusual for a Tuesday morning. The cool, dim interior contrasted sharply with the brightness outside, yet the stained glass windows depicting the Stations of the Cross were in their full glory. Long out of practice and without thinking, Hannah dipped her fingers into the holy water and crossed herself as she entered. She looked around. There were a few parishioners kneeling in the first two rows and another toward the back. None of them looked up from their rosaries or their folded hands when she stepped into the nave.

Hannah didn't recognize the woman who approached her, an older woman who carried herself like a nun, all modesty and subservience. *She could even be one,* Hannah thought;

they didn't all wear habits any more. "May I help you?" the woman asked in suitably hushed tones.

"I'm looking for Father Aloysius."

"I'm afraid he's making a hospice visit right now. Would you care to leave a message for him, or would you like to speak with Father Michael?"

"No, it has to be Father Aloysius." Father Michael gave fine sermons, as far as Hannah could remember, but otherwise he was a cipher to her, a pleasant male face above a collar that somehow entitled him to a degree of respect. When he first arrived at St. Agnes, Father Michael had been popular with the pre-teens for his guitar playing, pop-style hymn singing, and rock-star swath of thick, wavy dark hair. Natty had developed an innocent crush on him until she was old enough to label the very same features as deeply uncool and the idea of harboring affections for a priest as totally gross. His hair was salt-and-pepper now, and just as thick, but Father Michael was no longer anyone's idea of a heartthrob.

"If you like, I can leave Father Aloysius a message."

"Yes; please ask him to call Hannah Murrow."

"Come with me to the office; I'll take your number."

After leaving the church, Hannah remained dissatisfied and out of sorts. Somehow, she found the weight of the news she was carrying, as joyful a burden as it was, to be exhausting. Or maybe it was just the pregnancy. Whatever the reason, nothing seemed more important at the moment than getting back home, where she intended to lie down for a while.

But back at the house, Sadie stared at her with such intensity, such longing, such tension in her energetic little body that Hannah knew she would get no rest. While a long walk seemed beyond her, she compromised and decided on a visit to the dog park, where there would be a bench for her to collapse onto. Sadie needed no encouragement to jump into the car. It was a fifteen-minute drive to the park: two grassy, fenced-in acres with spigots and water bowls, and a separate area for smaller dogs and puppies.

Her head hanging out the window, ears blown back, eyes closed contentedly against the wind, Sadie seemed to know exactly where they were headed, even though their visits were usually limited to the odd weekend. Hannah marveled anew at Sadie's intuition and decided that there would be an extra biscuit with her dinner tonight, maybe even a little bit of meatloaf. She deserved a reward: for without the gentle nudging of her perceptive nose, who knows how long Hannah might have gone without discovering her miracle?

HANNAH 1:3

Dinner.

Nervously, Hannah checked the clock, again. When Ryan had called as usual from the office to say he was on his way home, she had let it go to voicemail. She didn't trust herself to talk to him, to pretend today was a day like any other. Although, she mused with wry amusement, even after twenty-eight years of marriage, she doubted that he would pick up on a change in her voice over the phone. How many haircuts, new outfits, and changes in décor had he completely missed? Last year she had bought a plush, deep-red Turkish rug for the dining room, where for four years the wood had been bare under the table, and after three months he still hadn't noticed. When she'd pointed it out, he had only shrugged and commented that it looked like it had always been there. And then he'd complained for twenty minutes about the expense.

He was due home at any minute now, and she still hadn't decided when or how to break the news. As soon as he got home? Over dinner? After dinner? Should she just pour him a glass of wine? Hannah would ordinarily be on her second glass already, but now she was abstaining and even that added to her nerves. Christ Almighty, she felt like a teenager going on her first date.

The garage door roared open and the car door slammed. Ryan, carrying as he always did both a soft-sided leather briefcase and the faint antiseptic smell of his dental practice, came into the kitchen and kissed Hannah on the right cheek. Same action, same spot. Every single time. Hannah thought that she must have developed a divot there from the repeated pressure. As he went upstairs to change into his warm-up suit, Hannah set the salad on the table. She wondered if he would notice that she wasn't eating with him. Or, perhaps more tellingly, that she wasn't drinking with him.

Ryan sat down at his place at the table, simultaneously digging into his salad and checking the texts on his phone. Usually Hannah would have prodded him to put the phone away during dinner, but tonight she decided it was best if he got all his distractions out of the way: texts, headlines, stock market prices, football scores. She waited silently through the salad, and when he was done, replaced the dish with his dinner plate. Meatloaf and roasted potatoes with a side of green beans. Hannah had cooked with a deliberate eye toward normalcy and predictability, as if for a final few minutes she could maintain the fiction that everything was the same.

It had the desired effect: Ryan hardly looked up during the meal, even when Hannah asked him about his day and he went into ghastly detail about a particularly bad case of gingivitis that had walked into his office. How he could relate such a story while eating dinner was beyond her. "Worst case of neglect I've ever seen, let me tell you. Never mind visiting a dentist—I'd lay odds the man hasn't even brushed his teeth in years," he said, his mouth half-full of potatoes, nodding his thanks as Hannah refilled his wine glass. "Taylor could barely give him an effective cleaning, there was so much bleeding. Good thing she was on duty this afternoon; she's got a strong stomach. I don't think Harlee would have gotten through it."

When at last the dishes were cleared away, Hannah sat down next to Ryan rather than across from him, and this break in their routine got his attention. She let her eyes flick affectionately over his familiar face: the soft brown eyes, now behind rimless progressive glasses; his long, thick eyelashes, the envy of every woman she knew—most notably of a flight attendant of Kuwaiti extraction who had once said flirtatiously to Ryan, "You have eyes like a camel," and meant it as a compliment; the receding hairline of thin gray hair that had once been dense and nearly black; the warm-toned skin that tanned so easily and that now was decorated with age spots and crow's feet. She had loved the contrast of his coloring against hers, the whiteness of her skin against the warm Mediterranean olive of his—a gift from the Sicilian side of the family.

And at sixty-one, Ryan was still fit, a result of a daily treadmill regimen as well as thrice-weekly indoor tennis games in the winter, golf in the summer. Although he had developed a bit of a gut as he'd aged, a testament to his fondness for wine and chocolate chip cookies, it was nothing compared to the paunches of his peers. His cholesterol ratio was enviable too, and though no one could predict the future, Hannah felt comforted that he was likely to be around for a long time to come, something that suddenly mattered more than ever.

"What's up, kid?" Ryan asked, his eyes wide and frank. "Something wrong?"

This was it. Up until this moment, Hannah had succeeded in keeping her excitement from showing on her face, but she finally gave in. Inhaling deeply through her nose, she said:

"I went to see Dr. A today." Ryan's wine glass stopped midway to his mouth. "Everything okay?"

"Actually, it's kind of funny."

"What's funny?"

"I'm ..." There was no stopping now. She grinned, unable to contain herself a moment more. Her hands flew up as if they were throwing confetti. "Well, I'm pregnant!"

Ryan smiled weakly as if Hannah had just told a joke in a foreign language that he was expected to get but was only pretending to understand.

"Wha ... ? You're what?"

"I. Am. Pregnant."

The smile came and went again, this time replaced by a frown. "You're kidding, right?"

"Nope."

"I don't understand."

"I don't blame you, honey. I don't understand it myself," she replied, her voice warbling unevenly with excitement. "But I had some symptoms, and I was nervous that maybe it was—I don't know, ovarian cancer—so I went to see Dr. A. She did an ultrasound, and here, look!" She pressed the black-and-white printout into his hand. "I'm pregnant. About ten weeks along." Because he had made little attempt to look at the picture, she tapped it with her finger. Finally his eyes focused on the image. "Look, Ryan! It's our baby! Well, it doesn't look like much now, kind of like a big kidney bean, but there it is. Isn't it amazing?"

"Yeah, amazing," Ryan said faintly. "Wow." He smiled now, but Hannah could tell it was forced. It kept slipping and recovering, like a person trying to regain their balance after nearly falling on a patch of ice. Realizing he still had his wine glass, he drained it, then put down the ultrasound to pour another. After a moment, Ryan cleared his throat. "But how ... ?"

Hannah laughed. "In the usual way, I'd imagine. And if I were going to guess, I'd say it was the night we split that bottle of pricey merlot Jules Feria gave us as a thank-you after you came in on a Sunday to fix his crown." The wine, and the sex, had both been far better than Hannah was accustomed to. Sadly, neither had been repeated.

"I haven't been on hormones or anything, Ryan, I promise! It just ... happened."

"Wow," he said again, and the lackluster repetition didn't give Hannah any more reason to believe he was enthusiastic about her announcement. The thought irritated her, but she remembered what Dr. A had said about the news being a lot to take in, and she acknowledged to herself that it certainly was. She would have to give Ryan more time to get used to the idea. And then they could celebrate properly. Not with champagne, of course, but maybe with a nice dinner out.

"It is a *huge* surprise, I'll grant you that, but Ryan ... it's a whole new beginning for us." She got up and paced around the table. "I'll have to tell Mom and Dad; I'll do that tomorrow. Can you imagine what they'll say? Here they've been badgering Natty to get married and make them great-grandparents, and now ... Good thing their hearts are strong; news like this could do a person in, you know?" She laughed lightly and, turning on her heel, paced in the other direction.

"And then there's Natty. I'll have to figure out how and when to break it to her. She's always in a mood, and I haven't exactly been in her good graces lately, and ... what?"

Hannah had never seen Ryan's face so white, or at least, not since that time in South Carolina when he'd gotten out of a hot tub too quickly and fainted on the spot. That had been frightening, but this ... She suddenly got the feeling he was not merely shaken by her pregnancy but unhappy about it, in a way she had failed to anticipate.

Ryan played with his napkin, crumpling and uncrumpling it. "Christ, Hannah, you're almost fifty-five. I mean, in another couple of months. *Fifty. Five.*"

"I'm aware," she replied defensively, annoyance giving a sharp edge to the reply. Trying to see it from his point of view, though, how shocking it must be, she sat at the table next to him and, laying a hand on his forearm, tried again. "Dr. A says I'm practically a medical miracle."

"Well, so you are."

The two of them sat in silence. Finally Hannah withdrew her hand. She hadn't known what she'd hoped Ryan's reaction would be, but she was pretty sure that this wasn't it. After all the negative results and all of their failed attempts, she thought he'd be happier about it. Certainly not as happy as she was—this was her dream, not his—but still.

"But you're going to be fifty-five," Ryan repeated, and now Hannah was genuinely exasperated. "And I'm almost sixty-two." He paused, then added in a petulant voice, "And we're so close to retirement."

Hannah stared. "What do you mean, retirement? Since when were you planning to retire so soon? I thought you planned to work well into your seventies."

"Plans change."

"*What?*"

"Well, maybe I will, maybe I won't," Ryan said curtly. "But I don't want to feel like I *have* to work that long." He wrinkled his brow and stared down at the table. Then he ventured, more subdued, "For that matter, you don't have to, you know."

"Don't have to what? Work into *my* seventies? What are you talking about?"

"No," he interrupted, still not looking at her. He drummed his fingers nervously on the table. "I mean … you don't have to, you know … have the baby."

Hannah's mouth sagged open. "What do you mean, I don't have to have the baby?" Her voice rose in pitch, giving the strident edge to it that her mother had always labeled "shrill."

"Hannah, I mean you're too old to have a baby! For God's sake, who knows what kind of, I don't know, genetic problems we're looking at? Down syndrome and what have you. And the kind of sacrifice that calls for, the expense—not to mention how unfair it would be to bring a child into this world under those circumstances." He paused. "You don't have to have it, Hannah," he repeated. "It's still early. You could have an abortion."

There it was. Dr. A was obligated to say it, but Hannah never dreamed she would hear it from Ryan.

"You! You, Mr. Catholic. Mr. Altar Boy. You've always given me grief about being pro-choice. And now you're telling me to have an abortion?"

Ryan quickly backtracked. "No, I'm not *telling* you to have an abortion, and Lord knows I could never *tell* you to do anything you didn't want to do. I just want you to be reasonable and to think this through. We don't have to make any decisions right away. There's time, several weeks at least, maybe even a couple of months. Right?"

"Ryan, I don't understand. Why in the world wouldn't I want to have this baby? Aren't you happy for me, for *us?*" She flung her hands out in supplication. "It's what we've always wanted. We tried so hard; don't you remember what it was like? I was miserable; it was agony. And now, against all odds, it's finally happening. Don't you want to be a father? Why aren't you happy? Why can't you be happy?"

"Why can't I be happy?" Ryan slapped his hands down on the table, startling Sadie. "Because this isn't something *I* want, Hannah, it's something *you* want. When we couldn't have a baby, after all the pain and grief and expense, you wanted to adopt and I said 'fine,' because it seemed like a good solution. We adopted Natty and *I moved on.* I've *been* a father for twenty-two years, to Natty, and that's been good enough for me.

"This," he continued, waving his hand vaguely toward Hannah's midsection, "this is … weird, unnatural. It shouldn't be happening, not now, not at your age. It doesn't *have* to happen." Ryan softened. "Hannah, it's a bad idea, and you must know it, too, deep down. The time for having babies is long past. Too much can go wrong and it's simply not the right time for us. We raised Natty—that was enough of a challenge. She's in her last year of college, there's only one more semester to pay for, and we're supposed to be saving for retirement. And," he concluded, "it's not what I want."

"But how can you even say that? You know how much I've always dreamed of being a mother."

"Hannah, you've been a mother. *Are* a mother. To Natty. *That* was what you wanted, wasn't it? Not for nothing, you know, because it practically broke us then—all the adoption fees and your trip to Russia on top of all the fertility testing which, by the way, put the ball squarely in *your* court."

Not true! Well, yes, the testing had given Ryan a clean bill of health, but it had hardly cast Hannah as the problem. There had been no blockages, no ovarian cysts, no ectopic pregnancies, no endometriosis. No reason at all why two healthy young people couldn't have gotten pregnant. "Well," Hannah said decisively, "I am pregnant now, whether you're happy about it or not. In another six-and-a-half months or so, you're going to be a father, again. And this time it will be someone with your genes and my genes. Maybe with my hair, and your eyes." Tears filled her eyes again. *Damn hormones*, she thought, but with gratitude rather than anger—and she smiled the inexplicable smile of someone given a great gift. "Don't you understand?" she said, gripping Ryan's hands. "Now I get to be a *real mother*."

Ryan looked shocked. He pulled his hands away from hers. "Oh, so is that what you're planning to tell Natty? That you're going to be a *real* mother now? Huh? What does that make her?"

Hannah's mouth fell open. How could she say something so awful? Of course she loved Natty! She loved her with the same passionate, unending devotion she would give to a child of her own womb. Of course she did.

"Oh, no, no, no. That's not what I meant to say. Of course Natty's my child—*our* child. I'm only saying that I've always wanted to experience life growing inside of me, Ryan, and now I do. And I am so grateful."

"No, what you are is selfish."

"*I'm* being selfish? Me? Why can't you see? I ..." Hannah was at a loss for a way to make Ryan understand. She looked around the room as if the right words might be in the sink, where the meatloaf pan lay soaking, or on the counter, where the wine bottle awaited recorking. But at the moment she could think of nothing to say. Eyes filled with tears of anger and frustration, she left him there at the table, staring at his now-empty wine glass.

THAT NIGHT, HANNAH LAY AWAKE, staring at the dim outline of the ceiling fan—a huge gray orchid looming over the bed. Ryan snored softly next to her. She envied his ability to fall asleep within five minutes of his head hitting the pillow and wondered, as she often did, whether it was an innate sort of thing or whether she could learn to do it. Sleep was going to be a precious commodity soon enough.

Selfish? After everything they'd suffered together? HE was the selfish one to even suggest ending this pregnancy. Her hand drifted to her belly. Logically, she knew it was far too early to feel any movement, but it didn't stop her from imagining what that might feel like, the "quickening." Several of her friends had described the first sensations as flutters, a butterflies-in-the-stomach feeling. A blink-and-you'll-miss-it moment. She wondered if she would recognize it when it happened and then decided absolutely she would. She would know her baby.

Hannah got out of bed and moved to the window, pulling back the curtains. It was a clear night and a few stars were visible despite the interference from the street lights. The moon was waxing, not quite full. A gibbous moon, she thought, dredging up a word she'd learned in some high school science class.

She remembered that night in 1969, watching in awe on a tiny black-and-white screen at her best friend Sharon's house as a man first walked on the moon. "Is that it? Is that it?" she'd whispered urgently to Sharon. The picture was grainy, and she could barely distinguish Armstrong or his crab-like lunar module ... but Sharon had fallen asleep. How could she sleep, Hannah wondered for years after that, when a human being was setting foot on another world? Didn't she want to see history made? Wasn't she excited? At the time, it seemed the most amazing thing that could possibly happen.

Until today.

HANNAH 1:4

The following morning, Ryan was already gone when Hannah's alarm went off. In itself that wasn't unusual—he probably had gone to the gym early—but Hannah was sure he was avoiding having to speak with her.

She sat up, her head and mouth fuzzy. Almost immediately, she felt nauseated, her stomach sending out an urgent warning. Tossing off the blankets, she made a beeline for the bathroom, grateful to make it just in time before her morning sickness asserted itself in the most graphic way. Morning sickness! As miserable as she felt sitting there on the cold tile with a damp washcloth to her lips, she couldn't help but smile. She wasn't terminally ill; she was pregnant. Not cancer. A baby.

Not death. Life.

At length, leaning heavily on the toilet, she got to her feet and brushed her teeth the way Ryan had instructed her to years back. She stared at herself in the mirror, looking for visible changes to match the internal ones. There didn't seem to be any, at least not yet. Her eyes were still the same unremarkable hazel, the lines and wrinkles around them kept at a minimum from a lifetime of protecting her pale Irish skin against the sun. She spit into the sink, then rinsed her mouth. She pulled at her slightly wattled neck, poked at the flesh beginning to sag on her jaw. Where was that glow she'd heard so much about? It had yet to make an appearance.

Although she wanted to shout the news of her pregnancy from the rooftops, Hannah knew she'd have to resist the urge. Because there was still a possibility of a miscarriage, she would have to wait a few weeks to tell the world at large and besides, such an unexpected and unlikely development was likely to cause some upheaval. Better it be done in bits and pieces.

Today she would tell her parents. She tried to imagine the conversation but she really couldn't. As a unit they were resistant to anything that would upset the status quo. Dolores was vocal about it. There was no pleasing her mother, never had been, but her father ... It was getting harder to know what he was thinking. A quiet man by nature, he was starting to disappear completely, like the fade-out at the end of a song: his body diminishing, his voice dimming. As a lifelong "Daddy's girl," always trying to make him happy, she was saddened by his increasing frailty.

Telling Natty would be an even bigger challenge, one Hannah wasn't sure she was up to facing yet. She wouldn't think about it today; one thing at a time.

After her shower, she stepped into the small walk-in closet and surveyed her options, which had recently become limited. Good thing she had resisted giving away her "fat" clothes, the ones she'd acquired during a brief weight gain three years ago. Her everyday slacks and jeans were beginning to pinch, leaving a painful red band around her midsection as if to divide her in half; the button-down blouses were straining at her swollen breasts. She'd have to wear sweaters, T-shirts, pullovers instead, until she grew large enough to merit real maternity clothes.

Sadie watched her with intelligent eyes, knowing she would be getting fed after the morning routine was complete, however long it took. Hannah was grateful that she didn't have to try to explain the delay to the dog. Sadie, at least, always seemed to know what she was thinking.

Sipping her decaf tea at the kitchen island after breakfast, Hannah made a mental note of the items she needed to bring with her to Best of Times Senior Living, the assisted living facility where her parents had been placed over their own strenuous objections two years prior. The shopping list read like a cliché straight out of a sitcom, but it was just the reality of her parents getting older: denture cleaner, Metamucil, assorted greeting cards and stamps for birthdays and anniversaries, prunes .... They could of course take the facility's bus to the local CVS or supermarket, but more and more they relied on Hannah to bring them whatever they needed.

Hannah liked Best of Times. It had a warm, welcoming feeling, high ceilings, plenty of organized activities, an exercise room, a library well-stocked with mildly scandalous romances and World War II memoirs, and a dedicated and concerned staff. There was old pop music playing in the hallways (the Four Seasons and Neil Diamond seemed to be favorites of whoever was doing the programming), free coffee and fresh fruit all day long, and a bistro where one could buy anything from a cup of soup to a sandwich. This was in addition to a dining room that served nutritionally complete lunches and dinners restaurant-style on white-clothed tables. It was a far cry from the nursing facility where her grandmother had passed the last two years of her life, an appalling place: stark and hospital-like, smelling strongly of disinfectant and urine, where barely conscious residents would be wheeled out into the hallways in the mornings and wheeled back in the evenings. Hannah had hated visiting there and had kept her visits as brief as possible, without guilt. It wasn't as if Nana had recognized her anyway. Or so Dolores told her.

At Best of Times, Hannah could almost pretend they were in a high-priced retirement condo development like the ones Ryan always eyed with interest—if not for the mass of walkers sitting, like a flock of large black birds, outside the activity rooms. Or, more tragically, if not for the emergency vehicles all too frequently parked out front, the paramedics wheeling their gray-faced, oxygen-masked patients on gurneys through the brightly painted hallways or the sunny atrium. After the initial shock of seeing such a crisis twice in her first three visits, Hannah quickly learned to avert her gaze, to avoid staring wide-eyed in dismay at someone else's misfortune. Sadly, such ambulance visits were a fact of life here, as they were in any residence where the average age was eighty-four.

It had only been a week since Hannah had seen her parents, but every time she visited, she assessed them with a critical eye for signs of decline. Was Mom's hair in need of a comb-out? Was that a new stain on Dad's shirt? Was the apartment messier than usual? She hoped this week in particular there would be nothing out of the ordinary.

Hannah knocked, and Dolores answered the door. An unsentimental, no-nonsense woman who had so far lost none of her faculties, Dolores Cavanaugh was still—as she had always been—sure of the way everything should be, and not shy about expressing it. Raised in a frugal, plain-speaking household, Dolores lacked the conspicuous motherly warmth expected of a woman of her era. From the beginning, acquaintances whispered that they found her to be "somewhat of a cold fish," a visual that Hannah as a child had found first confusing and then amusing, only seeing the truth of it as she entered her teens. However devoted Dolores was to her family, she was scant in her praise and lavish with her criticism, and Hannah grew to envy her friends whose mothers publicly admired their artwork, bragged about their academic accomplishments, cheered on their athletic successes. The best Hannah could expect from her mother was an approving nod and a brisk "well done."

At eighty-two, Dolores remained predictable as ever. Never one to be caught in a housecoat, she set her alarm for 6:30 a.m. and was fully dressed, complete with coordinated jewelry, by 7:30. Her white hair was carefully coiffed once a week by the resident hairdresser and was lacquered to stay in place until the next appointment. While Dolores's sense of what was considered proper attire had remained robust, her fashion sense had weakened as she aged. Today she was dressed in a lavender long-sleeved tee and deep-purple polyester slacks that were meant to match but were just off enough to clash; black flats with Pilgrim-hat buckles; big faux-gold button earrings; and the 14K-gold necklace Hannah and Ryan had bought her for her eightieth birthday, right after they'd moved them into Best of Times. At the time, Dolores had responded to the gift with, "Oh, isn't that lovely! Can't imagine where I'd wear it, though. What will I have to get dressed up for in this place?" Nevertheless, as she seemed to have found it suitable for everyday wear, Hannah knew Dolores was secretly delighted.

Hannah gave her mother a hug and a peck on the cheek, which Dolores returned with a one-armed embrace and a careless kiss that had no doubt left a smudge of Marvelous Mauve lipstick in the vicinity of Hannah's left eye. It was followed by a quick once-over. Nothing escaped her mother, though it always surprised Hannah how quickly she still picked up on subtle details.

"Back in your fat jeans?" Dolores asked in her straightforward way. Hannah swung the plastic bags she had brought with her onto the tiny kitchen counter, withholding the sigh with which she would have ordinarily responded. "I thought you were aiming to be in tip-top shape for your fifty-fifth?"

"Good to see you, too, Mom," Hannah answered. Long resigned to Dolores's rough-edged version of affection, Hannah chose to take no offense. She bent over to press a kiss on her father's forehead.

"Good morning, Hannah," Frank responded with a wan smile. He waved the Sunday crossword at her, and she nodded.

It was their weekly routine, one that had been declining bit by bit during the past year like the man himself. It used to be *The New York Times* puzzle. Now it was from the local rag. And he was having trouble even with simple clues and big squares, the empty spaces echoing the gaps in his memory. It saddened Hannah, but for his sake she maintained the fiction that he had lost none of his abilities. "In a minute, Dad."

During the rare times when he was on his feet, Frank's bent stature perfectly mirrored the curve of the wooden cane he used to help him get around. But when Hannah arrived, he was reading the newspaper while reclining, feet up, in a brown leather recliner, his favorite position. Frank Cavanaugh was fond of saying that scoring a desk job while his friends went off to fight in the infantry during the Korean War had introduced him to the advantages of being sedentary, and he been loyal ever since to the notion of remaining seated. He often joked that he had become a CPA chiefly because it enabled him to spend his entire career in increasingly large and comfortable chairs.

Frank, too, was fully dressed, no doubt at Dolores's urging, but with less fussiness: a soft green plaid flannel shirt over a white undershirt, jeans, and well-worn slippers that needed to be replaced. Given her father's customary lack of locomotion, he had to have owned that particular pair for a very, very long time. The apartment, Hannah noted with senses newly heightened by her condition, smelled much like her childhood home—of her mother's hairspray, her father's after-shave, their fondness for fried eggs over easy—but closer, stuffier, and overlaid with a vaguely medicinal odor, the sharp chemical-candy smell of a full bottle of capsules. It made her slightly queasy. She forced the feeling down.

"I spoke to your brother last night," Dolores announced. "He calls every week, like clockwork, you know."

"Yeah, I know. And I visit every week, Mom. You'd think that would count for something." Hannah remained in competition with her younger brother, Jason, long after it had ceased to be an appropriate thing for siblings to do. He was now approaching fifty-two and the two sniped at each other as if they were still fighting over whose turn it was to take the garbage out. Hannah was generally grateful that he lived far enough away to make regular family meals impossible, and both were content with the annual Christmas card and twice- or thrice-yearly phone call.

"That's different. He's busy. He's a lawyer. You're …" *Don't say it, Mom. Don't.* "Retired."

Hannah blew out a breath. At least Dolores didn't say "housewife." Once Ryan's dental practice had become well established ("taken root," he liked to say, in one of his typically bad puns) not long into their marriage, Hannah had not been unhappy to quit her unfulfilling position in HR at a large local company to stay home and raise Natty. Dolores, who considered motherhood as consequential as any high-powered job, had been supportive at the time but clearly expected her to re-establish some sort of career, or at least obtain some sort of employment, as soon as Natty was in high school. When that didn't happen, she defaulted to disapproval. "Why did we even bother giving you a college education?"

Frank, as was his habit, steered clear of the conflict and said little.

"I've been plenty busy, Mom. Who else would take you to all your doctors and do your shopping?"

"I was right," Dolores sniffed immediately. "You resent us. That's why you stuck us here, with all these old people." It was a familiar gripe, one that was gone through almost by rote. Hannah marveled at how her mother could separate herself from the "old people." True, there were many at Best of Times who could no longer fend for themselves and required aides and oxygen and other types of care. But there were also those like Tonio who, at 100, was irked he couldn't get a foursome together for golf or order a decent T-bone steak. Hannah wished her parents could be more grateful for their comparative good health.

Yet despite the grievances she heard weekly from her mother, Hannah knew from the director of the residence that

Dolores and Frank had settled in remarkably well and had several friends with whom they ate their lunch and dinner, and played cards and bingo. Dolores's complaints were almost as toothless as that affable Mr. Bookbinder on the second floor.

With the groceries put away, Hannah pulled up one of the vinyl-covered kitchen chairs next to her father's recliner and motioned Dolores toward the floral loveseat she and Ryan had purchased for them when her parents had moved into the apartment. Dolores gave her what Natty called a "side-eye," staring at Hannah suspiciously through lowered lashes caked with mascara.

"Listen," Hannah began, "I have something to tell you, and don't worry, it's good news, but it may come as a little bit of a shock." Her parents stared at her expectantly. "You're going to be grandparents. Again, I mean."

Dolores's eyebrows, thin arches almost completely created by her favorite shade of Maybelline "Define-A-Brow," rose of their own accord. "Really? Why didn't Jason tell us directly? Why are we hearing it from you?"

"Because it's not Jason; I mean, it's not Missy. It's me. *I'm* pregnant."

There was silence at first while Dolores and Frank took in this information. True to form, it was Dolores who responded. "What kind of a joke is that, Hannah?"

Hannah gave a half laugh. "Believe me, Mom, that was my first response, too. But I promise you, it's absolutely true."

"But you're too old!"

"Apparently not."

"And infertile."

"Well," Hannah said as she folded her arms defensively across her chest, "that is clearly no longer the case."

"I can't believe it." Dolores smacked her husband on the arm. "Frank, can you believe it?"

Shaking his head, Frank remained mute. He hadn't been a talkative man even before age had debilitated him—Dolores having done most of the talking for the two of them for the entirety of their fifty-seven years of marriage. Now, his words were even fewer.

"So, what are you going to do?" Dolores prodded.

Hannah shrugged. "Watch my diet. Get some maternity clothes. Rethink the rest of my life."

The three sat together in silence. Hannah couldn't imagine what her parents were thinking. So she asked them.

"Naturally we're very happy for you," Dolores said eventually, though her tone made Hannah think that the opposite was true. "What did Ryan say?"

"He's taking some time to, um, process the information."

"Which means he's not happy about it. I could have told you."

"Mom!"

"It's true. The man has been talking about retirement for the past two years. He's been looking at brochures. He can probably taste it. A baby is the last thing on his agenda, you mark my words."

Hannah stared dumbly at her mother. Dolores apparently knew Ryan better than she'd given her credit for.

"And what about Natty?"

"Oh!" Hannah said, "if you happen to speak to Natty before I do ..."

"What are the odds of *that* happening?"

"Well, Mom, in case you haven't noticed, miracles seem to be occurring more frequently than usual these days. So if you happen to talk to Natty, please don't say anything. I haven't had a chance to tell her yet."

"You haven't told her." Dolores looked significantly at Frank, who pursed his lips. "She hasn't told her daughter. That's going to be an interesting conversation."

"We'll be all right."

"I'm sure you will be," her mother replied, once again sounding doubtful.

"Daddy?" Hannah appealed to Frank directly as she rarely did these days. "What do you think? Isn't this amazing news? Aren't you happy for me?"

"If you're happy, Hannah Banana," he said hoarsely, "I'm happy." The old nickname never failed to drive her perilously close to tears. And though Hannah had the very strong impression that her father might not completely understand the significance of what he had just been told, she would take what she could get.

HANNAH 1:5

Ryan was still pointedly not talking about the baby, which left Hannah unsettled. He went to work as usual, went to the gym as usual, and ate his dinner as usual. They talked about whether the roof might need to be replaced soon; about the passing of one of Ryan's patients (92 years old but he still had his own teeth!); about what Natty might be up to. But no opening she gave him would make him have the most important conversation of their lives.

Unable to bear it any more, Hannah finally said, "We really need to talk," during an evening when Ryan had said very little at all, though she knew bringing up the subject during Monday Night Football was probably a mistake.

"If you're talking about what I think you're talking about, I'm pretty sure I was clear on my opinion," Ryan replied without taking his eyes off the 55-inch high-def screen he had bought himself two years prior. Although they had argued a bit about the cost at the time, Hannah had to admit it had a beautiful picture. And she was now addicted to binge-watching shows on Netflix. *Thanks for nothing, Ryan.*

"Yes, you were quite clear on your opinion, Ryan, but that doesn't change the fact that in a little over six months we're going to have a baby."

Ryan turned to look at her, but only for a moment. "You're right," he replied, his eyes turning back to the TV. "It certainly doesn't change anything. You're the only one who can do the sensible thing, and you're refusing to do it."

"*'The sensible thing …'*?" Hannah stared at him, horrified. "You still want me to have an abortion? Can't you see what you're asking of me? Don't you see how selfish you're being?"

His mouth set in a grim line, Ryan pressed "pause" on the remote and turned to face Hannah directly. "Hannah. Sweetheart. *We. Are. Too. Old. To be having children.* At the very most, we should be preparing ourselves to become doting grandparents, though Natty doesn't seem to be anywhere near ready for that kind of responsibility, thank God. We don't have the energy or the money to be having a kid at this point in our lives.

"And you," he continued, "you're going to see soon enough that your post-middle-aged body can't take the kind of stress pregnancy puts on it. And yes, before you ask, I did a Web search about that. For one thing, you'll be susceptible to high blood pressure and preeclampsia, which can threaten your life. Aren't you worried? Because I sure am; the idea scares the hell out of me.

"What's more, if both you and the baby are lucky enough to survive the pregnancy, you'll be a fifty-five-year-old woman with fifty-five-year-old bones and muscles and joints trying to keep up with an infant … and then a toddler and then an adolescent … a child who may or may not have cognitive or developmental disabilities. I read somewhere that the risk of autism increases with *advanced parental age*. Are you hearing me? We went through hell with Natty, but her problems are nothing compared to what happens on a daily basis with some kids. And even you have to be aware that this particular child is more likely to have those disabilities than not.

"And let's say, by some miracle, since you seem to believe in those these days, the child is normal. Do you know it costs approximately $300,000 to raise a child to adulthood in today's economy?" The timbre of his voice rose so high it cracked. "Where is that money supposed to come from, Hannah? We're coming up on Natty's last semester; how are we supposed to pay for another round of college? And where's the guarantee that either of us is going to live long enough even to see this child grow up? So you tell me: Who's being the selfish one here?"

And with that, Ryan picked up his remote, pressed "play," and returned to the football game.

Hannah stood there for a few moments with a dull ache in her chest that reached all the way up to clutch her throat. Clearly this conversation was at an end, but now what? Though she and Ryan had had arguments before, and some pretty serious ones, she had never felt this far apart from him. *Well, maybe a little distance is exactly what we need*, Hannah thought, turning on her heel and marching directly to the master bedroom.

Methodically, because when Hannah was angry or upset, she, like Dolores, always did such things methodically, she emptied her drawers and carried piles of neatly stacked clothes into the guest bedroom, where she filled the armoire she had inherited from her parents when it was deemed too large for their bedroom in Best of Times. She retrieved clean sheets and towels from the linen closet and made the bed up in a matter of minutes.

If Ryan didn't want to be part of this family, this *new* family, Hannah was certainly not going to snuggle up to him in bed. She was sure a few lonely nights on his own would bring him around, as it had in the past. In the meantime, she had a comfortable queen bed with an en suite bathroom, very convenient for both her morning sickness and her increasing frequency of urination.

AN HOUR TICKED BY. Hannah was sitting in bed, counting stitches on the argyle cardigan she was knitting for her father when she heard Ryan let Sadie in from the backyard. She listened to the dog make her way upstairs and then the familiar sound of her claws click-clacking against the hardwood floor in the hallway. It didn't take long for Sadie to find Hannah in the guest room, nor to jump onto the bed beside Hannah and, after circling three times, make herself comfortable on the quilt.

The argument, like previous ones between her and Ryan or between her and Natty, had made Sadie anxious. Always exceptionally sensitive, not only to Hannah's mood but to the atmosphere in the household, Sadie paced, whined, barked, or asked to go outside whenever voices or tensions were raised.

She had entered their lives as a nine-week-old pup intended to fill Hannah's "empty nest" when Natty moved out for the first time at age twenty. Hannah had studied up on the breed, researched the best food and toys, and made sure the puppy got plenty of stimulation and loving discipline. By the time

Natty, having broken up with her boyfriend Jake, had moved back home a mere two months later and had begun to shower the dog with affection and treats, Sadie had not been tempted. She had already decided where her loyalties lay, and that was with Hannah.

Stroking Sadie's soft fur as the dog let out a contented sigh, Hannah smiled. It was hard to stay angry when she was this cozy. So when Ryan's footsteps stopped at the master bedroom threshold, hesitated, and then arrived at the door of the guest room, Hannah was feeling benevolent. She would let him apologize and maybe even come into bed. Not for sex, not now. But a little cuddle and some pillow talk could be just the thing for them both.

Before she had the chance to slide over to "her" side of the bed from the middle, though, Ryan appeared to change his mind. Hannah listened to him walk back to the master bedroom; heard the door close with a decisive click.

Disappointed, Hannah put her knitting back into its tote, reached over, and turned off the lamp. Sadie would be her only company tonight.

HANNAH 1:6

Natty agreed to meet Hannah at a café near the local college where she was taking classes in business management. While she was waiting, sipping her herbal tea, Hannah thought about the little gold crucifix Natty used to wear, the one Dolores and Frank had given her for her First Communion. Hannah had marveled at the quality of the workmanship, the detail on Jesus on such a tiny pendant, and Natty had crowed to her friends about having something made of *real gold*. When had she stopped wearing it? During middle school? Hannah wondered whether it had been sold years ago, a victim of Natty's early but thankfully short-lived experiments with alcohol and pot, and hoped that it had instead been innocently lost somewhere along the way.

The café door opened and Hannah watched as Natty swung into the café. That's how she moved, Hannah mused with a fond ache in her chest: with a flowing, forward gliding movement as if she were still on the swings that used to entertain her for hours. It was beautiful to watch. Natty was taller than Hannah and had the classic body of a Russian ballerina, lean and long-limbed. But she had broken her mother's heart at the age of eight when she had refused to continue the ballet classes Hannah had arranged at great expense with Miss Vladlena, preferring to take art classes instead.

She was wearing a shabby pair of jeans and a washed-out pink T-shirt that had probably been red at one time. Hannah had never seen the shirt before and assumed it had come from a thrift store. Was this her way of asking for money? If so, she was in luck, as Hannah was in a particularly generous mood today.

"Hey, Mom," Natty said, going straight for the chair opposite Hannah and slouching into it, dropping a densely packed key chain noisily onto the table as she did. Hannah deflated a little in disappointment. But she reminded herself, as she often had to these days, that this attitude was just another bump in Natty's long road. Surely it wouldn't be long before Natty would be glad to see her mother again, would grace her with a hug or a kiss on the cheek, the way she used to when she was a little younger. Maybe this was only the price of her daughter becoming an independent adult. At least, that's what Hannah chose to believe. "What's up?"

"How's your week going, Natty?" At her daughter's raised eyebrows, Hannah amended, "Excuse me, *Natasha*." Remembering to use Natty's full given name was going to take some getting used to. "Everything okay?"

Natty shrugged. "Well enough." She plucked up the receipt resting on the table in front of Hannah and started folding it idly. Straight creases, pressed down with her fingernails. Hannah noted with approval that the nails were neatly shaped and polished, although she wasn't so happy that they were painted black, a holdover from Natty's brief Goth phase. At least she wasn't dressing all in black anymore.

"How's school?"

"Eh, you know; boring as usual."

So, that's the way it was going to be today. Why couldn't they put their differences aside and for once talk to each other the way they used to? Maybe Hannah's news would put a crack in the wall that Natty seemed determined to erect around herself.

"Well, I have something to tell you that is decidedly not boring. In fact, it could be considered fairly mind-blowing."

"Let me guess: you and Dad are retiring early to a little golf condo development in South Carolina and leaving me the house so Jonathan and I can move in?" Natty replied sarcastically.

Jonathan Holyoke was a recent addition to Natty's life, four months at the most, and Hannah didn't know yet whether she liked him or not. They had moved in together after only two months of dating, too soon in Hannah's book. He was tall, skinny, and attractive except for a bushy bro beard that seemed a misguided attempt to minimize a strong nose. And the man-bun, *well* ... Hannah had only met him once, when she and Ryan had helped Natty move in to a tiny studio apartment, little more than a single room, in a sketchy part of town. Still, he seemed a step up from her previous boyfriends, who were stoners or slackers or both. Jonathan was a graphic designer or web designer or something, and if he didn't currently have a real job, at least he had real skills. Or so Hannah hoped. He had an expensive-looking laptop anyway, which seemed at odds with his threadbare T-shirts and hole-spotted jeans.

"Not exactly, no."

"Then I'm not interested," Natty said as she sat up, making as if to grab her keys as Hannah reached out, covering her daughter's hand with her own.

"Nat … Natasha, please. This is important."

"All right," Natty said as she relaxed back into the chair, a dancer at rest. Even her slouch was graceful. Her hair was long enough now to be pulled back, away from her face, accentuating her elegant cheekbones—a facial structure Hannah envied from the time Natty's face had lost its babyish curves—and velvet brown eyes. Hannah thought her daughter was stunning and could have been a model; in fact, she had once offered to find Natty an agent. Of course, she would have to get rid of that nose stud she'd acquired at sixteen. Natty rejected the idea outright, and wisely, Hannah never pursued it.

She likewise was proud of her efforts to keep quiet about her distaste for tattoos, despite a brief period in which Natty apprenticed to a tattoo artist, lest Natty think it would be funny to subject her smooth, unblemished skin to some big, ugly piece of "art" on the spur of the moment. Hannah had been relieved when that chapter in her daughter's life had closed and she appeared to have emerged unscathed.

Though, to be fair, there were areas of Natty's body she hadn't seen in a very, very long time.

"Okay, Mom," Natty prodded, curious despite herself. "Surprise me."

Hannah had the same feeling of anticipation and dread a swimmer gets standing at the edge of a cold lake on a hot day. There was nothing for it: she took a deep breath and jumped in. "I'm pregnant."

Natty blinked rapidly, but otherwise her face remained remarkably impassive. "Say WHAT?"

"I'm pregnant." It seemed she had to repeat this sentence twice to get any conversation moving forward.

"You're shitting me."

"Honest to God, honey, I'm telling you the truth. Why would I lie about something like that?"

"I have no earthly idea. But those may be the least likely two words you've ever spoken."

"I get that; boy, do I ever. But listen: I had some symptoms, and I managed to convince myself I had ovarian cancer like Nana Dolores's sister Connie, who died when I was young. So I went to see Dr. A on Tuesday. She did an ultrasound, and well, I'm pregnant. Nearly eleven weeks now."

Natty's eyes betrayed her surprise, but her lip rose up in a smirk. "Pics or it didn't happen," she demanded.

Anticipating her daughter's skepticism, Hannah had come prepared: she reached into her handbag and pulled out the plastic baggie that held this most important piece of paper. She spread the plastic carefully in front of Natty to cover the table and placed the ultrasound down on it, daring her to challenge it.

Natty stared down at the blurry black-and-white image. She gaped at Hannah. "I can't believe it."

"I know."

"I really can't believe it," Natty repeated. "I mean, it's incredible: you two are still having sex? At your age? Eww!"

Hannah burst out laughing, the tension of the past week finally finding an outlet. Natty did not join in her mother's laughter, instead shaking her head in chagrin. She looked around to see if anyone was staring at the racket her mother was making.

"Mom!" she whispered under her breath. "Aw, c'mon, Mom, get a grip!"

"Okay, okay, fine." Wiping her eyes, Hannah finally restrained herself after a minute of hilarity. "It's true, you know."

"I guess it is." Natty returned to her little piece of paper, folding and re-folding. Hannah wished she would look up, wanted to gauge what she was thinking. "So. How do you feel?"

"Different. I knew right away that something had changed, but I couldn't tell what. Isn't that funny? Yet how would I know, since I've never been pregnant before? I get a little morning sickness right after I get up, but it doesn't last long. Lots of things put me off. But mostly I feel just … different. Happy, from deep down inside. It's … "

"… what you've always wanted," Natty finished the thought for her, head still bowed over Hannah's receipt. "You've said it often enough."

Had she? "Have I?"

"All the time." Fold, unfold, re-fold. "How did Dad take it?"

Hannah frowned. "Not great. He wasn't as thrilled as I was, oddly."

"'Oddly'?" Incredulous, Natty stopped mid-fold and looked up. "You mean you really didn't know how he'd take this bombshell? And you've been married to that man how long?"

"Well, as you said, I've never made a secret of wanting to be pregnant, and at my age it's practically a certifiable miracle, so you'd think he'd be happy for me, but he just … "

"He just what?"

Suddenly Hannah realized she didn't want to share Ryan's opinion with Natty. He'd accused her of being selfish and Natty would more than likely agree with him, as she did so often. For Natty, too, had always been a Daddy's girl; had always taken his side. So Hannah was selective about what she chose to reveal: "All he could talk about was how it would affect our retirement. Couldn't help talking about the money; the inconvenience. Don't you think that's selfish? I mean, why couldn't he just be happy for me?"

Natty took Hannah's hand and placed on her palm a lovely origami flower, a water lily. "Here, *I'll* be happy for you, Mom. Congratulations. You're *finally* going to be a mother." And, standing up, she grabbed her fistful of keys and strode to the door.

Hannah gazed at the flower. Natty surprised her: this skill was a new one. Or was it? How long had she been doing origami? What else didn't she know about her daughter? It wasn't until she had fully admired the artistry of the creation, the perfect symmetry of the petals and the crispness of the folds, that Hannah realized how much she had just hurt her daughter.

HANNAH 1:7

" **W**elcome! My name is Ke'isha; can I help you find something?"

Hannah had no intention of entering the maternity boutique and had, in fact, stood outside on the sidewalk for several minutes, simply staring at the window. "B. Fruitful," it was called. Such specialized retail outlets had barely existed during the time when her peers had been getting pregnant, and they certainly weren't on her radar at all in subsequent years. The window display was filled with fall and winter clothing for women of ever-increasing girth, yet none of it was dowdy or even obvious. Instead, the tailored career-wear and sparkly holiday dresses, in particular a sassy red jacket with a belt placed boldly above the expanded belly of the mannequin, could have been created for any fashion-forward woman. They were a far cry from the oddly-patterned smocks and ugly elastic-paneled polyester slacks women of her generation had worn. She told herself it was only curiosity that drove her inside.

Ke'isha—she pronounced her name the way natives said "Hawai'i," with a pause—the petite young saleswoman, smiled with blindingly white teeth that only a dentist (or a dentist's wife) could recognize as the product of good genes rather than a chemical process, the contrast sharp against her smooth, dark skin. Her hair, too, was natural: tight, glossy spirals that virtually exploded from the top of her head like the earthward-trailing tendrils of a fireworks blast. Her slender hands ended in long, lilac-lacquered nails.

"Um, just looking right now, thanks," Hannah said, her hand pausing on a rack of trousers and leggings. She could have stopped there, of course; she certainly didn't owe the saleslady any sort of explanation. But the temptation was too strong; she simply *had to* try something on. So the first thing Hannah tried on was a little white lie, and she found that it suited her perfectly. "For my daughter, that is." She allowed herself a conspiratorial smile. "Our first grandchild is expected in the spring."

"Oh, how wonderful! You must be so excited! Well, you just let me know if there's anything I can do for you." Ke'isha beamed at her, and Hannah slipped into that luxurious, warm feeling of being on the receiving end of genuine enthusiasm as if she were slipping on a heavy fur coat with a satin lining. It was a feeling that had not yet been granted her by her nearest and dearest, and it emboldened her.

"Say, y'know what?" Hannah asked. "My daughter and I are exactly the same size ... at least for the next month or so, haha! I think I'll surprise her. How about we choose a few things, casual, everyday stuff—some tops and a couple of bottoms—to get her started?"

Ke'isha's face lit up even more, charmingly creating dimples on each cheek, and Hannah reflected the glow back to her. *Screw it*, she thought, if no one else was going to treat this pregnancy as the astonishing marvel it was, Hannah would do it herself. Having no idea how maternity clothes were sized, she told Ke'isha that she, which was to say *Natty*, was ordinarily a size 8. (Natty, a size 2, would have been aghast.)

Within minutes Hannah was stationed in a clean and well-lit dressing room with a tri-fold mirror and an armload of clothes—shirts, sweaters, trousers—hung neatly on a set of hooks.

Hannah's hands trembled as she got undressed, her "fat jeans" already grown too snug and currently worn with the top button unbuttoned, and slipped into a pair of heather gray maternity slacks. Feeling close to tears, she turned sideways and pushed her belly as far outward as it would go in a futile attempt to fill some of the extra space. This is what it will look like, she thought. This is how *I will look*. Entranced, she stood like that, staring, until Ke'isha's voice interrupted her reverie with a cheerful, "How are we doing in there?"

How could she possibly answer that question? Hannah's mouth was dry; her eyes, damp. Finally, licking her lips and forcing her voice to be steady, she called back, "Looking good!" Knowing how odd it would be to remain in the little room much longer, having tried on just one item, Hannah pulled clothes on and off in rapid succession. Despite the speed, everything she saw in the mirror was beautiful because everything she saw reinforced what she had always wanted to see. She only hoped Ke'isha wouldn't notice that the clothes she ultimately selected were on the conservative side for a young, expectant mother.

"And that," Hannah said at home to a rapt Sadie, with her waving tail and unwavering gaze, "is how I ended up with $800 worth of maternity clothes in my first visit. But I'll have you know, I don't regret it." She ruffled the dog's fur, and Sadie snuffled contentedly in response. "Not one little bit." It would be a couple of weeks more until she legitimately needed the extra room the clothes afforded, so she hung them in the back of her closet, tags intact. Waiting.

By now, Hannah had told a handful of her closest friends the news and was stunned to discover that their reactions were much along the same lines as her family's: first incredulous and then half-hearted, filled with a great deal of practical concern and somewhat less enthusiasm than she'd hoped.

"Well, you're not going through with it, are you?" her oldest friend, Cathy, asked over tea, eyes and mouth wide open with shock. Cathy was not the only one to voice this question.

"Of course I am," Hannah replied, affronted.

"Don't you think it's unfair to Ryan?" asked Denise.

"… unfair to Natty?" asked Linda.

"… unfair to society at large?" asked Donna.

Hannah found herself forced to defend her choice again and again. She was starting to realize that the people she thought would be most excited for her were instead resistant to the idea of a pregnancy—or maybe specifically *her* pregnancy—this late in life. There were, though, a couple of very important people who had yet to learn of Hannah's astonishing situation, women who, she was sure, would give her momentous news the reception it deserved: "The Three Witches." They hadn't met as a group in over a year and a half and all blamed time constraints, family issues, anything but the weakening of the connection that had once held them together as close as any blood relations. Hannah haggled with her counterparts on the phone until she could establish a time convenient to all three, inviting them to her house for a midday coffee break nearly two weeks after Hannah's visit to Dr. A's office.

SADIE BARKED VIOLENTLY at the perceived threat posed by the doorbell as Hannah practically skipped to the door. There stood Marla and Amibeth, well-loved and greatly missed. Marla Hochberg: practical, solid; as blocky and deliberately unfashionable as the sensible shoes she'd worn since her forties; attired in muted colors with not a gray hair out of place; eagle-eyed and cynical. And Amibeth deWitt: dressed in a colorful tunic and shawl no doubt made with fair-trade labor by indigenous people somewhere in the developing world; her once chocolate-brown hair dimmed to a soft gray-streaked taupe but her face still full of an almost eerie inner peace that even a philandering husband and a lifetime of frustration couldn't dim.

"*When shall we three meet again? In thunder, lightning, or in rain?*" intoned Marla, grasping Hannah's outstretched hand.

"*When the hurlyburly's done, When the battle's lost and won,*" Hannah responded, reaching for Amibeth.

"*That will be ere the set of sun,*" Amibeth concluded, completing the circle by holding her friends' hands. The ritual done, the three came together into a group hug. The giddy joy they had once experienced at such gatherings, the laughter their incantation had once produced, was gone; their shared expectations were now tempered by time and distance and endless disappointments. No one laughed this time, but the embrace held longer than usual. Sadie high-stepped around the group, impatient and annoyed at being excluded, and was insistent upon herding the women inside.

Finally, Marla and Amibeth joined Hannah in the kitchen. ("Family doesn't use the living room," Marla had said with her trademark certainty all those years ago, and since then their kitchens had been their only gathering place. "Besides," Hannah had added drolly, "you'll never know when you want to stir up a batch of potion.")

Coffee served, cookies presented—and as Amibeth always baked and brought truly superior lemon cookies, fragrant and flavorful, there was never a need for store-bought—"The Three Witches" sat down to catch up. Hannah let the others lead, as she knew her news would be disruptive, but she could physically feel her own story tug and strain to be released, as if it were a dog pulling at a leash.

"And then Gene retired two months ago," Marla was saying, and Hannah realized she hadn't been paying much attention. She struggled to focus, overcompensating by arranging her face into an expression of intense interest. "Now he's around the house all day long, driving me crazy."

"I thought he had a couple more years left at least?" Hannah inquired, hoping she had her story straight. She hadn't spoken to Marla since the spring, and there was a danger she was conflating her story with someone else's.

"It was a forced retirement," Marla replied, biting into her cookie. She tapped the crumbs delicately off her lips with her napkin and took a sip of black coffee. "The firm was offering buyouts to the senior members and Gene could see the writing on the wall, so he took it. We figured that between my consulting work and the money we've put away, we'll be just fine financially, particularly now that Niko is on his own and doing well."

A small cloud passed over Hannah's sunny mood. Somehow Marla's life always seemed to be that much better than her own. Although Ryan was every bit as successful as Gene, and Hannah remained in far better physical shape than Marla, Hannah couldn't deny that the adoring way Gene gazed at Marla—albeit through thick aviator-style glasses best left in the '80s—and the way Marla gazed back in return, was lacking in her life. Hannah had once told Linda that she wished Ryan would look at her the way he looked at a set of straight, cavity-free teeth in a healthy pair of gums. A joke, yes, but one with some bite in it, pun intended.

Like Hannah and Ryan, Marla and Gene had opted for a Russian adoption when they failed to conceive, bringing home three-year-old Nikolai from the same orphanage shortly before Natty arrived. And like Natty, Niko had suffered through the cognitive and behavioral difficulties his early childhood deprivations had created. Through elementary and middle school, Hannah and Marla had spent hours on the phone in tearful commiseration over the calls from the principal's office: the restlessness and disruption in class; the lying and fighting; the unexcused and unexplained absences; the beer, the pot. And though the struggle, which Marla referred to totally without irony as her "labor pains," had turned Marla's hair completely gray far faster than normal, she refused to color it, embracing the change as her "battle scars."

Perhaps what Hannah envied about Marla most of all was the deep connection she had always felt to her child— something that had always eluded Hannah. It was *bashert*, Marla had said in Yiddish; *meant to be*. Niko had simply been destined for their family. She claimed to have dreamed of this serious, dark-eyed boy six nights in a row before they were informed of his availability. And despite his challenges, the problems he had attaching and communicating and showing affection, his parents never wavered. Not Marla, not Gene. They remained a united front of unconditional love in the face of the forces buffeting their Niko.

Through a combination of intense parental intervention, plain good luck, and perhaps some mystical link to his parents that Natty lacked, by tenth grade Niko had abruptly switched gears. After re-dedicating himself to his studies, he received a scholarship to State and graduated with honors, becoming a financial adviser. He now had his own apartment and was engaged to marry a lovely girl who was in law school. By comparison, Natty's lax attitude toward school and life in general, not to mention her less-than-stellar choice of companions, had always been an embarrassment to Hannah.

"So what is Gene going to do now?" Amibeth asked in her usual unruffled, almost lazy, way, seemingly always placid no matter what turbulence surrounded her.

"Not sure yet. He's thinking of volunteering somewhere, possibly with at-risk kids, or maybe he'll teach. He's always wanted to teach math, and I'll say he did an amazing job with Niko. But anything to get him out of the house, frankly. I love the man to death, I do, but he's so bored and unhappy. You know what I mean?

"What about Dorian?" Marla asked Amibeth. "He's getting to be about that age, too, though I imagine it's a different story entirely with doctors."

"As of three weeks ago, Dorian is no longer my problem." This major announcement was related by Amibeth in the same serene tone of voice she had used when offering her friends the lemon cookies, and it took both Hannah and Marla a moment to catch up with her meaning.

"What? He *left* you?" Hannah blurted out. Marla looked at her, incredulous, as if the affront were personal to her instead of to Amibeth. Hannah shrugged defensively. Well, why not? A man who had had that many affairs might have finally decided there was no reason to stay, or even found a younger woman who could give him children. Money, of course, would have been a powerful motivation for him to stay: twenty-nine years of marriage to a radiologist would have, no doubt, built up a nice nest egg for Amibeth that Dorian would be reluctant to abandon.

"I left *him*," Amibeth clarified, and Marla nodded vigorously with a sharp look at Hannah. "I'd had enough. He hasn't been fully present in our marriage for years, and this last affair was the straw that broke the camel's back. It was his *secretary*, for God's sake! A girl quite literally half his age. I mean, how cliché can you get! I can forgive a lot, but his lack of imagination was too much to bear."

Amibeth had, as usual, put a good face on a difficult situation. Her inner poise was a gift Hannah had admired since the day they'd met in support group. Unlike Marla and Hannah, Amibeth had suffered the devastation of early-term miscarriages—four of them. Once it had been established that she was unlikely ever to carry to term, Amibeth and Dorian had declined to go the adoption route, deciding instead to enjoy the relative freedom of not having children. Amibeth filled the void with travel and language classes. She had become fluent in both Spanish and French, and had made good progress with Italian. A lengthy trip to India had resulted in a lifelong devotion to meditation, which only served to deepen her already innate tranquility. Marveling at Amibeth's smooth, relatively unlined face now, Hannah saw a vision of what she guessed "transcendence" was supposed to look like. If only they could bottle it.

Unfortunately, "freedom" had a very different meaning to Dorian, whose series of affairs had troubled Amibeth's friends for years. Why it had taken her this long to kick him out of their marital bed was a mystery to Hannah, and Amibeth had always been coy on the subject. Privately, Marla suggested that Amibeth's classes and clothes and travels didn't come cheap.

The unspoken question hung in the air: *What will* you *do now?*

"Don't worry about me, kids," Amibeth continued as if in answer. "I've got a good lawyer and expect to live in comfort for the rest of my days." She stirred her coffee sedately. "I think I'll move to someplace warm, like Sedona, and get a fresh start. Maybe take up painting or pottery. Or photography."

"That sounds perfect," Marla said, and when Hannah didn't concur immediately, a jab from Marla's sharp elbow was enough to rouse her to agreement.

"Good for you, Amibeth," Hannah managed. "You deserve to be happy."

The three sat in thoughtful silence. Hannah itched to break it, but the consequence of her news made it more difficult than usual.

"Ladies, I have an announcement, too." Marla and Amibeth looked at Hannah expectantly. "There's really no easy way to say this, so ... here goes." She took each friend by the hand as she had done at the door, and they both gripped hers in response. The tension among the three was palpable, as the other two Witches were no doubt anticipating the disclosure of a serious illness just as Hannah had, not too long before.

"I'm pregnant."

Amibeth's jaw dropped, and Marla drew back in disbelief. "You're kidding."

Hannah blew out a frustrated breath. "Why is that everyone's first reaction? No, I'm not kidding. I could not possibly kid about this. I am, in fact, nearing the end of my first trimester, according to Dr. A's calculations." She looked eagerly from one to the other, waiting for the inevitable congratulations. "Pretty wild, huh? Dr. A has never seen anything like it, particularly after everything I'd gone through."

After everything they had *all* gone through, Hannah thought, too late.

"Wow." Hannah could feel Amibeth's hand go limp in hers, and she dropped it. "That's amazing, Hannah. Congratulations." Her pale skin flushed slightly and she stared down at the table. Amibeth's closely monitored but nevertheless failed pregnancies had never lasted past nine weeks.

"Yes, that's ... some incredible news, Hannah," Marla added, her usual nimble wit dulled. "But ... how? *How* is that even possible?"

"Who knows? Faith? Fate? Dr. A is as puzzled as anyone." Now that the dam had broken, Hannah couldn't resist overflowing with her joy, and she brought out the ultrasound, passing it first to Amibeth. "And here's the evidence." Marla reached into her purse for her reading glasses.

"That's ... that's really wonderful," Amibeth said, and Hannah could see her eyes were moist. Marla took the sonogram next, her thin lashes lowering over gray eyes. "Well, *mazel tov*, Hannah. You've got a miracle there. A little late in the game, true, but let's call it what it is."

"That's exactly what I've been thinking. And when I spoke to Father Aloysius, do you know what he told me ... ?"

HANNAH 1:8

As anxious as Hannah had been to speak to Father Aloysius, he still hadn't returned her call days after her visit to the church. He probably had other, more loyal parishioners to attend to, she thought wryly. They hadn't said a word to each other without the confessional screen between them in years. She decided to phone.

"St. Agnes Church, Heather speaking." Hannah searched her mind trying to picture Father's secretary, Heather, and finally remembered her as a slender, youngish woman, perhaps in her early thirties, with a pleasant if unremarkable face. She had the kind of innocuous presence that, Hannah realized now, had made her forget that Heather had actually been in the church office the day she'd received her earth-shattering news, blending into the background like the dusty certificates and photos on Father's dark wood-paneled walls.

"I'm sorry, but unless this is an emergency, Father's calendar is completely booked for the next couple of days," Heather said with the mechanical assurance of a gatekeeper, one who had said the same thing many, many times before.

Hannah closed her eyes in frustration. "Will you please tell him it's Hannah Murrow and that I have some very important news for him? Tell him," and here she read off a Post-it note she had written herself, to make sure she got it right, "*1 Samuel 1:19–20*. Please tell him that. It might not be what you'd call an emergency, but it is urgent."

"1 Samuel 1:19–20," Heather repeated. After a moment of silence on the other line, during which Heather was presumably writing down the Bible passage, Hannah received an assurance that Father would call her back as soon as a break came in his schedule. Apparently this Old Testament reference was enough to get Father Aloysius's attention. He called Hannah back not two hours later.

"Hannah, it's been a very long time," Father said. Hannah pictured him sitting in his office, bald and bent, his ears prominent. He was a tall man, and thin, with long arms ending in knobby fingers, a figure who struck fear in the children of the parish when they first met him—precisely because he looked like everyone's concept of a mortician or maybe even Death Itself. After they got to know him, though, they grew first to respect and then to love him. He was always fair and wickedly funny, occasionally looming silently like the Grim Reaper behind a boastful child or swearing teen as their friends struggled not to laugh. His deep voice was a shadow of what it once was, but it was still capable of delivering both a powerful homily to a congregation of hundreds and comfort to an audience of one.

"I'm hoping all is well with you and Ryan."

Hannah paused to consider how best to phrase this. She wasn't going to bring her arguments with Ryan into this particular discussion. She settled for: "Our lives are full of surprises, Father."

"Well, I suppose that's a good thing, isn't it?" How glad she was he didn't care to pursue that line of questioning! "And how is Natty?"

"Well enough," Hannah said. "Finishing up her business degree, a little late. And still trying to find her place in the world, I guess."

"It's not unusual for young people these days, I understand. Natty is a lovely girl. All she needs is time."

"I hope so. But listen, Father, that's not why I called."

Father Aloysius gave a short laugh. "There was a time when Natty was the only reason why you called. But yes, your message. I must admit you intrigued me. I didn't know you'd recalled our discussions from so very long ago."

"Of course I did. But I didn't expect them to be suddenly relevant."

"How so?"

"Father, I'm pregnant."

Once again there was silence on the line, and Hannah suspected she had Father's full attention.

"Forgive an old man, Hannah," he said finally, with an apologetic cough. "But I must have misheard you. Could you repeat that?"

She obliged. "Father, I'm pregnant."

"Oh, my."

Silence again, and this time Hannah feared for Father's heart. The priest was in his early eighties and had been hospitalized with two cardiac "episodes" already during the past three years. There was a faction in the parish that was pushing him to retire, but they were outnumbered by those who adored him.

She pressed her ear harder against her phone and held her breath. "Father?"

"Hannah." His voice was small and hesitant, a far cry from the unexpectedly full sound he produced when sermonizing. "I'm sorry to have to ask this, but are you absolutely certain?" She knew what Father meant. Over the years she had heard of more than one case of "false pregnancy" among women with her history (and her intense maternal longing). She could hardly blame him for doubting her story. "I mean, do you have confirmation from a doctor?"

"Yes, I do. And even better than that, Father," Hannah said proudly, "I have an ultrasound to prove it. I can email you a copy if you want."

His gasp was satisfying. Hannah smiled. "My word! Then this is indeed a miracle! Well, congratulations to you and Ryan on this amazing if somewhat belated blessing!"

"Thank you, Father."

"But Hannah," he said, his intonation gaining in strength and volume as he returned to more familiar ground. "You do understand: it is clear that our Father has blessed you in this remarkable way for a reason. It is not for us to know why He has willed it. You must therefore accept this gift of grace with a full heart and without questioning. It is not to be taken lightly."

"I know," Hannah said. She still did not know where she stood on the question of God and divinity and faith, but she did know that she was more than willing to demonstrate her gratitude for the universe's largesse when it came calling.

"Will you be coming back to the Church? You belong here, now more than ever."

She sighed, shaking her head though he couldn't see it. "I don't think so. I mean, at least not on a regular basis. Maybe. I don't know. Certainly for Christmas, at least. Will it sound weird if I say this changes everything, yet it doesn't change anything?"

"I do understand. Look, I know we don't always see eye to eye, Hannah, but I have always had your best interests at heart. I very much appreciate your letting me know."

"Thank you, Father. I have to say, I'm still in a state of disbelief. I hardly know what to do next."

"In such a situation, with such glad tidings, I would usually say that you should pray the rosary every day until the healthy birth. In your case, however, given the, ah, temporary hiatus you have taken from the Church and your exceedingly special circumstances, I would recommend for you exactly what the Hebrew matriarch Sarah did when the Lord blessed her with a pregnancy in her old age. Genesis 18:12."

"And what's that?"

"*'Sarah laughed.'*"

⁓

HANNAH WAVED GOODBYE to her friends and went back into the kitchen to clean up the table and put the dishes into the dishwasher. She didn't quite make it. Instead, she sat down at the round pine table and stared hard at the ultrasound, heaving a deep, blissful sigh. Resisting the silly urge to kiss the piece of paper, she put it back in the Ziploc bag where she had been keeping it safe since her return home from Dr. A's office, and placed the baggie in her handbag.

Hannah popped the last half of lemon cookie into her mouth—there would be time to worry about calories later, months later; these cookies were that good—and stacked the coffee cups and plates. Grabbing the used napkins with one hand, she cleared the dishes with the other, pleased with her own efficiency.

But somehow she was less than satisfied with the way the meeting with the Witches had turned out. Marla and Amibeth were every bit as shocked as Hannah had expected, yet their enthusiasm was lacking. They had questioned her at length.

"When are you due?" This first came from Marla, ever pragmatic, and was the only easy question to answer. According to Dr. A's calculations, her due date was May 15th.

Naturally, Amibeth was the one who asked, "How are you feeling?" Hannah could only respond in the same vague way she had to Natty. In the few intervening days, she still had not been able to put her overwhelming emotions into words.

The questions continued. There was more, much more, they wanted to know: Did she notice any differences in her mood, her appetite, her skin, her hair? What did Ryan say; what had Natty said? Her parents? Only once did the three of them share a laugh. It came when Marla asked, in typically bold fashion, "Tell me, and be explicit: Did you and Ryan do anything differently the night of conception?"

Hannah almost spit out her decaf. "This is Ryan we're talking about, Marla!"

"I guess we have our answer, then," Marla responded with a shrug.

"I mean, it was good, maybe even great because of the wine, but I wouldn't say it was *different*."

And that was that. Once again, Hannah had misjudged people she thought she knew well. Where were the whoops of joy, the warm hugs? The celebratory dances around the kitchen? Perhaps they were too old for that now. Too serious. Or too jealous, she acknowledged with a frown. Hannah had nabbed the brass ring, won the lottery. What had she done to deserve it?

Was this baby some kind of divine reward? And if so, for what? Hannah wasn't much given to introspection, but she figured she was neither as good nor as bad as anyone else. If whoever was doling out rewards based them on behavior, Amibeth would have won: Amibeth the kind, the generous, the tolerant. Recycler of plastics, baker of cookies, rescuer of kittens, forgiver of all sins ... well, almost all, at least until recently. Hannah had always thought Amibeth, with her endless well of patience, would have been a wonderful mother—better than she had been, certainly. Who knows how Natty might have benefited from a mother who was so nurturing and virtually imperturbable, instead of someone who had an admittedly short fuse?

Or if the reward was for devotion, this prize should have gone to Marla and Gene, who still walked hand-in-hand; who kissed under the mistletoe on a holiday they didn't even celebrate; who giggled like adolescents at each other's jokes and would name each other as their best friends. Look at the job they'd done with Niko! They had turned him around and their marriage was somehow the stronger for it. Surely they deserved this happiness more than Hannah and Ryan.

Instead, somehow this treasure had landed in Hannah's lap, or to be more precise, in her womb, and now she was forced to confront the notion that it wasn't perhaps the ideal situation, what with Ryan being totally against it and Natty feeling more alienated than usual.

And why now, dear God? Why now, when her body had started down the road to old age, when an everyday blessing was viewed as freakish, when friends and family looked askance instead of celebrating?

As Hannah expected, God was silent. She suspected He—or She—was having a good chuckle at her expense.

HANNAH 1:9

After dinner, Hannah enjoyed a cup of decaf tea and a ladyfinger while reading a brand-new copy of *What to Expect When You're Expecting (Fifth Edition)*. She had given up wearing even her "fat jeans" now and was much more comfortably attired in her very first pair of maternity slacks from B. Fruitful. So deeply engrossed was she that Ryan's matter-of-fact voice startled her when he sat down beside her and spoke.

"You wanted to talk, Hannah. So let's talk."

This was a surprise: he had been avoiding her for nearly two weeks, and she had pretty much settled into the guest bedroom as a permanent location. They had been cordial to each other and she still cooked his dinner, but there was little interaction beyond that. He stayed late at the office, visited the gym, went out for drinks with his friends. There were no cuddles, certainly no sex, practically no conversation at all. Strangely, it didn't disturb her as much as she would have thought. Hannah was so focused on the changes taking place in her body, and the anticipation of what would come next, she didn't notice that Ryan was drifting away.

"I've been wanting to have a conversation about this, but it never seemed to be the right time," Ryan continued, "and then the pregnancy happened."

Ryan's tone was disconcerting. He seemed agitated and wasn't even trying to be conciliatory. This was not typical behavior for him, even when a major fight was brewing.

Hannah pushed her mug and plate away and reached for his hand. "What is it, Ryan? Will you tell me what's wrong?"

And waited.

By way of response, Ryan placed a well-thumbed manila folder on the table, tapping his fingertips on it. He was clearly reluctant to speak.

"These," he finally said with a heavy sigh, "are our finances. The most recent ones, anyway."

Now Hannah knew something was definitely wrong. Ryan had always taken pleasure in handling their finances: researching stocks, reading *Forbes* and *The Wall Street Journal*, watching their assets accumulating. He had once told Hannah it was like a game, rearranging the pieces to see how far they could take their family. His goal had always been a comfortable retirement, one in which they could buy, as Natty already put it, "a golf condo in South Carolina" and still take the trips they had never taken—to Europe, to the Holy Land, maybe even on an African photo safari.

"Remember back when the recession started, Hannah? When the internet bubble burst in 2008 and the housing market tanked?"

"Sure, I remember it. It was awful. We lost a ton of money in the stock market."

"Right. The thing is …" And here Ryan stopped, deliberating. "The thing is, Hannah, it was worse than I let on."

"Worse than you let on? You barely slept for weeks. It was a couple of years before our situation recovered."

"Yeah, about that. Our situation didn't exactly recover."

"I don't understand. What do you mean?"

"It means that I was investing on margin."

"On margin?" The term was foreign to Hannah.

"See, things were going so well in the market up until 2008 that I was investing more than we actually had, with a loan from the brokerage. I overreached because I couldn't see a downside. The market was going up and up, every single day. And when the market started heading down, I invested more, thinking it was a temporary setback that I could use to our advantage. A once-in-a-lifetime buying opportunity. Then everything collapsed so quickly that I didn't have a chance to extricate myself."

"But … I don't get it. Where did the money come from?"

"I refinanced the office."

"Refinanced? You already owed money on the practice from buying out Herb when he retired, right? And then you bought new equipment in 2010; didn't you still owe for all of that?"

"Yes. And now I owe more." He looked down at the table. "And on the house, as well."

"But …" Hannah was baffled. "But we don't have a mortgage on the house."

"We do now. I'm sorry, sweetheart."

Well, that certainly explained their ever-increasing arguments about money. Bracing herself, Hannah asked, "How much … how much do we still have?"

"That's the thing, Hannah. It's not really a question of how much we still have. It's a question of how much we still owe."

"We're in debt."

"In a word: yes."

Clearing her throat to clear her mind as well, Hannah said, in a weak voice, "Well, how much do we still owe? I mean, it's been years, hasn't it? It can't be all that bad."

"The good news is that I've been paying it down, and it's gotten manageable. In round numbers, we only owe about $50,000 on the house."

"Oh, my God," Hannah said, letting out a long, uneven breath. "So how can you even think of retiring now?"

"Well, the house has to be worth at least $450,000, based on the sales I've seen in our area. Actually, the Wilkers just sold for $385K, and our house is much nicer than theirs and on a bigger piece of property. As far as the practice goes, it's always been profitable, and it's in a good location. I brought a broker in, casually at first, y'know, to crunch the numbers and assess the value and, well, I was planning on surprising you, maybe for your birthday: it turns out that he found me a buyer. Young guy named Morales."

"A buyer for the practice?"

"Yes, and it's a really good offer, Hannah. Better than I expected, frankly. After selling the house and the practice, we should have no problem getting ourselves a little condo and having plenty of money to live on comfortably for the rest of our lives, if we're careful."

Live comfortably if we're careful. Hannah could feel the blood rising to her face, like the red line in an old mercury thermometer. "But Ryan, we owned the house outright! And the practice was so doing well! How could I not know about all of this? We're *partners* in this marriage. Why didn't you tell me?"

"Why? Because, Hannah, I was trying to make it all work, and I didn't want to worry you. It was a tough time: we were still catching up from all the infertility treatments, and we had a young child to support! You weren't working, which, don't get me wrong, was actually a very good thing, considering how much attention Natty ended up needing. You had plenty on your plate without this adding to your burden.

"But since you asked," Ryan added, apparently prepared to go all in to defend his decisions, "I didn't *have* to let you know. My parents left the house to me, not *us*." Another point of contention, an old argument. Ryan's parents had never liked Hannah, always treating her as an interloper. Hannah hadn't shed a single tear when Mr. Murrow passed away at the age of fifty-seven from a massive heart attack a couple of years after they married. "And the practice is also in my name. I didn't need your *permission*."

So much for their partnership. "When you put it that way," Hannah said numbly, "I suppose not."

Looking a little chagrined, Ryan switched tacks. "Look, Hannah, we don't need a lot to live on. Once we sell the house and the practice and get out from under all the expenses and taxes, all we'll owe is maintenance and utilities on the condo and the usual monthly expenses: food, insurance, whatever. We'll be okay."

He stopped, took a breath. "That is, if we don't have another child."

"Well, Ryan," Hannah replied, "everything you've just told me notwithstanding, I think you'd better get used to the idea that we're having another child."

Ryan set his jaw stubbornly. "And what if I don't want to get used to the idea? Another child affects my life as well as yours!"

"Your life!" Hannah felt the words lodge in her throat and coughed to get them out. "You put us into debt without consulting me—hell, without even mentioning it to me *for ten years*. Doesn't *that* affect *my* life, too?"

She stood, hurt and anger welling up inside her. "I was upfront with you, Ryan. I told you about the baby *the day I found out*. We would have had plenty of time to plan for the unexpected expenses. You don't want to have this baby? Fine. I'll go it alone, then." Hannah's voice began rising, and Sadie howled. "Once the baby is born, we'll sell this house, pay off the mortgage you created, and you can take your half of what's left and do whatever the fuck you want with YOUR life!"

Hannah grabbed the folder from the table with both hands and flung it, as hard as she could, directly at Ryan, scattering the meticulously organized papers all over the kitchen floor. Raising her chin, she walked purposefully out of the room and headed upstairs to the guest bedroom with Sadie nipping at her heels, barking at the disturbance. When she reached the haven of the bedroom, she slammed the door as hard as she could, wincing as she inadvertently twisted her shoulder.

Sitting on the bed, breathing heavily, Hannah waited with balled fists for the tears to come. Yet surprisingly, she didn't feel like crying at all. Instead, she felt deeply angry: at Ryan for his years of deceit; at herself, for not bothering even to ask about their finances or to notice that he was keeping something significant from her. Her heart ached, and she questioned herself, as she had in the two or three times during their marriage when it seemed likely they wouldn't make it to their next anniversary, whether she and Ryan had ever been really on the same page. Not for the first time, she acknowledged that deciding to marry him within six months of their first blind date, while she was still hurting from her breakup with the Category 5 hurricane that had been Andy, hadn't been the best idea. A little too desperate for stability, she'd walked right into the first relationship where sturdy dependability was the primary attribute, taken a quick look around to determine that its walls would hold and that its old-fashioned upholstered furnishings were unlikely to wound her tender spots, and had decided to set up house.

Hannah's love for Ryan had been and still was very real, yet it never was a raging fire to begin with and had cooled considerably over the years. Now it burned roughly with the heat and ferocity of a child's Fourth of July sparkler—a warm glow that spoke more of their history together than their future. They were pleasant companions when they were getting along, had been a good parenting team to Natty. But what was left to salvage now?

And for the very first time, Hannah considered the possibility that she might just have to make a go of this pregnancy on her own. But was she up to it? To become a single mother at fifty-five? Whether he had planned for it or not, Ryan would have to support the baby financially, regardless of his wishes. Surely he wouldn't try to fight child support; he was better than that. Or so Hannah thought. But then, she'd also thought he was fiscally responsible and irreproachably truthful. It turned out she didn't really know him that well at all, after almost thirty years.

The finances were only one aspect. Leaving this house, the only home Natty would ever remember having, was going to be a hardship. And Sadie, dear Sadie ... well, Sadie was *her dog*. Unquestionably, Hannah would have to find a place where she'd be allowed to keep her.

Would she get lonely, worn out? Hannah always gave Ryan credit for being a wonderful father to Natty: attentive, caring, the proper combination of indulgent and strict. Hannah had always been the disciplinarian and Ryan, the nurturer. When the high school phoned to say that Natty had skipped out three days in a row in her junior year, Hannah was the one who had answered the call and enforced the punishments: the month-long grounding, the withdrawal of her iPod and her allowance. But it was Ryan who had coaxed her back, however reluctantly, not only back to school but to making up missed work. It was a gift he had. Now Hannah wondered how this new child would fare with only one parent to provide both the nurturing and the discipline—and how she would fare, as well. Would she burn out without anyone to provide her respite? As difficult as Natty had been, this situation had the potential to be a lot worse.

For Hannah knew full well what continuing with this pregnancy could mean. She had done her research, hours of it, and had stared, grimly but unflinchingly, at the data and the photographs. She told no one of the nightmares she had started having: giving birth to monsters, to chimeras; watching panicky exchanges between the attending OB-GYNs and horrified looks from passersby. Yet she kept thinking, "Just one more week, one more week." If it turned out that Dr. A saw any obvious anomalies, there would still be time to terminate. And even as she reassured herself of that option, she wondered if she could bring herself to do it. She had grown to love the changes her pregnancy had begun to make in her body—the fullness of her breasts, the new youth in her skin and hair, the certain knowledge that life was growing inside her—and could no longer imagine herself without them.

So, what now? The conversation with Ryan had an air of finality to it. How surprised would he be if she actually decided to get herself a lawyer! She had faith in Amibeth's judgment; she would call her tomorrow to get the name and number, just in case. If Ryan wanted to play a game of chicken, Hannah could give as good as she got.

There was a knock at the door, and Ryan poked his head in. "Seems to me, it's time for us to consider making this separation of ours official," he said, closing the door as he retreated.

A lawyer it is, then.

HANNAH 1:10

"What the hell, Mom!"

"Good morning to you too, Natt … Natasha," Hannah said calmly. (Weeks in, using Natty's full given name was still awkward.) While it was a surprise that Natty had called at 9 in the morning when Hannah assumed she would still be either asleep or in class, she had long ago become accustomed to her daughter's dramatics.

"What did you do?"

"What do you mean, what did I do?" Why did she always assume that it was her mother who had done something wrong?

"Dad tells me that you guys are separating."

"Well, that certainly was fast. I wish he'd be that quick fixing the garbage disposal."

"Mom, don't joke! He says you're being unreasonable about the pregnancy, and that he can't even have a conversation with you about it. *Are* you splitting up?"

Hannah sighed. "Yes, we're separating. We've actually been separated for a couple of weeks now, anyway, if you want to get technical. And truth be told, it was your father who wouldn't discuss the pregnancy. Every time I tried to talk with him about the baby, he shut me down. He wouldn't say anything about it except that we shouldn't have it. And do you know why he doesn't want to have it?"

"Well, for one thing, he thinks you're both too old to be starting out as parents again."

"Well, partly that. But the real reason is because he doesn't think we have the money to do it. When the stock market crashed in 2008, we were overextended, way overextended, and apparently now we won't be able to have the retirement we'd planned. Dad has calculated what he thinks we can afford, and a baby doesn't enter into the equation."

Natty was quiet for a moment. Then she exclaimed, "But he also said there are going to be problems with the baby, serious birth defects!"

Hannah bit her lip. She needed to be careful not to say anything definitive one way or the other. "He doesn't know that for a fact. No one knows that for a fact. Yes, the probability of birth defects at my age is higher, but then again, what was the likelihood I would even get pregnant? Astronomical. Unthinkable.

"Isn't it possible, Natasha," Hannah said softly, though she knew Natty would resist the idea, "that something bigger than the two of us is at work here, and that there's a real reason for this baby to be born?"

Sure enough, Natty, a declared atheist, snorted. "You know, Mom," she added, "it's still early enough to end the pregnancy."

Hannah wasn't surprised Natty had taken this route. In fact, she was proud to have raised her daughter to believe in a woman's agency over her own body, considered it a triumph that Natty's politics were more like her mother's than her conservative father's. Nevertheless, she said, "I am not having an abortion. End of story."

"I don't see why not. You're, like, the perfect candidate: unexpected pregnancy, high-risk, first trimester, unwilling partner. You've been pro-choice your whole fucking life. Don't be a hypocrite!"

"That's right, I'm solidly pro-choice. But you know what that means, Natty? Being pro-choice means that *I get to choose what I want to do.* Continuing the pregnancy and having the baby is a choice, too. And that's what I intend to do.

"And as for your father, I told him that if he doesn't want to be part of this child's life, I'll go it alone."

Natty went silent again for a moment. When she spoke, her voice sounded younger than it had in years. Hannah's heart ached a little for her.

"I can't believe he wouldn't want to raise the baby with you, Mom. That doesn't seem like him at all."

Neither did getting us into debt, Natty, but here we are, Hannah thought sadly.

"So what are you gonna do?"

"I'm going to take things one day at a time and hope for the best. In the meantime, since there's plenty of room in the house for the two of us, there's no reason for me to go anywhere else. I'll be at home, like always. Your dad will, too, at least for the time being.

"And please, don't take Dad's word for everything without asking me, as well. Sometimes the situation is more complicated than it first appears. Okay?"

"Okay. I'll talk to you soon?"

Hannah smiled, anticipating at least some contact with her daughter in the near future. "All right, Natasha. Soon." The impossible was becoming increasingly possible.

From her permanent residence in the guest room, speaking as little to Ryan as possible, Hannah found to her shock that—absent the occasional intimacy—it didn't make much difference in their relationship at all. Between his work and his visits to the gym, and their lack of common ground on any subject ranging from movies to politics to what constituted an interesting news item, she was amazed they had managed to stay married as long as they had. Now that Natty was grown and very nearly on her own, what was there to talk about, anyway? The weather? She wondered how many couples divorced late in life from the sheer boring sameness of their interactions, when they didn't have life-altering news like an unexpected pregnancy or a concealed debt to derail them.

There were new elements to Hannah's routines now: greater attention to her diet, longer but more sedate walks with Sadie, a nap in the afternoon. In between, she met all her local friends for lunch and coffee, telling her story over and over, having a glass of sparkling water instead of a glass— or two—of wine. She had mental lists of the people she had told, the people she had yet to tell, and ticked them off one by one. Once the latter had become short enough and as she safely hit the three-month mark, with the baby still healthy and growing, Hannah posted the news—along with the ultrasound—on Facebook.

"Call *Ripley's Believe It or Not!*" she wrote, aging herself even with her announcement. "I'm pregnant!"

The reactions she got there, from distant relatives, high school buddies, and long-forgotten friends-of-friends, weren't what she had hoped. There were "likes" and "loves," of course, but they were outweighed by the "wows," and even several that said "ha-ha," which she couldn't understand at all. What was even remotely funny? While nearly everyone who commented congratulated her, some of them asked for more of an explanation. Hannah provided it every time, at first gladly, and then with irritation. People began to challenge her decisions, second-guessing her, occasionally even insulting her. One "friend" she'd acquired somewhere over the years shared some very graphic and inappropriate thoughts about what Ryan might have done to cause the pregnancy. Another slammed her for daring to go against "the natural order of things." She ended up having to block eleven people.

After only one trimester, Hannah found herself wondering how she would manage the next six months.

TRIMESTER 2

HANNAH 2:1

"You need help with what, now?"

"I'd like to start a blog, Natasha, and I don't have the first idea of what to do."

"A blog?!" Natty giggled. "That's what it sounded like on your message, but I thought for sure I must have heard you wrong." She stopped herself, then said: "I don't know, Mom. It seems to me anyone who is that clueless about setting up a blog has no business writing one!"

Hannah, embarrassed, stayed silent.

"Okay, Okay, it's actually really easy; I can walk you through it no problem. Can I ask what it's about, or should I take a stab at it?"

"What do you think?"

"Your 'miracle' baby, right?" Natty's tone was neutral, lacking the edge Hannah had feared.

"Yes."

"Uh-huh, no surprise there. But why?"

Hannah had asked herself this very question. She had always found personal blogs self-indulgent and had said as much to Natty on at least one occasion that she could remember. Now she had a better understanding of what motivated the writers: a need to connect with others, even strangers, who might be interested in what she had to say. A need for validation, a desire to be heard. She was, admittedly, feeling isolated when she thought she'd be on top of the world, and she didn't like the feeling.

"I guess I want to share my story, spread the news?" It came out as a question; her lack of confidence showed. "Even if I'm just shouting into the void. Maybe someone else will want to listen." She paused. "Maybe someone else will relate."

Natty's response came after a couple of beats, during which Hannah held her breath. "Okay, that's legit. There are tons of mommy blogs out there; I suppose the world can handle another one. At least you've got a fresh angle. Do you want me to come over and show you?"

"Yes, please," Hannah said eagerly.

When Natty arrived at the house later that afternoon, she was all business. "So where do you want to do this?" she announced as she walked in.

Hannah sat her down at the kitchen table with a laptop and a plate of fresh chocolate chip cookies, pretending not to notice how Natty's eyes lit up.

"So here's a site a lot of people use," Natty said with her mouth full of cookie, typing in the URL and brushing away the crumbs that had fallen onto Hannah's laptop. "It gives a nice, contemporary look with plenty of style options, while being generally user-friendly." She took another bite, then looked up at Hannah. "First things first, though: you have to choose a name. What are you going to call your blog?"

"What am I ..." Hannah echoed, the question taking her by surprise. She sank down into the chair next to Natty. "I guess I hadn't thought about it. I don't know; should I use my name? What do other people use?"

"Well, it varies. Some people use their names if they're trying to be professional; others come up with a short but catchy title, capturing what they'll be discussing."

"So what should I do?"

"For you, I think go with short and catchy. You're not really looking for name recognition; you have something to say." Natty squinted at her, then at the screen.

"How about ... 55 and Pregnant?"

"But I'm fifty-four."

"Duh, Mom," Natty sighed with dramatic exasperation. "You're going to be fifty-five soon, and for the rest of your pregnancy. And it plays off that TV show with the expectant teens."

"I don't know. I'm not sure that's the association I want. What about, um, Hannah's Miracle?"

"Really?" Natty made a disagreeable face, a face Hannah knew too well: the one made by the little girl who didn't want to put on the "ugly" sweater Hannah had spent weeks knitting; who refused to try the "icky" coquille St. Jacques Hannah had sweated over for Ryan's birthday. It was the same face Natty had worn as she got older, when Hannah insisted on homework being finished before TV time, or tried to enforce a curfew. The reminiscences made her eyes fill.

"I'm sure we could come up with something better," Natty continued. "But if that's the way you want to go, I'll make sure it's available."

Hannah watched as Natty's fingers flew over the keyboard, reserving the blog name in a matter of seconds and sealing it with a decisive tap of the "Enter" key.

"I'm not even going to ask you to choose a design template; I think you'll get overwhelmed," Natty continued as she scrolled through the options. Hannah opened her mouth to object but closed it immediately. Natty was right; there were too many choices, and she had no idea what to base her selection on. "I'll pick one for you; something clean and easy.

"So, now you're set up and you've gotta start writing. Here's how you enter text," Natty instructed, typing in *Look at me, everyone, I'm pregnant!* "And this is where you choose a font.

"Blogging is all about content. Be yourself; develop your own style. But if you don't really want to be 'shouting into the void,' as you put it, you also want people to follow you, so make sure everyone you know is aware of the blog. Post about it on Facebook, for starters. And you'll want to research 'mommy blogs' to get an idea of how successful bloggers operate; figure out how they get followers. You have an interesting story and I won't be surprised if you get some traction."

Natty glanced at the time on the screen and said with exaggerated surprise, "Oh, wow, will you look at the time? I'm outta here." After quickly folding the remaining cookies into a napkin, she scooped up her mass of keys from where they sat splayed on the table like an octopus stranded on the sand and hustled to the door.

"Good luck with the blog," she called out over her shoulder as she let herself out.

"Thank you," Hannah said in a whisper, to the empty hallway and the closed door.

Sitting back at the table, she pulled the laptop toward her and, full of doubts, stared at the words on the screen. Natty had set her up with the site, chosen a format, showed her how to input text … and now what? How does anyone know what to write on these things? How do you share your most intimate joys and sorrows with complete strangers?

Where do you start? *Look at me, everyone, I'm pregnant!?* Not with that, certainly.

Hitting the "backspace" key, Hannah watched Natty's sentence disappear one letter at a time. Then, with her index fingers resting lightly on the "F" and "J" of the keyboard, the others lined up alongside, Hannah sat up straight and willed the words to come.

They didn't. Hannah had never managed better than a B minus in her English classes, and even then she had often pulled it out more on the strength of her presentation skills than on her sentence structure or vocabulary. She'd never thought of herself as a strong writer, even when she had something important she wanted to say. Like now.

Feeling a need to break the inertia, which was starting to make her itchy, she typed the first thoughts that came into her head:

"My name is Hannah Murrow. I've been infertile my whole life, but now I'm pregnant for the first time. I am 54 years old. It's a miracle. *My* miracle."

It wasn't elegant—hell, it wasn't even good—but it was a start.

HANNAH 2:2

" I lied."

"I'm sorry, what?"

Burdened by an outsized feeling of guilt, Hannah had returned to B. Fruitful to speak to Ke'isha and set the record straight. She pretended to look through a stack of deliciously soft cashmere sweaters while she waited impatiently for the saleswoman to finish speaking to the only other person in the store: a tall, immensely broad young man roughly the size of Hannah's armoire, who looked out of place among the feminine trappings. They were discussing the prices of coats, their tags draped over his fingers, resting like tiny white flower petals on the warm, dark earth of his huge hand.

Finally separating herself from the man, Ke'isha approached Hannah, smiling broadly until Hannah blurted out, "I lied."

"Oh, I remember you," Ke'isha said, recognition dawning. "Hannah, right? Didn't you come in to buy your daughter her first maternity clothes?" Her face fell. "Oh, no. Is everything all right?"

Hannah shook her head: first yes, then no. "I lied. I came in here and told you my daughter was having a baby. But it's not her. It's me!" She held her palms up and shrugged, a smile breaking through. "I'll be fifty-five in January, and I'm pregnant for the first time!"

"Well, isn't that something!" While Ke'isha seemed genuinely surprised, her hands raised to her face—her long, curved nails, now painted red, acting as parentheses around her eyes—at least she didn't ask if Hannah was kidding. The two stood there together as Ke'isha absorbed the news.

Finally, Hannah said, "I wanted to let you know because … actually, I have no idea why I wanted to let you know." She laughed.

"I'm glad you did. Can I assume that congratulations are in order?"

"Oh, yes. Yes; it's a dream come true."

"That's wonderful; I'm so happy for you! So, can I help you find something to add to your wardrobe today?"

"Not right now. I …" B. Fruitful's line was pricey, and having already indulged once before, Hannah felt she needed to show restraint. "Not right now."

Ke'isha nodded. "Well, at least stay and have some tea and a macaron." She led Hannah to the corner opposite the try-on rooms where a small table bore a coffeemaker, a selection of teas, and a tray of tempting pastel macarons. Hannah, who'd never met a cookie she didn't like, supposed it had been exactly in the same place during her previous visit, but she had been too excited and overwhelmed to notice. She sat down in one of the floral upholstered chairs, sighing with pleasure. After devouring a pink cookie, she had a yellow one, not realizing how hungry she'd gotten. Ke'isha watched with an indulgent smile.

Hannah smiled back, yet because she had no intention of making a purchase, it felt as if she was freeloading. "How did you come to work here?" she asked awkwardly.

Ke'isha laughed. "I own the place." Bowing dramatically, she added, "Ke'isha Gibson, entrepreneur."

"Wow, really?" She hoped she didn't sound or look as incredulous as she felt. Thinking of Natty, Hannah couldn't imagine a young woman her age so focused and motivated. And successful. Her respect for Ke'isha increased.

"Yes, really! Eric!" Ke'isha called to the young man who was now refolding a stack of sweaters with a speed and delicate grace that belied his size. "Come meet a special customer."

He crossed the store in four long strides. "Eric Dieujuste," he said, extending his hand down to Hannah, who found hers completely swallowed up in his. It was like putting on a boxing glove.

"Hannah Murrow."

"Nice to meet you."

"Eric is my fiancé," Ke'isha explained. "He works for me."

"Works *with* you," Eric corrected.

"Oh, please!" Ke'isha shook her head, her hands on her hips. "Eric currently works *for* me. As soon as he finishes his MBA, I'll be taking him on as a partner. But not before." Eric rolled his eyes in a way that said they'd had this conversation—or maybe this mock argument—many times before. "Hannah here is pregnant for the very first time."

"Hey! How about that! Congratulations!" He grabbed her hand again, shaking it heartily.

Hannah nodded her thanks.

"Now," Ke'isha said, putting on a frown that was clearly meant to mean the opposite, "get back to work!"

"Okay, okay!" Eric laughed. He bent down to give K'eisha a peck on the cheek, which she received with a glow of delight. "Nice to meet you, Ms. Murrow."

"Hannah, please. And it was lovely to meet you. I'm sure you two have a bright future ahead of you."

Eric strode back across the store and resumed his repetitive folding with an almost Zen-like patience, more than Hannah would expect from someone who was working on an advanced degree.

"An MBA, huh? What did Eric study in undergrad?"

"Math. Man loves his numbers; everything logical and in order. And he's so good at it. He's going to be great for the business. He was good at football, too: really good. A real star in high school, a defensive guard—quick on his feet, smart with his hands. State offered him a full-ride scholarship to play but his mom said, 'No way I'm going to let a brain like that get scrambled playing football.' They argued about it a lot; ooh, did they ever! His dad wanted him to play, too, but Mom won out. I think ultimately Eric's relieved. I know I am."

Ke'isha certainly seemed to have her life in order. *I'll bet her mother is proud*, Hannah thought. A business of her own; a smart, ambitious fiancé … She was already thinking of Natty and Jonathan, her latest, and wondering what kind of future they could possibly have together—if it lasted. Natty's track record wasn't encouraging.

⁓

HANNAH WAS SURPRISED WHEN, over the course of the next week, Natty started calling with inconsequential questions, then showing up around the house. What was more surprising was that she seemed to be doing it to spend time with Hannah rather than to pick a fight or fill her own fridge. All the while she was pleasant and even attentive. In return, Hannah made a special effort to be understanding and sympathetic and to call her daughter "Natasha," as she preferred.

On one of those visits, Natty was accompanied by Jonathan. Hannah greeted him with a wary smile, which he returned with a much warmer one that appeared genuine. He had a nice smile, Hannah decided, though he might want to take care of those rotated incisors.

They had seated themselves somewhat formally in the living room and, as she always did, Hannah fretted about the antique walnut coffee table that had been her paternal grandmother's. It was a magnificent piece from the 1920s, with a distinctive burl and intricate carvings around the sides and legs. When Dolores and Frank had moved into Best of Times and distributed their belongings among the family, Hannah and her sister-in-law, Missy, had nearly come to blows when the table was gifted to Hannah instead of Jason. It was easily the nicest piece in Hannah's entire modest house, and Missy always maintained it belonged in a more compatible environment, like her own tastefully designed home. On the rare occasions when Missy visited, she always eyed the piece enviously, which made it even more treasured in Hannah's eyes.

Hannah kept an eye on it when Jonathan drew his laptop out of his backpack, unsure if he knew the value of nice things. From a couple of frightening near-misses, she was aware that at least one of Natty's previous boyfriends had not. Natty's large clutch of keys was also a concern, but at least Natty knew how her mother cherished the piece and sensibly set them down on the rug at her feet. Thankfully, Jonathan's laptop stayed on his lap.

"So, Mom," Natty said, with the ingratiating smile and businesslike tone of a saleswoman. Hannah stared at her quizzically.

"Jonathan and I have come up with a brilliant way to help you with this, um, unusual change in your physical circumstances."

Hannah's brows shot up.

Natty went on: "I mean, a way to help you out financially. I know Dad's being a dick, and you'll probably need more money once the baby is born ...."

"Your father will support his child," Hannah insisted, embarrassed Natty would bring up such a sensitive topic in front of Jonathan. "I'm sure of it." If Ryan didn't come to his senses on his own, the courts would ensure he did. "We just haven't worked the details out yet. You should know at least that much about him."

"True, but aren't you going to need money for college? God only knows what it's going to cost by then."

Jonathan took over. "So here's the thing, Mrs. Murrow. Natasha and I have been following your blog, and we're impressed with how many followers you've managed to amass with your, let's say, *unpolished* style and total lack of promotion or sponsors. Just shy of 23,000 followers now! That's no small feat. We think you have something really special which could be huge, and profitable, if positioned correctly. And Natasha and I can take care of everything.

"Here's a quick rundown of what we think you'll need, as a start." His eyes gleaming, he ticked off on his fingers: "First, a new Facebook page; naturally it'll be a different one from the one you use every day.

"Then there's the blog. If you want to keep writing it, that's cool, but we'd really like Natasha to take over, with input from you, of course. Do you have any idea how well she writes? And you'll want to be on Instagram and Twitter, of course," he continued, "and you'll need a retail website, linked to the blog, for all the merch."

"Wait, MERCH? What's merch?"

"*Merchandise*, Mom. For heaven's sake, keep up!" Natty exclaimed. "We'll do T-shirts, definitely. Maternity clothes, obviously. Something hot and trendy, something the hipsters will take to. Jonathan and I will make up a logo. Give us a few days, we'll come up with everything. Jonathan's a genius at these things."

"I don't understand ...."

"I think we need to claim your domain name and your Twitter handle right away," Jonathan continued, "before someone cybersquats on them." At Hannah's deepening confusion, he clarified, "Cybersquatting, Mrs. Murrow, is when someone buys a domain that's likely to be needed by someone in the future and just sits on it until the potential owner comes along and wants to use it. Then the cybersquatter asks for a ridiculous amount of money to give it up."

"What *in the world* are you two talking about?"

"Your brand, Mom!" Natty said, her enthusiasm bubbling over. "We're talking about your *brand*."

"My brand."

"Yes," Jonathan agreed, nodding vigorously. "Your brand. And we're planning to call it," and he and Natty exchanged a mischievous look before he delivered the clincher, "*Saint Hannah*."

"What? Are you kidding? But that's ... blasphemous!" Hannah shouted, leaping to her feet.

Jonathan grinned. "That's what makes it hip!"

"No, no, no!" Hannah covered her face with her hands. *What the hell were they thinking?*

"Mom," Natty said, more gently, "you have an amazing story, a fairy tale, a miracle—isn't that the whole basis of your blog? People are hungry for it. Trust me, we have to jump on this, make it official before someone else does, and you're left negotiating for a percentage of something you already own. You don't want someone else profiting off your life, do you?"

"That's not going to happen," Hannah said faintly, settling back into her chair.

"You'd think it wouldn't," Jonathan said, shaking his head. "But all it'd take would be some smart entrepreneur, maybe a screenwriter looking for the next feel-good chick flick, and suddenly everyone is telling your story, except without your input."

Hannah shook her head. "Look, I've got the blog and a few thousand followers who are willing to listen to me rant about ... oh, the effects of prenatal vitamins on a middle-aged stomach or whatever, and send me nice messages to cheer me on. Why would the wider world care about some anonymous fifty-something woman from nowhere in particular getting pregnant?"

"You're kidding, right?" Jonathan said, staring at her in disbelief.

"Would everybody *please* stop saying that!"

Jonathan glanced at Natty, who gestured urgently for him to continue. "Human interest, Mrs. Murrow! Your story gives hope to the hopeless! That's why they'll care. You weren't on hormones; you weren't paying out a fortune for in-vitro fertilization.

"You're not ... I don't know, carrying a child for your daughter who can't do it herself. Think about it: you're the faithful believer who had her prayers answered. Who wouldn't be interested in that?"

There was a certain amount of truth to what Jonathan was saying. Hannah fidgeted with the hem of her shirt. She had already noticed a slight shift in behavior among the friends to whom she had told her news: they had begun to call more frequently, looking for updates. Hannah had to acknowledge that this might be just the sort of story that *People* magazine— and God help her, even the *Enquirer*—would eat up. So perhaps it *was* better for her, as Jonathan put it, to control the narrative.

"All right," she said reluctantly. "I'll think about it. *BUT* I would get approval on everything: logos, photos, what kind of information goes public. You got that?"

"Yes, ma'am!" Jonathan said, grinning.

In return, Hannah muttered, "Lord only knows what I'm getting myself into."

"There's just one more thing, Mom. From a brand perspective, that is ... How would you feel about letting your hair go completely gray?"

HANNAH 2:3

Turning right and then left, Hannah surveyed her new hairstyle in the mirror and, as much as she hated to admit it, acknowledged that Natty and Jonathan had been right. At first she had balked at the idea of going gray. Her whole idea of herself at fifty-five was that she would still be young, vital—in other words: *not old*. Unchanged. Vigorous exercise and a sensible diet had kept her from the excess heft that plagued so many of her peers, though she couldn't help the inevitable unsightly sagging or the redistribution of weight that, like continental drift, made permanent changes in the landscape (with the southern hemisphere becoming more prominently represented). She had long ago given up the idea of wearing a two-piece bathing suit, and she was quickly approaching the time when she might cease to go completely sleeveless. But Jonathan had made an excellent case for the gray, and she found she had been unable to argue with him.

"It's for the brand, Mom," Natty repeated.

"Go gray? Why would I want to do that?"

"You do whatever you're comfortable with, of course, Mrs. Murrow," Jonathan said. "But if you're in the market for a new look to go along with your new life, why not consider letting your natural gray come through? Your brand is all about a modern-day miracle and at the base of that miracle is your age. It's a unique and completely transformational event. Why would you hide or try to disguise it? If you look like you're in your forties, there's something a little less impressive about what you're selling. It's not uncommon enough. Many women well into their forties are having children these days; lots of celebrities are doing it. Yet if you embrace your age, if you juxtapose the glow of your complexion with the silver of your hair, then we really have an amazing message. Think about it, okay?"

"I think you missed your calling, Jonathan," Hannah laughed. "You should have been in sales. You can be very persuasive."

"I'm self-employed," he smiled. "So I have to be! Most of my working life is devoted to marketing myself, and any time I have left over is for actually doing the project."

TRUE TO THEIR WORD, Natty and Jonathan jumped into their roles with gusto. By the following day, StHannah.com and half-a-dozen variations were all under Jonathan's control, as were the appropriate Twitter and Instagram accounts. Hannah found herself appreciating this new, enthusiastic Natty and thought with some pride that her daughter had learned quite a bit in her business management classes.

It had taken Hannah a bit longer to jump on board, but once she had made an appointment with her colorist, Camille, and her stylist, Marinna, she became excited to make the change. When she was younger, Hannah had had the kind of naturally bright locks (not red, not orange, but that rare and desirable color her amateur numismatist father lovingly referred to as "1963 uncirculated penny") that dishwater blondes and mousy brunettes would have traded their 36D's for. As she'd aged, as her hair had mellowed into a duller color, like watered-down iced tea, she had first augmented it with highlights and then started dyeing it when gray roots appeared.

She was surprised to find the ladies at the salon equally enthusiastic, as they both independently admitted to Hannah that after seven years, they had long been eager to try something different for her. The new cut was exciting and flattering: her once shoulder-length hair now parted just to the side, curving around the edges of her ears and ending about two inches below her lobes.

Getting the gray right was another story. After being reassured several times that there was no danger to the baby, Hannah made a separate appointment for the time-consuming bleaching and dyeing process. Camille had her do a deep conditioning treatment the day she came in for her cut, but it wasn't until the following week that the two of them spent the better part of the day together as Hannah's beloved copper hue was stripped out and the gray was layered on.

It was … a statement. She felt unexpectedly powerful. Like singing "I Am Woman"—a reference, she thought ruefully, that would be lost on Natty and Jonathan. Why had she never considered this before?

Natty gasped when she saw the new look. "Mom! That. Is So. Cool." Hannah could actually hear the millennial punctuation being spoken aloud. She basked in her daughter's approval.

Jonathan whistled. "It's perfect," he agreed. "And it gives me an idea for a logo."

~⟍◌

Dr. A continued to be impressed by Hannah's progress, though her optimism was muted. "I would not have guessed that your pregnancy would be moving along so well, with so few complications. But I still need to caution you against taking too much for granted. It's very common to feel good, even uncommonly energetic, in your second trimester. At the very least, you might find your morning sickness is abating. But frankly we are in uncharted waters here.

"And you still have a long way to go. The upcoming months, even if everything continues to remain normal, will be challenging for you. Even young women experience new aches and pains. I would imagine you might find those magnified."

Given the extraordinary circumstances, Dr. A joined Daphne for Hannah's next ultrasound. Together they watched, fascinated, as the tiny fetus floated in its amniotic fluid. If Dr. A was jaded by the thousands of times she had seen the very same thing, she didn't let on. Hannah, for her part, was completely enthralled.

"Everything looks good," Dr. A continued. "There are no *visible* abnormalities, which, of course, does not mean that there are no hidden ones. We did the NIPT a couple of weeks ago, and now it's time we discussed doing some more advanced fetal testing."

"No."

"No?" Dr. A turned to Daphne, who, without being asked, stood up and left the room.

"Now, Hannah, you must consider ..."

"No," Hannah said again, more firmly. "It doesn't matter. I don't want to know."

Dr. A shook her head, her mouth a tight line. It was not an expression Hannah was accustomed to seeing on her doctor. "This is a very dangerous pregnancy, Hannah. You knew that from the outset. Just because everything appears fine from the ultrasound and the NIPT, that does not guarantee the child is going to be normal.

"The procedures are generally safe and ordinarily they're optional, but in your case, I have to strongly recommend you do at least one."

"Why?" Hannah asked, struggling up to her elbows. "I mean, you're testing for abnormalities. For Down syndrome and the like, right?"

"Chromosomal abnormalities, yes, and neurological defects. So you see ..."

"But you said the NIPT screens for Down syndrome." Noninvasive Prenatal Testing, in which her own blood was used with no risk to the pregnancy, was the only type Hannah was interested in having. "You said everything looked good. Isn't that enough?"

"Yes, NIPT *does* screen for a few of these conditions," Dr. A said. "And it is generally very accurate. But as I explained to you when you were first tested, NIPT can only tell you the *likelihood* of your fetus having certain issues. Your age lowers those odds considerably."

"But you know what?" Hannah replied. "It sure looks like someone wants me to have this baby, doesn't it? It's God's plan for me, if you believe in that sort of thing, or my destiny, my fate, my karma, if you want to look at it that way. I believe it. And no test result is going to change my mind. I'm not risking this pregnancy on the chance that something's wrong.

"Look, I understand your concerns, Dr. A. Really, I do. And I also understand your obligations. If you need me to sign a waiver of some kind, I have no problem with that. Send a whole team of lawyers in if you have to. But I'm not having an amniocentesis or any other invasive test. Not now. I'm going to carry this pregnancy to term, and I'm going to have this baby. I'm willing to take the risk."

"Even if it means you might give birth to a child with severe disabilities? Because that is …"

"I know, 'a greater than usual possibility' in my case," Hannah broke in, showing Dr. A that yes, she had been listening. Indeed, Hannah had already read that the chances of a child being born with Down syndrome, for example, leaped from 1 in 1,200 at age twenty-five to 1 in 100 at age forty. Who even knew what the odds were fifteen years later? It would give anyone pause.

Anyone *else*, of course.

Hannah wasn't afraid of Down syndrome. It was hardly the bogeyman it had been when she was growing up. There were of course other, more daunting outcomes. Yet she set her jaw, which now quivered slightly.

"If you insist. But yours is an unusual case, so I am going to refer you to Dr. Suzanne Felcher. She's at the university and is the region's top perinatologist, a maternal-fetal specialist. I spoke to her earlier today and she's expecting your call."

"Is that really necessary?" Hannah said, uneasily. Other than with Ryan, she had never had as long a relationship with anyone as she had with Dr. A. And the idea of introducing someone else into this pregnancy was as foreign to her as bringing a third party into their bedroom.

"I believe it is. Now, shall we continue? I promised you the fetal Doppler."

Hannah lay back down and Dr. A took out the device, both knowing this fight would likely be fought again and again in the next months. But for now, Hannah allowed herself to be carried away with her joy, the watery sound of the fetal heartbeat giving voice to the wonder she was feeling: a steady murmur of *wowowowowowowowow*.

HANNAH 2:4

Except for the inevitable exam table with stirrups, Dr. Felcher's exam room was so different from Dr. A's as to be nearly unrecognizable as serving the same purpose. For one thing, as Hannah gratefully noted, it was warm enough for a woman to be comfortable while naked. There was no dated knotty-pine paneling: everything was white, chrome, and black. It was modern, slick, high-tech, with brand-new equipment, some of which she had never seen. Hannah supposed that younger women would find all of it impressive or reassuring, but to her it lacked a certain human element. There were posters decorating the walls here, too, but they were also slicker and of newer vintage (© 2012), none from AnnaTomMichael Products. She wondered fleetingly if they'd gone out of business. And although Hannah could now examine the poster of the fetus without despair, she found she missed the hominess of the old poster back at Dr. A's.

Dr. Suzanne Felcher, too, was the polar opposite of Dr. A. She was tall and substantial—what her mother would euphemistically label a "big woman"—about Hannah's age or perhaps a bit younger, and wore well-tailored and clearly expensive clothes. She had unusual aqua-colored eyes, which Hannah, given her close proximity, immediately identified as contact lens-enhanced. Her wheat-blond hair was, to Hannah's fascination, blow-dried and lacquered into a helmet-like coif of the kind that Hannah thought had gone out of style years ago, and her too-wide mouth sported lipstick the exact shade of her deep blood-red sweater.

Most remarkable, though, was her precise, overly enunciated manner of speaking. Hannah got the strong impression that Dr. Felcher had had some diction training, perhaps to rid herself of an undesirable regional accent. Hannah thought briefly about Eliza in "My Fair Lady," but then realized the overall effect was more akin to an aged-out Fox News blonde seen through a fisheye lens. It was slightly terrifying.

"You might be interested to know that we don't like to call pregnancies like yours 'geriatric' anymore," Dr. Felcher explained as she finished Hannah's preliminary exam. "Those of us who choose this especially rewarding field of obstetrics refer to women like yourself, having their first child after the age of thirty-five, simply as being of advanced maternal age." She sat back and removed her exam gloves.

Hannah gave an unenthusiastic laugh. "I'm not sure that's much better."

"You are, of course, an outlier, an extreme example," Dr. Felcher said—meticulously articulating each word as if dotting a series of "i's" as she dropped her used gloves into the bin—"and therefore your case is very important to document for future study. I'm so glad to have been brought on board, Hannah. I've been following your extraordinary pregnancy from the beginning through my dear friend Dr. Anandanarayan." Hannah admired the practiced ease with which the difficult name flowed off her tongue, although its very pronunciation implied that the two doctors did not have more than a nodding acquaintance. Nobody who knew her at all, neither patients nor colleagues, called her anything but Dr. A.

"Let me assure you that our team here will deliver the finest care available anywhere in the country."

"But Dr. A will still be my primary OB-GYN, right?"

"Of course; for now." The doctor smiled, aiming for warmth and sincerity and widely missing the mark, hitting somewhere in the neighborhood of patronizing. "Understand, Hannah, that there may come a time when Dr. Anandanarayan and her little practice will no longer be able to provide you and your baby with the kind of specialized care necessary to see you both through a successful birth. There's a reason she recommended me. The months ahead will likely provide many challenges. I've devoted my career, my life really, to helping high-risk mothers have healthy babies. I consider it the most important job in the world, a true calling.

"Now, there are two tests we could look at doing for you: an amniocentesis and a CVS, which is a chorionic villus sampling. I'm sure you're aware of the amnio."

"Yes, but ..."

Dr. Felcher stood up and moved across the room to stand next to the detailed poster illustrating a fetus in utero. "An amnio, of course, samples the amniotic fluid," she said, drawing a circle around the fetus with a finger. "A CVS is done a week or two earlier, right around now would be the time, and takes genetic material from the chorionic villi, these little growths over here, in the placenta." She wagged her fingers in an area of the uterus to which Hannah had never given much thought. "The genetic material in here is identical to the baby's. There's also the cordocentesis, which is, as its name implies, a blood sample taken from the umbilical cord. That's typically done at eighteen weeks." Still staring at the poster, Dr. Felcher added delicately, "But we'd rather not do that test, due to its risks."

"Speaking of risks," Hannah interrupted, "I'm not interested in any test that might endanger the pregnancy."

Her eyebrows raised, Dr. Felcher nevertheless spoke calmly. "Hannah, the risk of miscarriage as a result of a CVS is extremely low, around 0.7% to perhaps a high of a little over 1%."

"Too high."

"Really? Well, an amniocentesis poses an even lower risk, topping out around 0.1%. Perhaps we'll consider an amnio in a few …"

"No."

"Hannah."

"I just had this argument with Dr. A. You said yourself this is an extraordinary pregnancy, an extreme example." She felt herself growing angry. *Why wouldn't anyone listen?* "Any risk at all is too much. Bearing this child is the most important thing in the world to me."

"Then you'll understand why it's important to let a specialist handle it."

Hannah mulled this over as Dr. Felcher made notes on a tablet. She could never see being as comfortable with Dr. Felcher as she was with Dr. A, though she guessed that her feelings were no longer the point.

Minutes ticked by as the doctor continued to focus on her tablet. This, too, was different from the way Dr. A conducted an exam. Hannah drummed her fingers on the paper covering the exam table, wondering if Dr. Felcher had forgotten there was a patient in the room. In an effort to fill the silence, Hannah asked: "Do you have any children, Dr. Felcher?"

The question seemed to take Dr. Felcher by surprise, and she paused as if composing an answer. Her forehead tried to furrow, but Botox had apparently paid a visit. Finally she said, in her very measured way, "No; I have not been that fortunate. I was busy building my career and did not even meet my husband until I was in my late forties."

"Oh, is he in medicine, too?"

Dr. Felcher's body language indicated that she found this line of questioning overly personal. It hadn't occurred to Hannah, who knew all about Dr. A's husband—who was literally a rocket scientist with a doctorate from MIT—as well as their children and six grandchildren.

"No," she said, her lips stiff in obvious reluctance. "He's in television production."

Well, Hannah thought with amusement, that explains a lot: her clothes, her hair, her precise way of speaking.

"So you see," Dr. Felcher added briskly, "it was obviously too late for me. Too late for anyone." She smiled again. "Until I met you, of course. You're the game-changer." Turning away from Hannah, she murmured, "You can get dressed now. I'll see you in my office."

Game-changer: that was a new one. Hannah pulled on her clothes mechanically. Of course, the success of the blog had clued her into the intense interest in her pregnancy, and the responses she'd been receiving from her followers seemed to indicate that some other women saw her unexpected fertility as a symbol of hope for their own futures. But no one, Dr.

Felcher included, was going to use her as some sort of guinea pig or test case.

⁓

"Is THAT SUPPOSED to be me?"

Hannah looked at the logo doubtfully.

"Of course," Jonathan said. "It's stylized, but it's you all over."

It was, admittedly, a professional piece of artwork, and Hannah chided herself for underestimating Jonathan. His minimalist drawing used a few dashes and swoops of line to give the suggestion, the *impression,* of a gray-haired woman sporting Hannah's stylish new bob, with a halo perched jauntily just above her head like a beret. Behind a set of reading glasses, the woman was giving a saucy wink.

Hannah pursed her lips. "What's the wink for?"

"It's a wink at the impossibility of it all. It's a wink at those who don't believe miracles can happen. It's ... engaging and maybe a little provocative. What do you think?"

"What can I say?" Hannah smiled. "No wrinkles, no bags—I wish I looked that good."

Jonathan and Natty grinned at each other. His eyes flicked over her. "So, how are you feeling?"

"Amazing. The morning sickness is completely gone, as long as I remember not to take my vitamins on an empty stomach. Have you seen those things? They're huge! With enough iron in them to build a skyscraper."

"Good, good. That means you'll be feeling up to a little promotional activity?"

"Promotional activity? I'm not following."

"Mom," Natty jumped in, "there's a possibility that if this really takes off, we'll ask you to do … um, public appearances. Nothing strenuous, of course; just showing up."

"Showing up—to promote what?"

"Let me show you, Mrs. M," Jonathan said, flipping through some visuals on his tablet. He turned it around to show Hannah some mockups: T-shirts, beanies—even, good Lord, was that a nursing bra?—with the St. Hannah logo on them. "Here's some merch, the apparel side. At first we'll be selling it exclusively online, but as we get closer to the big day we might try to get into some brick-and-mortar retail outlets. It's always a struggle to get shelf space, but if we can make enough noise, we might be able to get a foot in the door."

Hannah thought about Ke'isha and B. Fruitful. She opened her mouth to mention it, then closed it. The whole enterprise might fail spectacularly, so it hardly seemed worth dragging Ke'isha into it. Hannah liked her too much.

"Or we could do a pop-up store," Natty interjected. "I've been scouting out some places locally for a good site."

"All right," Jonathan continued. "That's the clothing line. We could also offer the usual mugs, pens, stickers, and other accessories if you want to."

"Well, I certainly don't want anything cheesy." Hannah frowned.

Jonathan nodded at Natty, whose I-told-you-so smile Hannah knew so well. "Natasha has been saying the same thing. It will be all quality stuff, American-made. And of course, you'll have approval on everything, as we agreed."

Look at them, Hannah thought, *so full of excitement and hope*. It wasn't so much that Hannah was a pessimist, but she did consider herself a realist. There was no way she was going to dampen their enthusiasm with real-world facts about how many small businesses fail. And speaking of real-world facts ...

"Jonathan, how are you ... how are *we*," she amended, "funding this little enterprise?"

The question didn't seem to faze him at all, and in fact it was as if he had been waiting for Hannah to broach the subject.

"I have some money put away that ..."

Hannah reached out a hand and stopped him.

"No, forget it. I can't let you do that," she said. Based on the hole-in-the-wall studio apartment where he and Natty were currently residing and the threadbare clothes he wore every day, that nest egg could be the only thing standing between him and homelessness. Hannah couldn't help but think of Ryan and the difficult position he had put them in by taking such extravagant chances with their money. Of course, Natty and Jonathan were just starting out their adult lives, and without many financial responsibilities were in a better position to take such leaps of faith, but decisions they made now could plague them for years. *If, of course, they even stayed together that long.*

"I can't let you gamble your rainy-day fund on such a risky investment."

Natty's eyes swiveled from her mother to Jonathan, but she stayed silent. Jonathan grinned broadly and with surprising affection.

"No worries, Mrs. M. My, um, "rainy-day fund" will be sufficient. I'm in no danger of destitution. This is a chance I'm willing to take, because I have a good feeling about it. And about Natasha." And as he turned his bright smile on Natty,

Hannah was overcome with a wave of emotion she couldn't blame on her hormones.

She had seen Natty with many boyfriends, starting around age fifteen, but this was the first time one had looked at her daughter with such genuine love and not just lust or affected indifference. Maybe there was hope for this relationship, hope that it could outlast even the financial burden it was likely to put on them. Her heart ached for her own relationship with Ryan and what might have been. On the verge of tears, she sat up straighter and forced herself to get back to business.

"You know you're taking all the risk? I don't know if Natasha has told you, but I'm not in a position to make any kind of financial contribution." At Jonathan's nod, Hannah continued. "Suppose, against all odds, there are actually proceeds from this little venture. How do we plan to split those?"

"If there are profits after our expenses, I plan to split it evenly, if that works for you: a third each for me, you, and Natasha."

Was that fair? Hannah wasn't sure. What could Natty possibly bring to this enterprise?

"I'm going to manage the business, Mom," Natty volunteered as if in answer. She opened her laptop, tapped something on the keyboard, and turned it around to show Hannah a spreadsheet. "Jonathan and I will share the social media responsibilities, but other than that, I'll keep the books, contract with vendors, run the website, schedule appearances, write press releases, contact the traditional media, and do anything else that comes up."

"Wow." Hannah was impressed. "That's really amazing, Natasha. I'm blown away, seriously. It looks like you two have thought of everything. I really don't know what to say. Thank you."

"You're welcome."

"I guess you've really learned something at those business classes you've been taking."

"So, are you in?" Jonathan asked. "All we need is for you to give us the go-ahead, Mrs. M."

Hannah shrugged. "I guess I'm in."

"Well, then. Let's go."

⁓

"ABSOLUTELY NOT."

Dr. A was adamant, and Hannah wondered what she could say that could change her mind. She spoke slowly, choosing each word with care.

"Dr. A, you know how much I respect you. I understand and appreciate that you're only looking out for my benefit. I'm not asking you to issue a statement or to be available for interviews or anything like that," Hannah said. "All you need to do is confirm the basic details of the pregnancy."

"To whom?"

"Well, to whoever asks. It's my understanding that there is interest in my story. Reporters may want to confirm that the pregnancy is real, the ultrasounds are real, and that I wasn't on hormones, doing IVF, or having any other sort of assistance. That this is a genuine, natural, one-in-a-million pregnancy of a nearly fifty-five-year-old woman who had been previously and demonstrably infertile."

"It is not anyone's business but yours, Hannah." She had never heard Dr. A's voice so harsh. Hannah swallowed around the lump in her throat. "Among other things, it's a violation of HIPAA rules and hardly something you want to be broadcasting all over town."

"All over town" was an understatement if their plan worked, of course, but Hannah felt it would be best to start small, particularly when talking to a reluctant Dr. A.

"I get that you're bound by HIPAA privacy laws, Dr. A. But I'm willing to sign whatever you'd like to free you from that responsibility."

Dr. A studied Hannah coolly. "You are willing to sign away your privacy. You are willing to sign away the chance to be a more informed parent by not having an amnio. I know how badly you want this baby, Hannah, but I'm not sure you are approaching your pregnancy with the degree of caution it deserves."

Hannah rubbed her hands over her face. How could she make Dr. A understand? She opened her mouth to try to explain, to capture some of the excitement Jonathan had created, but Dr. A spoke first.

"Perhaps it would be better if you made these requests of Dr. Felcher. She is more ... flexible than I am and will no doubt be more amenable to them." She pushed away from her desk and stood up, somehow appearing much larger than life. "In fact, I think at this time perhaps Dr. Felcher should take over your case completely."

Hannah gasped. "No, no, no. Please don't do that, Dr. A. I like Dr. Felcher just fine, but you've always been there for me. I need you more than ever now."

"What you *want* is someone who will agree to all your requests without question. That is the exact opposite of what you *need* right now. No one is more dedicated to the success of this pregnancy than I am, Hannah; it is my job to bring you and your baby safely through a very dangerous journey, and I take my job seriously. Yet as I cannot support the decisions you are making, I will turn your care over to Dr. Felcher."

She moved to the door; opened it. Hannah stood up and gathered her coat, numb.

"Goodbye, Hannah," Dr. A said, her voice firm. "I will follow your case through Dr. Felcher. Perhaps I will even consult on it again if I find that I can truly be of use to you, in my own way, on my own terms. I wish you the best of luck, and hope you will have a successful birth and a healthy baby."

It had once been fairly common, but it had been years since Hannah had left Dr. A's office with such a sense of sadness and loss.

HANNAH 2:5

Although Hannah had announced her pregnancy to her friends and acquaintances, by the middle of her fourth month she still had a degree of privacy: being a woman of a certain age with a belly would be chalked up to a slowed metabolism and a fondness for wine and tiramisu. Yet now that Natty and Jonathan were busy planning the official launch of St. Hannah, Hannah realized that she was about to kiss her anonymity goodbye.

She wasn't entirely clear on how it would all work, so Natty and Jonathan set aside some time to go over their business plan.

"Okay, Mom, look here: we're starting out by sending press releases to the local newspapers and radio stations, to the reporters who specialize in human interest stories. If we make a real connection with a reporter, we send over some swag." At this point, Jonathan held up a black T-shirt and beanie cap with an embroidered St. Hannah logo. Hannah had only seen mock-ups before. Pleased with the result, she had to admit they looked pretty stylish.

She then glanced over the press release, nodding. It was unsurprising that Dr. Felcher had immediately agreed to help with the publicity push. Though she said it was because she "wanted to ensure that Baby Murrow would have the resources needed to guarantee a fulfilling life," Hannah knew that Dr. Felcher was also eager to promote her fertility clinic at the university hospital, and if someone mistook Hannah's pregnancy for something made possible by the latest advances available at the clinic, well, that would be just fine with Dr. Felcher.

Attached to the release were an inoffensive photo of Hannah taken by Jonathan, a copy of the ultrasound, and a high-resolution copy of the St. Hannah logo.

"Simultaneously, we're going to make a push on Twitter, Instagram, and Facebook," Natty continued. "We've already amassed several thousand followers on each platform with some clever teasing and judicious following; that's in addition to your blog. We've also identified some receptive major players among the mommy bloggers who have agreed to help us along in exchange for cross promotion.

"There are also a handful of minor local celebrities we think we can pull in if we get a big enough following. We think we're ready to make a big splash." Natty stopped and looked Hannah in the eye. "Are you, Mom?"

Though she didn't understand everything Natty was saying, Hannah listened with interest. And, with a certain degree of nervousness. As many did while growing up, Hannah had dreamed of being "famous," like Farrah Fawcett or The Rolling Stones. Her concept of fame had, at that time, been nebulous. It consisted of having plenty of money, wearing the latest clothes, going to parties every night, and being admired by millions around the world. Being in the right place at the right time had once won her a split-second appearance on a TV commercial in her senior year of high school, which had brought her some measure of celebrity among her peers. By the time she had become old enough to accept she had no talent for music, art, politics, acting, or anything else that could actually make her famous, the thought of being loved around the world had given way to the idea of being loved by one man and by several children. Her efforts to become a mother had been all-consuming.

So she asked herself if she wanted to be famous now, and it gave her pause. What did it mean to her these days, when people were becoming famous for the most ridiculous reasons, for sex tapes and embarrassing viral videos?

But when her mind helpfully reworded the question as, "Do you want to be famous now, *for this?*" To become famous for becoming a mother? The answer then came quickly and unequivocally: "yes."

Hannah was ready.

IT WAS NO COINCIDENCE that Natty and Jonathan had scheduled the launch of St. Hannah for the beginning of November, in time for Thanksgiving discussions of gratitude, blessings, and the meaning of family … and in time for Christmas shopping on Cyber Monday.

For the launch, Natty had sent out dozens of press releases and as a result had made contact with the local weekly newspaper and the regional ABC-TV news affiliate. One three-paragraph article and a two-minute segment on the 5 o'clock news was a very modest start, but Natty told Hannah not to be disappointed. Once they had made those initial steps into the public eye and got the print and video, she assured her, they could spin them endlessly on social media and gain momentum.

Before long, they discovered that Natty was right.

With help from well-timed tweets and Instagram posts, Hannah was soon fielding questions from ever-larger media outlets (first county-wide newspapers, then state-specific cable shows). Jonathan schooled her on how to talk to reporters and publicists, how to get her message across regardless of the questions they asked her. They found she was very comfortable being in the limelight, "a natural," as one producer labeled her.

"Loved your piece on 'Simon at 6,'" Natty told her one day after she'd appeared on a local early-morning talk show. Hannah had griped about getting up at 4:30 a.m. to make it in time for hair and makeup, but they'd even sent a car for her. "You really held your own against the other panelists on that 'Best Years of Your Life' roundtable: the rest of them came across as old farts, with their boring recommendations for eating lots of fiber and taking chair exercise classes. You came in there and knocked their compression socks right off.

"Really, Mom, who knew you could be so charming and witty?" Natty concluded.

It was another rare compliment, and Hannah soaked it in, even as she pretended not to. She put on a fake scowl so obvious that even Natty could see right through it. "I've always been charming and witty, Natasha. How did you not notice?"

"And relatable," Natty said, ignoring her. "Particularly when you told the story of your struggles with infertility. Pure gold. And you know what? Even though I know the whole story backward and forward—I mean, I'm the one who put it on the website and in the press releases—I don't think I've ever heard the whole thing coming from you, with all the emotion behind it. It was powerful."

She added, more thoughtfully, "There wasn't a dry eye at the table," and Hannah wondered if Natty's own eyes had remained dry. She thought perhaps maybe Natty now could appreciate what her parents had suffered before she'd arrived on the scene.

"Anyway," Natty continued, "I think everyone who watched today will want to have you over for tea. Or brunch. Or whatever it is you old ladies do. Hopefully, what they'll really want to do is buy your merch."

Shortly thereafter, Hannah was invited as the special guest at the grand opening of a new toy store. Although all she needed to do was to cut the big red ribbon with the giant scissors, she also shook hands, kissed babies, fielded questions about her pregnancy, and carried it off as well as any seasoned politician. Next, she was asked to do a guest spot on the local weather forecast, and somehow managed to ad lib a comment about "a large front slowly moving in" that had the news crew high-fiving her afterward and inviting her to return with her own "large front" for a repeat performance.

Women of all ages began stopping her on the street to ask for selfies and autographs, which she always provided with aplomb, carrying a black Sharpie in her handbag should the occasion arise. Where this confidence had come from, she had no idea. But within a couple of weeks, it became as natural as walking the dog, and Hannah relished this sweet spot of minor celebrity, one where she could feel popular without feeling hounded.

Unfortunately that's also when the "pilgrimages" began.

Or at least, that's what Natty called them. And the "offerings." Two days after the launch of the St. Hannah brand, Hannah came out to the front porch in the morning to pick up her daily newspaper and found small bouquets of flowers, prayer candles, and rosaries. Jonathan and Natty celebrated the gifts, pointing to them as evidence that Hannah's story had touched people in a very deep, personal way. Some came with handwritten notes—prayers that they, too, should be as fortunate as St. Hannah. Hannah alternately thought the gifts sweet and creepy.

Ryan thought they were the last straw.

"I'm moving out."

This declaration, made shortly before Thanksgiving, did not come as a complete surprise to Hannah, but it did disappoint her. Hannah had continued to hope they would come to some sort of understanding that would keep their family together in some form, however platonic, to raise the new baby.

"I don't want to be part of this circus you've created."

Hannah shook her head. He still didn't understand. "It took both of us to create this baby, Ryan."

"Yeah, but *you*, you and Natty and her latest boyfriend, you created the circus. The wackos leaving presents and messages and statues of the Virgin ... Did you see what was out there this morning? I counted a dozen votive candles, three statues, and three boxes of 'I'm-not-sure-I-want-to-know.'

"I don't want any part of it, Hannah," he reiterated, frowning deeply. "It makes me uneasy. It's an invasion of my privacy."

"But where do you plan to go? I thought it was more important for us to conserve resources. Paying rent in addition to a mortgage makes no sense at all, particularly since I've been living in the guest room anyway. I'm staying out of your way, aren't I? We barely see each other."

Ryan shrugged. "Mitch has a second bedroom in his condo, and he says he'd like the company, whether I pay him rent or not. Guess he's lonely."

"It's been four years since Cathy left him. The man should start dating again."

"Whatever. Maybe he enjoyed the peace and quiet. I kind of get that."

"I'm sure you do," Hannah said, stung.

"So I'll stay there until we sell the house."

Sell the house.

"Goddammit, Ryan, I'm going to have a baby, and I'm going to have it while living in this house!"

Shaking his head, he sighed heavily. "We're going to need to sell the house, Hannah. You do understand that, right?"

Hannah remained stubbornly silent.

"Like it or not, it's going to happen sooner or later. We're going to need the money. It really wouldn't have been an issue if it was just the two of us: retiring, playing a little golf, living within our means, but now …"

"So, we're really going to do this, then?" Despite their quarrels and differences, the idea of breaking up their marriage permanently brought Hannah no joy.

"Looks like it."

She tried one more time. "And you're absolutely positive you don't want to be a father to our child?" For emphasis, Hannah put her hand on her belly, longing to put his hand there too, to make some kind of physical connection between him and his baby, one he couldn't deny.

"You might not believe this, Hannah, but I've given it a lot of thought," Ryan said. "I'll accept my responsibility and provide whatever support we can agree on, but that's as far as I'm willing to go."

"Well, in the interest of conservation of resources," Hannah said, defeated, "what do you say we think about using mediation instead of lawyers? If you and I can be civil about this, and come to some kind of agreement around distribution of assets and child support, we can save ourselves some money. A lot of money."

Ryan cocked his head thoughtfully.

"Jason tells me we live in an equitable distribution state, which means there are already some standards in place about how assets are shared. If we ended up in court, the state would dictate parameters to us. If you'd rather make this a mutual decision rather than something the state imposes, we should go with mediation.

"Can we do this, Ryan? Can we make this less of an ordeal for both of us?"

"I guess we could give it a try."

Hannah nodded. It was the best she could hope for in a bad situation.

"But I want to choose the mediator," Ryan added.

Of course he did. But she was happy to hand that responsibility off to him, as it would reduce the likelihood of his arguing over the results and give her more time to focus on her brand.

"All right, Ryan. If that will make you more comfortable, go ahead."

The next step, according to Jason, was to make the separation official in the eyes of the law. After Thanksgiving, they would have to shut down their joint bank accounts and credit cards, and Hannah would have to open accounts of her own, something she hadn't done in years. What was her credit rating? Hannah had no idea, and only a vague understanding of how it was calculated or improved. She was only now beginning to understand how little she was prepared to be on her own.

At fifty-five, she would be starting from scratch.

HANNAH 2:6

Thanksgiving wasn't going to be the same without Ryan. This year the holiday was supposed to have been at the Murrow house with his sister, Maria, her husband, Henry, and their two teenagers making the three-hour trip. Ryan pre-emptively decided on the reverse, texting Hannah from his new location to say that he would be with Maria's family. Hannah had no idea what he had shared with his sister and two brothers, or his grown nephews and nieces, about their recent remarkable news and their even more recent troubles, but she was relieved not to be the one making all those explanatory phone calls. Ryan's widowed mother was in a nursing home with dementia, having lived long past the capabilities of assisted living. But his family still tried to remain close via phone calls, Skype conversations, text messages, Facebook posts, birthday cards—the whole gamut of communications options.

Sometimes Hannah looked upon such families with wonder. How did they get along so well? Did they actually enjoy each other's company that much? They seemed to. Sure, they might have the occasional blow-out argument, but their love was obvious to anyone who spent even a half hour with them. This was a family that played board games together, shared uproarious inside jokes, sent thoughtful gifts for all occasions—not just for birthdays and Christmas, but for anniversaries, new jobs, promotions ...

She considered her relationship with Jason, his wife, Missy, and their children as cordial, approaching but not ever quite reaching "warm"—the sort you'd have with a pleasant coworker in a remote office. Hannah supposed that much of it was due to the leftover baggage from their childhood when Jason was the golden child who could do no wrong, the honor roll student, while she struggled to keep her grades above a C. And of course, he had married Missy, who took "perfection" to an even higher level.

Missy was one of those mothers who seemed to be able to do it all: have a career as an interior decorator, keep an immaculate house, maintain a slender figure. Her sleek auburn hair could even do the rare "messy bun" that struck the ideal balance between casual and chic. And having children, oh, but she was good at that! With a minimum of fuss and barely a bead of sweat during the world's shortest labors, she turned out three perfect kids: two boys and a girl, now ages eight, thirteen, and fifteen, all athletic, artistic, smart, and impeccably polite.

Natty, unimpressed, called them "the Three Little Prigs."

Though she scolded Natty for saying so, privately Hannah agreed with her. The kids *were* insufferable. Missy, too, she found irritating: whatever praise she offered was condescending, and her criticisms were couched as coming "from love." Of a new outfit Hannah was wearing for the first time, Missy might say, "Oh! That's a bold choice for you! Do you love it?" the implication being that *she*—and therefore the world at large, which naturally agreed with her—did not.

Her example was hard to live up to. She remembered every occasion, no matter how minor, acknowledging it with a card arriving no fewer than two days before the event, a Facebook post, and a phone call. Taken on the surface, Missy was the model of a generous, caring sister-in-law; underneath, however, Hannah was sure she was looking down her perfect, gently turned-up nose at the Murrows. Or laughing at them.

Hannah thought about the way her sister-in-law had fought over the years, with various excuses, to keep Natty away from her children, the implication being that she would be a bad influence over her younger cousins. She now bristled at the thought, ashamed in retrospect that she had not defended Natty more vigorously. It had always seemed easier to let Missy have her way and not make waves.

The less-critical, family-oriented Ryan took Missy and the children at face value and thought the whole crew was terrific, accusing Hannah of overreacting or, at the very least, assigning a malign intent to innocent remarks. Hannah, having grown up in a family where criticism was more common than affection, thought she knew better.

Hannah's frustration about not being able to produce either kind of family—the loud, messy, affectionate kind or the quiet, perfect variety—had plagued her for years, and Natty's difficult childhood and adolescence hadn't helped. Her need for discipline and attention had drained Hannah and Ryan, too, she acknowledged. Many families crumbled under that sort of strain, and she had been proud that their marriage had endured despite its challenges. Somehow, though, having merely "endured" didn't seem to be much of a success.

In retrospect, their love and mutual respect had thinned out too much, like paint too diluted to cover the dark flaws underneath, and eventually wasn't hardy enough to sustain itself. It was sad.

So, Thanksgiving turned out to be a simpler affair. Natty retrieved her grandparents from their apartment while Hannah put the finishing touches on the sweet potatoes, green beans, and the world's smallest turkey. Natty had lately decided she was a vegetarian (though privately Hannah doubted she would be able to survive long on the vegetables she actually *liked*), and the combined amounts her parents ate would barely fill a single dinner plate. Jonathan was spending the holiday with his own family, promising he would join Natty at Christmas.

Dolores insisted they eat in the dining room and use the good china, claiming it wouldn't be a special occasion if the four of them used the everyday stoneware in the kitchen. Hannah agreed, thinking wistfully that it might be the last time they would use the dishes, the old-fashioned floral pattern she and Ryan had chosen together when they were engaged, for some time. Perhaps ever. Would that be split up, too, in the divorce? Would he demand half the dishes, a gravy boat and sugar bowl of his own?

Likewise, Dolores reminded them to say grace, though she knew full well it was something Hannah and Ryan had stopped doing on a regular basis years ago. Natty rolled her eyes but had the good sense to keep her opinion to herself.

"Bless us, O Lord, and these, Thy gifts, which we are about to receive from Thy bounty. Through Christ, our Lord. Amen."

Hannah found herself saying "Amen" and meaning it for the first time in a long time. She glanced around the table, grateful for having her parents alive and in relatively good health; grateful for having Natty engaged with the world and doing something constructive; grateful especially for the unexpected life growing inside her. Her eyes, seemingly of their own accord, kept returning to the seat that Ryan would usually occupy. It generated a little pang in her chest, and she hoped if she could get through this holiday without him, she would do just fine.

As it happened, she did. The meal itself was, as usual, over in a flash, with everyone pleased with the food except for Dolores, who complained that the white meat was dry. (Hannah noticed she did, however, clear her plate.) They lingered over their store-bought pumpkin pie as Natty introduced her grandparents to the St. Hannah brand, showed them the website, and gave them each a St. Hannah enamel lapel pin. ("They sure as hell aren't going to wear one of your T-shirts or beanies, Mom.")

"Is this supposed to be your mother?" Dolores asked as she examined her pin.

"An artist's rendering," Hannah replied with a bit less of her usual defensiveness, deciding for once not to care what her mother thought. She loved the logo and had become personally attached to it.

"Well," Dolores said, pinning it onto her blue cardigan, "anything to support the cause." Frank put his on, too, with a little help from Natty. "It's cute."

Hannah was touched. In Ryan's absence, having the rest of her family supporting her meant a lot. Having her mother on her side was practically another act of God.

"Ooh, Mom, you're going to love our numbers," Natty said to her over decaf coffee after logging into the website and checking the online store. "We're close to our goal for the month, and we haven't even hit Black Friday or Cyber Monday yet. I can't wait to see what will happen in the next few days, when holiday shopping really begins." She picked up her phone for the tenth time and texted Jonathan.

"That's ... that's great." Hannah was content to let Natty and Jonathan take care of the numbers and the website as a whole. The blog continued to grow in influence, and was now being ghostwritten by Natty from Hannah's point of view. Natty also kept track of a database of several thousand fans, who received an email once a week with updates and special offers on featured merchandise.

Hannah's responsibilities extended only to giving interviews and making appearances. She had, on her tablet and synced with her phone, a calendar that reminded her with a *ping* when she was an hour away from talking to the Church of the Blessed Virgin Expectant Mothers' Circle or the Active Seniors Club at the local YMCA.

Although she was still nervously watching her pennies, Hannah allowed Natty and Jonathan to persuade her that with her higher profile, she might want to add a little low-key glamour to her warm and accessible public image. It didn't take a lot of arm-twisting to coax her into making Ke'isha's boutique her exclusive source of maternity wear.

~⟋⟍

"Whoo!" Eric shouted at the store when he heard the news, lifting Hannah completely off her feet in an effortless bear hug. For good measure, he next picked up Natty in one huge arm, sending her laughing. It was a rare sound Hannah never tired of, and she had already heard it more in recent weeks than she had in the past several years.

Jonathan did not get the same treatment, but the two men exchanged an enthusiastic fist bump.

"Just in time for the Christmas rush." Ke'isha smiled broadly. "We've already seen a nice boost in sales from the two times you stopped by."

"Here's what we propose," began Natty. "We'll give you exclusive advertising space on our website. Also, you'll be able to use approved St. Hannah images and logos for your advertising and point-of-purchase, and have Mom for weekly or bi-weekly meet-and-greets. In exchange, we'd like a minimum of 40% off retail price on any current season maternity clothing that Mom chooses for herself as well as self-standing display space in the store for St. Hannah merchandise such as beanies, nursing bras, T-shirts, socks, and hoodies. If you provide an outfit for an event or interview free of charge, Hannah will name B. Fruitful as her source. Does that all work for you?"

Ke'isha nodded. "Let's make it happen."

❧

REMEMBERING THAT DAY IN THE STORE, Hannah smiled. While it was still beyond her understanding why anyone would want merchandise with her likeness on it, according to the numbers Natty was relaying to her at her crumb-strewn dining room table, the St. Hannah brand was apparently selling very well. If they could sustain it through her pregnancy and make a little extra cash to put away for the baby, Hannah would be happy.

Yet Hannah also knew there were expenses beyond the raw data she was seeing. She wondered if they were profitable yet, and decided she was too afraid to ask. During her frequent sleepless nights, she had visions of taking in Natty, and Jonathan, too, after their little venture failed to cover the cost of the website, the manufacturing, the shipping, her wardrobe … Maybe setting up a GoFundMe page to help them survive once it all came crashing down …

No. Nope. She wasn't going to think like that, she decided. At least, not today, not on Thanksgiving. Today she would just enjoy the state of balance that existed in her household right now, with everyone—even Dolores, even Natty—smiling in contentment. It would be good if that mood could be sustained at least until she got her parents back to their apartment.

As Hannah rose to help Dolores and Natty clear the sticky remnants of the pie and the last few dishes off the table, she felt it: a slight fluttering in her abdomen. *The quickening.* Though it stopped as quickly as it had started, Hannah was certain. There was no mistaking it for too much turkey, a muscle cramp, or anything else. *She had felt her baby move.* A long, shaky whimper escaped her, and she sat down again, dishes forgotten, overcome.

"Mom?" It was Natty who noticed her odd behavior first. "You okay? Mom?"

"I felt it. I felt the baby move! Oh, my God. Mom!" she shrieked to Dolores, who had been ferrying the coffee cups back to the kitchen. "Mom, I felt the baby!"

Dolores came back into the dining room, in no particular hurry. She patted Hannah on the shoulder. "Oh, isn't that nice," she said. Frank clapped slowly and deliberately. Hannah wept into her gravy-stained dinner napkin.

"Natty!" Hannah cried. "Natty, I finally felt the baby move."

But Natty had left the room.

HANNAH 2:7

Ryan had already been out of their home a week when Hannah's story appeared simultaneously in the monthly AARP magazine and in *People*, which was a good thing, because it was around then that the "circus" that he had claimed drove him from the house added another couple of rings.

It was a real coup, getting into *People* magazine. Everyone knew it. Natty declared it the crowning achievement of her life so far, made through a connection of a friend of Jonathan's but a result entirely of her own persistence: "Eleven emails and eight phone calls," she laughed. Even though it was only a one-pager and wasn't the cover story—that was reserved for yet another Marvel superhero movie opening around Christmas—there was still a breathless cover line: "St. Hannah: Meet the 54-Year-Old Miracle Mom!"

Hannah had been anxious about the way she would look, the way she would be portrayed. Would they embellish details they found unsatisfying? Would they mock her and the fledgling St. Hannah brand? Would they judge her? When the magazine arrived, she stared at the glossy cover with its glowering, costumed superheroes for a long moment and handed it off to Natty.

"I can't look."

Natty, having no such problems, flipped the magazine open and scanned for the article. Quickly breezing through the text, Natty smiled and handed it back. "I think you'll be pleased."

Hannah took the magazine in damp-palmed hands. The first thing she saw was a large color photo of herself in one of Ke'isha's stylish pantsuits, holding an ultrasound of the baby. She breathed a sigh of relief. It was one of the most attractive pictures taken of her since her wedding day; thank God for good lighting and professional photographers! And there, in an inset, was the St. Hannah logo. Against Natty's wishes, she had refused to wear a St. Hannah maternity T-shirt for the picture and thankfully the *People* stylist had taken Hannah's side.

The article, which hit all the high points and hewed closely to the facts, was almost perfect in Hannah's view. Almost. She was only troubled, ever so slightly, by the quote attributed to Dr. Felcher. While Dr. A had insisted that she never be mentioned publicly with regard to Hannah's pregnancy or the St. Hannah brand, Dr. Felcher had been only too happy to grant an interview. Characterized as "an expert in geriatric pregnancies and perinatal care," Dr. Felcher told *People*: "The minute I examined Hannah, and saw the fetus in the ultrasound, I knew we were looking at a once-in-a-lifetime event. It's my honor to be the only one trusted to guide this amazing woman and her miraculous baby into their new lives."

"What's wrong, Mom?"

"I don't know. It's just that, well, it's almost as if Dr. Felcher is claiming credit for all my care, even for having diagnosed the pregnancy. It burns me to have to leave Dr. A out of it entirely."

"Her decision, remember; not yours."

Hannah was forced to agree.

"But hey, the issue went out to subscribers last week and hit the newsstands today, and we've already seen a huge uptick in hits on the website, and they're really into the merch. Orders are coming in from everywhere in the country now. We're on our way to becoming a full-fledged phenomenon!"

How much of a phenomenon became clearer after the magazine had been out for a week. The beanie caps were now best-sellers, accounting for over half the sales. Stickers, socks, scarves, and pins were popular stocking-stuffers. Either Natty or Jonathan called Hannah daily to give her updates on the amount and variety of merchandise being sold. With Christmas drawing closer and the campaign gaining momentum, Natty was busy signing new vendors who could promise December 24th delivery. Hannah had never seen her so happy, so full of purpose. Whatever her own role in this whole absurd enterprise turned out to be, it would be worth it to have her daughter back.

A FEW DAYS LATER, before Hannah had the opportunity to bring in the most recent gifts left on her doorstep—and in fact, before she had even finished breakfast—the doorbell rang. Instantly Sadie was at full alert, leaving her spot at Hannah's feet to dash to the front door, barking. Annoyed at the intrusion, she brushed the remnants of her toast to the center of her plate, drank a last sip of tea, and took her time getting to the door.

"Yes? May I help you?"

Two women beamed up at Hannah from the porch. One was probably in her sixties, if Hannah could judge correctly by the small amount of lightly lined face showing between her St. Hannah beanie and St. Hannah scarf. The other was a young woman in her early twenties, with bright green eyes and freckles. In addition to her own beanie and scarf, she sported a scuffed leather portfolio case with a St. Hannah sticker on it, clutched to her chest with St. Hannah–gloved hands. It was a sunny day in the high 30s, not unusual for early December, hardly the kind of weather that necessitated such bundling up. Hannah, comfortable enough standing in the doorway in a sweater, knew the display was for her benefit alone.

"Good morning, Hannah!" the older woman said. "My name is Emily Crane, and this is Mary Catherine McMillan. We're the Outreach Committee for the Midline Valley Right-to-Life Association, and I hope you don't mind my saying, it is *so* exciting to meet you!"

"Such an honor!" Mary Catherine gushed.

Oh, dear.

"I hope you'll forgive the early hour. It's just that ... we read your story in *People* magazine last week and spent the next few days catching up with your blog. We could not believe we had a real, live celebrity a short thirty-minute drive from headquarters! I said to Mary Catherine, 'We can't let this opportunity go by! We have to get St. Hannah on board before someone else does!'"

"Excuse me ... on board with what?"

Emily and Mary Catherine looked at each other with barely contained fervor. Finally, Emily said: "We'd like to invite you to become the celebrity spokesman—sorry, spokes*woman*—for our organization. We want St. Hannah Murrow as the face of Midline Valley Right-to-Life!"

Flipping open the portfolio at this cue, Mary Catherine held a page up for Hannah to see. It was a crude mock-up of an ad for their organization. Using a badly silhouetted photo of Hannah cribbed from the *People* article, surrounded by cut-and-pasted stock photos of babies, it was headlined: "St. Hannah Reminds You: Choose Life!" A St. Hannah logo appeared prominently in the lower right-hand corner.

Hannah bristled. Unconsciously, she took a step back, nearly tripping over a protective Sadie in the process.

"Of course," Emily said hastily, misinterpreting the look on Hannah's face, "the finished product will be a lot more, well, *finished.*"

"You'll have to forgive us, Hannah," Mary Catherine interjected, "we threw it together in a minute and a half." Hannah strongly suspected it was Mary Catherine who had thrown it together. She looked embarrassed. "But you get the idea."

"Oh, I certainly do." Hannah leaned against the door jamb and rubbed her aching lower back. She would have to look for some good stretching exercises before her center of gravity really shifted and exacerbated the problem. "But why me?"

"Why *you* ... ?" Mary Catherine echoed. The women looked at each other, puzzled. "What do you mean? You're the woman who never gave up her dream of having a baby, and who committed herself to ignoring the obstacles and naysayers and seeing her pregnancy through."

Recognizing her own language taken from the *People* article, Hannah groaned inwardly.

"Who better than a woman who truly knows the value of life to speak for us? And to speak for those who cannot speak for themselves," Emily said earnestly. "So, what do you think, Hannah? Will you join Midline Valley Right-to-Life in our righteous struggle to save the innocents?"

Hannah understood their point of view, she really did, particularly now that she'd been given the unlikely gift of feeling a baby growing inside her. She had a certain amount of sympathy for their sentiments, however misguided she thought them. Nevertheless, she had read enough, heard enough, and seen enough to know that not every pregnancy was as wanted, desired, prayed-for as hers. Who was Hannah Murrow, who were the Midline Valley Right-to-Lifers, to tell other women what to do with their bodies?

It was on the tip of Hannah's tongue to tell the ladies they were mistaken, that she supported a woman's right to choose. She wanted to send Emily and Mary Catherine off her porch with the message that she was, that all women are, more than an incubator, and that their rights to bodily autonomy should come first. She wished she could scorn them and tell them that the views mandated by their religion (and, not coincidentally, hers as well), by *any* religion for that matter, shouldn't be imposed on all women everywhere. She thought of showing them the receipts for her donations to Planned Parenthood.

But she couldn't. So she didn't.

Hannah had had enough experience on Facebook to know that there were certain topics on which certain people were immovable. This situation was, she felt, a textbook example.

Trying to explain her pro-choice position to the ladies on her porch—so full of zeal for their cause and admiration for her—would be a waste of time and patience, both of which she had little to spare these days. What's more, there was no upside that Hannah could see to getting drawn into an argument with them; hoping to educate them, she could only alienate them. (And by extension, any number of other St. Hannah supporters to whom Emily and Mary Catherine might air their grievances.) They were also quite literally on her doorstep, and should the encounter turn ugly, there would be nowhere for Hannah to go.

Fortunately, Jonathan had given her the perfect out.

"I can't tell you how flattered I am, ladies," Hannah said with her most sympathetic smile. "And that you would drive all this way to offer me this opportunity! I hope you won't be too disappointed when I tell you that my lawyers won't allow any outside organization to use my image or logo in their advertising."

"Blame the lawyers," Jonathan had advised. "Works every time."

The ladies' faces, so optimistic, fell as one.

"But this is different! Surely if you told them why it's so important, why you wanted to do it …" Emily began.

Hannah interrupted her.

"Emily, you can imagine how many requests I've had for this sort of thing." Until this morning, there had been exactly zero. Nevertheless, Hannah raised her hands helplessly. "I'm not allowed to play favorites."

"What cause could possibly be more important than the babies?" Emily insisted, her voice and face turning harder.

"I'm very sorry, but I can't help. Thanks so much for your offer, though."

As she watched Emily and Mary Catherine get into their old blue Chevy and drive away, Hannah blew out a relieved breath. This was the downside of her new-found celebrity, she supposed sadly. No doubt it would get worse.

With the visitors gone, Sadie was sniffing with interest around the gifts left the night before. "Hey! Get away from there!" Hannah stepped in to shoo the dog away. She never knew what would be left on her doorstep. In addition to the religious items and baby supplies, there was often food: she had already received dozens of cookies, several boxes of chocolate, and one memorable gift selection of cheese and hard salamis. Sadie, ever compliant, focused on shadowing Hannah as she started carrying the packages and letters inside.

It was going to take a couple of trips.

Corresponding to the growth of the brand, the offerings left on Hannah's doorstep had become grander, more expensive. This morning Hannah found a Moses basket filled with a complete newborn layette, tied up with a big yellow satin bow, as well as an entire case of Pampers for newborns. With Natty's help, Hannah had selected a local women's shelter as the beneficiary of her fans' generosity. The charity was grateful for the baby items, the occasional maternity outfit, and even for the food treats, which added a much-needed dose of variety to the bare necessities the shelter was equipped to offer. Natty's old bedroom now served as a staging area, and every couple of days she, Hannah, or Jonathan would make deliveries, which were becoming ever more frequent.

And as the gifts increased in size and value, the messages that accompanied them—like the visit from the ladies that morning—began to become more problematic.

"Marry me, Hannah!" she read off the tag of an enormous teddy bear left on her doorstep.

"There are a lot of desperate men out there," Natty said, grinning. She and Jonathan had arrived an hour after the visitors' departure and were now in Hannah's living room, working quietly side by side (and occasionally pressing their knees against each other's) while Hannah went through the morning's gifts.

"First of all," Hannah sniffed, "how dare you suggest that someone has to be desperate to want to marry me. Second of all, this proposal is from a woman."

They all laughed. "And, if you must know, it's actually my *third* from women, plus I've had four more from men. And those are only marriage proposals. There are other kinds of proposals as well," Hannah added with a sly smile. "Should I read them to you?"

"No!" Natty clutched her ears as Jonathan guffawed. "Nope, nope, nope, nope. Ugh, are they all like that these days?"

"No, those are actually in the minority. Most of the notes I get lately are like this one," Hannah said with a frown, holding up a #10 envelope and its handwritten contents. "They ask for miracles, for my blessing. For my personal intervention with the Virgin." She stopped, staring into space. "They seem to think I'm on some kind of inside track with the Holy Mother." She shook her head, uneasy for the second time that day.

Hannah moved on to open a box from Neiman Marcus that turned out to contain a collection of very expensive designer babywear. *Someone from New York has gone a wee bit overboard*, she thought with a glance at the enclosed card. Still, she sighed over the tiny cardigans, the festively decorated caps, and the miniature overalls, wishing she could in good conscience keep the well-meant presents.

"There's no going back now, is there?" Hannah said slowly. "I mean, even if something turned out to be dreadfully wrong with the baby, even if I got very sick, I'm still going to have to carry to term."

"I don't know, Mom," Natty replied. "Don't you think people would understand?"

"Well, does that really matter?" Jonathan joined in, concerned. He pushed his laptop aside. "Are you having second thoughts, Mrs. Murrow?"

Hannah thought about how she'd been fighting any attempt to persuade her otherwise. "Not second thoughts; never that. I mean, there was no way I was going to give up the pregnancy just because it was going to be challenging, or inconvenient, or expensive, or even dangerous. Or because Ryan didn't want me to do it. But not having the choice any more scares me. I always figured the deadline was at least a couple of months away and I'd have time to make a decision, just in case." She shrugged. "Time's up, I guess."

HANNAH 2:8

At her next exam, Dr. Felcher told Hannah she should plan to come to the office every three weeks, slightly more frequently than the average mother-to-be at this stage. Ever conscious of what she was spending, Hannah tried to explain her anxiety that her health insurance wouldn't cover the extra visits. Dr. Felcher waved away her concerns. "Don't let that worry you, Hannah. We are doing what's best for you and the baby. I will make sure that it's all taken care of." Hannah supposed there were codes the office could use that would satisfy the insurance company. Or perhaps, like B. Fruitful, the practice had gained enough in publicity to more than offset the costs. Surely the *People* article alone had sent mothers-to-be flocking to Dr. Felcher. She did seem pretty pleased with herself.

"All right, time to get dressed!" Dr. Felcher said briskly. "Everything looks wonderful. I've prepared some research I promised you on the relative safety of amniocentesis in first-time pregnancies of advanced age, including one of my own papers on the subject that was published last year in the *American Journal of Obstetrics and Gynecology*." She paused, perhaps waiting for Hannah to show some sign of being impressed. When Hannah merely nodded politely, she proceeded: "That will be, no doubt, a great deal more technical than you'll need or perhaps will even be able to comprehend, but I'll send you home with a packet so you can give it some good thought.

"In the meantime, though, meet me in my office when you're done. I have some thrilling news."

And then she winked.

Hannah was taken aback. She didn't know Dr. Felcher well at all, but the gesture seemed odd and out of character. Forced. Dr. Felcher wasn't the coy, winking type; far from it. Left alone in the exam room to pull on her clothes, Hannah puzzled over what sort of news would excite the doctor. It couldn't have anything to do with the baby or she would have mentioned it during the exam.

When Hannah reached Dr. Felcher's office, she was surprised to see two other people in there, a man and a woman, already seated in the guest chairs in front of the doctor's desk. Thinking she was interrupting a consultation, Hannah began to back away, saying, "Oh, sorry, I ..."

"No, no, come in, Hannah," Dr. Felcher said, getting up from her chair and leading her in. "Hannah, I'd like you to meet Robin Santino and Kelsey Morgan."

Bewildered, Hannah shook hands with the newcomers and sat down in the chair that Dr. Felcher offered her. Robin and Kelsey (Hannah was still trying to determine which was which) smiled at her with picture-perfect white teeth and barely contained enthusiasm.

Looking now at Dr. Felcher, who was once more seated behind her large, modern desk, her fingers knitted together,

Hannah was struck again by how much she resembled a TV news anchor. "Hannah," the doctor began, "when you gave me permission to speak openly about your miraculous pregnancy, I thought, what can I do to help spread the word besides just waiting passively for someone to approach me with questions? And once the initial interest dissipates, for instance after the baby is born, what will be left for posterity? A story in a couple of magazines? An interview on the local news? Ephemeral!" Dr. Felcher waved her hand dismissively.

"I needed to find a way to reward your trust in me. And I believe I have. Robin and Kelsey here," her broad, theatrical gesture toward them doing nothing to help identify the guests, "will be helping me document your journey."

"Document? What do you mean?" Hannah was feeling leery and distinctly off-kilter with this new tack.

"Dr. Felcher has reached out to me ..." said Kelsey. *Or was it Robin?* It was the woman, in any case, a petite and slender brunette in slacks, a pale-blue cashmere sweater, and the highest stiletto heels Hannah had ever seen outside of a fashion runway. "She's asked me to write up your case for a book to be published sometime after the baby is born."

Hannah's jaw dropped.

"And ... " said Robin. *Or was it Kelsey?* It was the man: one about Jonathan's age and size, but clean-shaven and buzz-cut, wearing black-framed hipster glasses. "I'll be bringing in a crew to film for a documentary."

"Isn't it exciting?" Dr. Felcher beamed. "You have a big, important story to tell, Hannah; one we've agreed has all the elements that will move the American public."

"I don't know," Hannah said in a small voice, "if that's something I really want to do."

She should have been elated; certainly Natty and Jonathan would have jumped at the opportunity to promote the brand with a book and a film, and to keep the momentum going after the birth.

On the other hand, wasn't this exactly what Jonathan had warned about: someone else taking control of her narrative? Would she even retain the rights to her own story? Alarm bells were ringing in her head. "Would I get approvals on everything that's used?"

Kelsey and Robin and Dr. Felcher all looked at each other. Hadn't they expected she would ask such a question?

"Now, Hannah," Dr. Felcher said, "you didn't exactly tell *People* magazine what they could or couldn't say, did you? Of course not. This isn't advertising; it's a legitimate news story, for the scientific community as well as the general public, and we will approach it with the gravity it deserves.

"Naturally," she added, and Hannah could practically see the doctor smoothing her ruffled feathers in the manner of an offended cockatiel, "your release gives me the permission to proceed with these projects whether or not you choose to work with us, though the finished product would suffer without your input. I promise you, you will be pleased with the result.

"Trust me."

It had been Hannah's experience that people who said "Trust me"—time-share hawkers, car salesmen, would-be investment counselors—were among those least to be trusted. So she paused to consider what was being asked of her. Hannah could, of course, tell Dr. Felcher to stuff it, and find herself another well-regarded perinatal specialist to guide her through the rest of her pregnancy. But, trying to think the way Natty and Jonathan might—of the future and not just the present—she contemplated what advantages Dr. Felcher's offer might bring her. Hannah had already acknowledged that she might not live into this baby's adulthood; on dark days, she admitted there was a small chance she might not survive the birth. Wouldn't it be helpful, even desirable, to have the whole extraordinary process recorded professionally so that Hannah—or Natty, if the worst happened—could show the child what it took to bring him or her into the world? And if others gained inspiration or hope along the way, wouldn't that also be a good thing?

So Hannah replied, "I'll talk to my lawyer." She hoped her brother wouldn't balk too much at helping her out. Just this once.

~⁓~

"As unusual as it is, in many ways Hannah's pregnancy is like most others," Dr. Felcher narrated. Strictly speaking, Hannah wasn't due for another exam for a few more weeks, but Dr. Felcher and her new media team were anxious not to miss any more of the pregnancy than they already had. So Hannah reluctantly agreed to come in for an exam that was largely performed for show as soon as a contract had been signed.

Robin (with a 50% chance of getting it right, Hannah had guessed incorrectly) recorded on a hand-held device and made notes on a tablet. It would take some getting used to, having others—and cameras!—in the room while she was being examined. Per Hannah's request, she would be attired in cotton gowns rather than paper ones; no more skin would be shown than could be revealed by a two-piece bathing suit; and her modesty would be further protected by judicious camera angles. Dr. Felcher had protested that the documentary was for scientific, not prurient interest, but Hannah was adamant, and it was now in her contract, courtesy of Jason.

"The development of the fetus is going along perfectly on schedule, exactly what one would expect, what one would hope, to see at this point in the early second trimester. Fetus is approximately 8.1 centimeters in length, a little over three inches. Perhaps slightly smaller than average but nothing to be alarmed about.

"The next step, particularly in what we used to undiplomatically call a geriatric pregnancy, will be an amniocentesis."

"Excuse me," Hannah broke in. "I thought we'd discussed this."

If Dr. Felcher was irritated by the interruption of her narrative flow or by Hannah's combative tone, she didn't let on. Instead, like a runner leaping nimbly over an unexpected obstacle in her path, she said without missing a beat, "We've had a conversation about your concerns, yes. But we also talked about my spotless record of zero fetal complications over the course of my career and the importance of knowing what, if any, troubles lie ahead of us. I'm certain you were reassured by the research papers I gave you to read during your last visit.

"Your amnio is scheduled for next Tuesday at 1:00."

"Can you imagine her nerve!" Hannah fumed to Natty on the phone that night. "Making an amnio appointment for me after I've made it *very* clear that I had no intention of having any invasive testing?" When Natty remained silent, Hannah added, "And then she had the gall to announce it on *camera*, as if it were a done deal! Don't you think she's on a bit of a power trip?"

"*I* think it's a good idea," Natty finally said.

"What?" Hannah felt betrayed. "Natasha! How can you say that?"

"Mom, it's a good idea," she repeated mildly. "You have to know that. We're in unknown territory here. More information has to be better than less. And I've read all about Dr. Felcher. She's *uber* qualified. Like her personally or not, she has an amazing reputation. You'll be in the best possible hands."

Hannah's resistance weakened. It was only recently that her daughter had begun to demonstrate such mature and well-reasoned concern toward her, and surely it should be rewarded. So when Natty prodded, "Promise me you'll consider it?" Hannah promised.

~⁀⁔

HANNAH SPENT THE NIGHT before the amnio awake and in a cold sweat, her hands running obsessively over her expanding belly. She had seen her baby's progress on the ultrasound and had felt the occasional stirrings of movement, each time a tiny bit stronger, a little bit longer. Tonight she wanted more, prayed for a sign that everything was going to be all right, some kind of message that she would carry a healthy baby to term.

Her deepest fear, the one she refused to reveal in front of Robin and Kelsey despite their coaxing her to do so, was that something awful would go wrong during the amnio and that she would lose the baby—right when she could finally feel the life growing inside her, palpable assurance that the pregnancy was progressing normally. Dr. Felcher's exceptional record was a comfort, of course, but no one could predict the things that could go wrong. What's worse, from what she had read in addition to the bits and pieces she understood of Dr. Felcher's own research paper, Hannah realized that she might not know that everything had gone south until days later.

But there was no sign, nothing to bring her comfort. The baby was quiet, the universe silent. And now there wasn't even Ryan to laugh at her and tell her she was being hysterical. She'd never imagined that was something she would yearn for.

Having read the available information on the subject, Hannah thought she knew what to expect when she arrived at her appointment.

And then, of course, she saw the needle.

Hannah was not a squeamish person, but by the time she was settled on the exam table, with a confident Dr. Felcher ready to begin, she was nearly ready to get dressed and walk out. Or perhaps throw up. Or faint.

Hannah had never missed Dr. A more than at that moment. Dr. Felcher's attempts to alleviate Hannah's fears fell short because, much like Dolores, she was not a naturally comforting person. Instead, she reverted to what she knew best, which was to describe the procedure in clear and impersonal terms, speaking more to the camera than to Hannah.

"After applying the gel to your abdominal area, we use the ultrasound transducer to accurately assess the location of the fetus." The sonographer, who had been introduced as Lori, was technically controlling the transducer, but Dr. Felcher was clearly controlling the proceedings.

"And there ... we ... are," she said as the image of Hannah's baby appeared on the screen. For a moment, Hannah forgot her anxiety as she watched the screen, suffused with love and longing.

"Now, after cleaning the skin with antiseptic, we prepare to insert the needle." The woman had no bedside manner at all. Dr. Felcher continued, as if reciting from a script she had repeated many times before: "Most women don't find the needle itself painful, Hannah, though you might experience some discomfort or cramping once it's inserted. Now, please lie still." Hannah's anxiety returned in full force, and she looked away, unwilling to watch the needle's entry into her womb and trying to shut out the danger it might represent to her baby.

"*Some discomfort.*" Hannah would usually have put this lie in the same category as "You'll feel a slight pinch" when given a painful shot. Yet no matter how uncomfortable she now felt, she was determined to remain completely unmoving to minimize any risk. Fortunately, the pressure she felt was mild, and it was only a matter of moments before the needle was withdrawn.

"The amniotic fluid will be sent for analysis to test for Down syndrome and a variety of other genetic abnormalities." Dr. Felcher handed the needle off to her assistant, who whisked it away. "It will give us other information as well, of course, including the sex of the baby." Dr. Felcher smiled jovially at Hannah, though she felt strongly it was not so much for her benefit as it was for the documentary. At that moment, Hannah hated her. "I'll bet Hannah can't wait to know!"

"Yes, I can," Hannah answered bluntly. How could Dr. Felcher even say this? They had discussed it before: if the doctor saw any tell-tale genitalia on the ultrasound, she was to avoid pointing it out to Hannah, who wanted to be surprised in the delivery room. "When the results come in, I only want to know if my baby is healthy or if we'll be facing some kind of difficulty down the road," she said, adding directly to the camera, "I'm going on record that no one is to reveal the sex of the baby, and that goes for everyone in this room. Got that?"

Dr. Felcher's face had fallen visibly, but she quickly returned to form as soon as the camera re-focused on her. "Of course, Hannah. We will all consider it our solemn duty to respect your wishes."

THE EIGHT DAYS it took for the results of the amnio to come back were the longest in Hannah's memory: longer, it seemed, than the waiting she had lived through during her infertility treatments. It was excruciating. She was constantly on the lookout for evidence, whether it be leakage or cramps, that the pregnancy was in peril.

Each day she went through her routine—her meals, her walks with Sadie, her meetings with Natty and Jonathan—but her heart wasn't in anything. Required to attend a meet-and-greet at B. Fruitful, Hannah put on a happy face for an hour, dropping it immediately after the customers left.

When she was feeling particularly low and frightened, Hannah locked herself in her bedroom and sobbed her apologies to the fetus into Sadie's fur. And, twice, finding herself near a Catholic church, she slipped inside and prayed to the Virgin and to the Holy Trinity. Just to cover all her bases.

As Hannah approached the end of the waiting period, her anxiety over possible complications caused by the needle faded. Yet she now began to check her phone obsessively on the chance she might have missed a call or a text from Dr. Felcher, giving her the results. No matter how much she'd insisted it didn't matter, how much she'd love her baby regardless of the results, she admitted only to herself her fears of the long line of any abnormalities the amnio might reveal.

And then the call came.

"Hello, Hannah," Dr. Felcher said, her voice giving nothing away. She was clearly on speakerphone in her office.

"Hello," Hannah croaked back. Her hands were clammy and shaking, and she was afraid she would drop the phone.

"I'm here in the office with Robin and Kelsey."

Of course they were all there. Hannah let out a long, silent sigh, heartily regretting having agreed to their intrusion into her life. But then she sat up straight and reminded herself of the goal: to have this pregnancy fully documented for her child and perhaps the generations of her family that might follow. The inconvenience, the irritation, the intrusions into her privacy would all be worth it.

"The results of your amnio are back, and I'm very pleased to say that everything seems perfectly normal."

Grateful tears trickled down Hannah's face. "That's wonderful news!" Hannah laughed with relief and, for good measure, crossed herself.

"Yes, it is. Although I would caution you once again that this in no way guarantees that your child will be 100% healthy, as there can still be many different kinds of unexpected complications. Yet it is an excellent indicator."

There was a brief pause. "We also have your child's sex identified, Hannah. Are you ready to hear it now?"

Hannah was struck by the phrasing of that question. Dr. Felcher did not ask, "Did you change your mind? Are you sure you don't want to know?" Instead, she came at it as if Hannah might, in a fit of relief over positive results, impetuously agree to hear the information. Hannah could picture the three of them sitting in the doctor's office: Dr. Felcher dangling this delicious tidbit in front of Kelsey and Robin, who were leaning forward in their chairs hungry to be allowed to share in the news.

They were going to be disappointed.

"No, I don't want to know." *How many times did this woman have to hear it?* "Thank you for the good report, Dr. Felcher. You've taken a load off my mind."

And Hannah hung up.

HANNAH 2:9

It was just the three of them in the claustrophobic little conference room: Hannah, Ryan, and their mediator, Charles Garibaldi. Upon first glance, Garibaldi did not make much of an impression on Hannah. With his thin gray hair escaping its comb-over, a white beard in need of a trim, and a striped shirt that was perhaps a size too small and pulling at the buttons across his expansive belly, he looked to her like Sigmund Freud on a bender.

When she got close enough to shake his hand, however, Hannah smelled ... vanilla. And cinnamon. She was unexpectedly charmed, wondering if he had accidentally used his wife's body wash in the morning or whether he thought smelling like a Christmas cookie would put his clients at ease. It certainly worked for Hannah.

"Oh, so you're *that* Hannah Murrow," Garibaldi said when they introduced themselves. His deeply set gray eyes lit up, and his smile showed a mouthful of straight if somewhat coffee-yellowed teeth. "I didn't make the connection when I saw your name on the paperwork. Delighted to meet you, despite the circumstances. My daughter is pregnant with her second, in her eighth month, and she's a big fan of St. Hannah." Hannah couldn't resist a smile. "Wait till she finds out I met you."

Ryan grimaced in irritation at the topic of conversation. He had brought his briefcase with him, and he now removed a pad of yellow lined paper, apparently with handwritten notes about what he wanted from their divorce, and set it on the round table in front of him as he sat. Hannah felt unprepared. She had thoughts of her own, but what little she wanted to take with her from nearly thirty years of marriage, or from the house that had been their home, would barely cover a third of a page.

A series of emotions began welling up—anger, sadness, regret—and threatening to bring tears; she pushed them away with a sharp, deep intake of breath and a resolute swallow.

"The point of mediation is to try to come to an amicable agreement to divide the marital assets, including cash, IRAs, real estate, and the like, in a matter that suits both parties instead of what the State dictates. In this case, there is also going to be a discussion of child support for the baby to be born, which is … ?"

"My due date is May 15."

"Sometime around May 15 of next year." Garibaldi made a note. "I understand you also have an adult child, Natasha, for whom you are no longer financially responsible?"

"In theory," Ryan said wryly, with Hannah nodding her agreement. "She's twenty-four, and we only recently paid off her last semester of college."

"We still help her along," Hannah said. "Sometimes."

"But she is no longer a minor, and we won't need to formalize support for her unless you want to.

"So, today we'll be discussing support for the unborn child, which I sense will take up the bulk of our time together. We're also going to be looking at the distribution of all the assets.

"But I would prefer to begin this session by asking for a statement from each of the parties, about where you're coming from, so I have a better idea of how to direct the proceedings." Garibaldi placed his own yellow pad and pen on the table, indicating his readiness to listen. "Mr. Murrow ... Ryan, what would you like me to know?"

Ryan leaned forward in his chair, and picking up his pad, looked at his notes. "I would like you to know that I am sixty-one years old. I would also like you to know that I have worked hard all my life, starting in my teens, first in school and doing odd jobs and then in my practice. I love my career, but I have lately started looking forward to my retirement.

"I would like you to know that I had a pretty good idea of how the rest of my life was going to play out: in a few years, three or four at the max, I would sell my dental practice and Hannah and I would downsize to a condo. We would use our free time to play golf and travel, and maybe someday enjoy a grandchild that Natty—that is, Natasha—would provide.

"Recently, I was given an opportunity to advance the schedule: to sell my practice in the upcoming year and start enjoying my retirement early. I accepted an excellent offer from a competent young dentist and will turn the practice over by Q2 of next year. Everything seemed to be falling into place. But then ...

"Last month Hannah told me that she was pregnant, and you can imagine my shock. Long ago, we had spent a great deal of time and money trying to make it happen and, despite our best efforts, we couldn't, so we adopted Natty. She was a difficult child with a lot of issues, and whatever resources that we didn't expend in trying to get Hannah pregnant, we used up while raising Natty. In addition to the usual expenses, for clothes and art lessons and field trips, we also had to deal with therapists, psychologists, and other types of interventions.

"I was satisfied being a parent to Natty, but apparently that wasn't enough for Hannah. *Isn't* enough. Despite everything—the danger, the expense, the myriad of things that could go wrong with the baby—she's determined to go through with this pregnancy. I think she's acting irresponsibly, particularly with this crazy St. Hannah thing Natty and her boyfriend cooked up. It's an intrusion into our lives and I'm not staying around for it.

"I acknowledge that the child Hannah is carrying is mine and I will live up to my responsibilities as I always have, by providing support as negotiated in this mediation. But I no longer want to be a part of this marriage."

Garibaldi nodded, his face impassive. "What would you like to say, Hannah?" the mediator asked.

Although she had no little speech of her own written down, Hannah knew exactly what she wanted to say.

"You know the St. Hannah story, Mr. Garibaldi?" He nodded again. "Then I don't think I need to tell you how desperately I wanted to have a child and how thrilled I am that this miracle happened. For his own reasons, Ryan doesn't want to take this journey with us. His objections seem to be about money and lifestyle. And that's largely because he overextended us years ago without telling me, and we no longer can afford both the retirement he wants as well as this child. I don't agree with him and I'll probably never understand it, but here we are."

"All right," Garibaldi continued, "all of that is clear. Did each of you prepare a list of the personal effects that you would like to take with you from the marriage?"

Ryan had. He listed the Audi; the Mini Cooper convertible; the treadmill; the pool table; his grandmother's two-carat diamond ring (still in their joint vault, still promised to Natty if and when she ever got engaged); the antique grandfather clock that had stood in the foyer of his parents' house since the 1950s; his tennis trophies …

"Seriously, Ryan," Hannah broke in, "you had to list your tennis trophies? What the hell would I want with those?" *How petty did he think she was?*

Ignoring her, Ryan plowed on: the HD TV and the recliner from the family room; his set of Craftsman tools (another item for which Hannah had absolutely no use or desire); his father's gold watch; his mother's marcasite necklace …

"Wait a minute," Hannah said, "you gave that to me."

Ryan looked across the table at her, stone-faced. "Do you ever wear it?"

"Well, no, but … "

"I'll have it back, then."

"Is that all?" Garibaldi interjected mildly, no doubt sensing a dispute in the making.

"My laptop. And the desk and chair in the home office." Ryan leaned away from the table. "That's it."

"Hannah, what do you think of Ryan's requests?"

She shrugged. "They seem sensible, I guess. There's nothing there worth arguing over."

"The marcasite necklace?"

"I can't imagine what he'll do with it, but let him have it. Natty isn't going to want it, and I certainly have no use for it."

"All right. So, how about you, Hannah?"

"Well, I don't have a *list* as such," she said defensively, feeling as if she'd somehow missed a memo even though she'd had plenty of warning. "All I know is that I want Sadie … "

"Who's Sadie?" Garibaldi paused mid-note.

"Our dog," Ryan responded.

"*My* dog," Hannah shot back. "The one I house-trained, and walk and feed every day, and take to the vet and the groomer. You know, *my* dog."

"Don't expect any child support for Sadie," said Ryan, without humor.

"All right, Hannah, your dog. What else?"

"The antique table in the living room, the one that belonged to my grandparents. The good china. The whole set. Service for twelve. Platters, serving pieces, the whole shebang." But Ryan said nothing, doodling in the margins of his pad.

"And my grandmother's silver-plate," she added for good measure. They'd used the cutlery too on Thanksgiving.

"Plus my Subaru, which is registered under Ryan's name, but has always been mine." And had over 125,000 miles on it, so it was unlikely to interest Ryan at all. Unsurprisingly, he nodded and made a dismissive gesture.

"Well, then, that wasn't so difficult, was it?" Garibaldi asked. Although the question was meant to be rhetorical, both Hannah and Ryan shrugged. Hannah would have smiled at their shared action if only Ryan had done the same. The meeting, scheduled for an hour, slogged on from there. Ryan supplied Mr. Garibaldi with a summation of his income and debts, and Hannah provided the latest St. Hannah financial reports; she had no other assets to call her own.

"I'll be examining these in detail," Garibaldi advised them as he checked his watch, a scratched old Timex, "and from them I'll develop a child support and alimony plan I hope will work for both of you.

"Even that will only be a starting place, of course. I'll mail you each a copy and you can email me your comments. I hope we'll be able to reach a consensus that will keep the lawyers out of your lives."

Ryan gathered up his papers and, silent, shook hands with Mr. Garibaldi. He said nothing to Hannah as he hastened out the door, checking his phone.

"Thank you for your time, Mr. Garibaldi," Hannah said, suddenly weary now, as she shook his hand. The meeting had made it clear to Hannah that Ryan was never coming back. It wasn't specifically the loss of Ryan she mourned; it was her fantasies of their perfect little family—Mommy, Daddy, big sis, and baby—that was never going to happen. "I appreciate your efforts to be fair to both of us."

"That's the job, Hannah. I do my best."

It was the most she could hope for herself, as well.

HANNAH 2:10

A thin layer of snow had fallen, and the town looked like it had been baked out of gingerbread, dusted with powdered sugar, and decorated with colorful sprinkles of festive lights. Hannah couldn't be happier; even the weather had cooperated to bring her a picture-perfect Christmas. Despite her withdrawal from weekly church life, Hannah had always loved and attended Midnight Mass on Christmas Eve and was determined that this year would be no different. To her surprise and delight, Natty and Jonathan volunteered to pick up Dolores and Frank and join them at Mass. She was grateful; it had been years since Natty had displayed any interest at all in going to church.

Dolores fawned over Jonathan, though Hannah could tell—with a grin she kept to herself—that her mother would be complaining loudly about his facial hair and earring the next time they were alone. Hannah had more than gotten used to his appearance and no longer allowed her inner critic any say over him. He was good for Natty, and as far as Hannah was concerned, he was now family. Frank was walking slowly, relying heavily on his cane and the arm Jonathan offered him, his one remaining good suit bagging at the ankles and hanging off his thin shoulders. But her father was beaming, looking happier than she had seen him in months. Hannah was warmed by her family, her church, and the celebration that would be even more significant tonight. That her marriage was coming to an end was the only low spot in an otherwise glorious evening.

The church, always packed for Christmas, was already crowded when they arrived ("I told you we should have left the apartment earlier," Dolores sniffed as she did every year), and not a few heads turned when Hannah walked in. Pretty much everyone in the church—and indeed, the entire town—knew about St. Hannah and "the inconceivable conception" as one wag had lately put it on Twitter. And for those who didn't, her state at five months was obvious and could no longer be mistaken for middle-age flab.

In another situation, at another time, Hannah would have been mortified by the whispers she caused. But not tonight. Tonight she glowed as brightly as the candles that illuminated the sanctuary, exuding a radiance that came directly from her womb; from the knowledge that she was bearing life at last; from being surrounded by the people she loved the most (Jonathan was recently added to that list); and from knowing she looked exceptionally well turned-out in a simple but obscenely expensive royal-blue maternity dress chosen by Ke'isha. The baby's movements were regular now and stronger, if still unpredictable, and Hannah felt she could take on the world.

So let them talk! she thought triumphantly and raised her chin a notch higher.

Before they could reach their seats, Hannah found herself accosted by Heather, the church secretary, better attired than usual in a possibly homemade but flattering hunter-green velvet dress, her eyes alight. "Mrs. Murrow, could I speak to you for a minute? Just a minute, I promise."

Hannah nodded, distracted. "Natasha," she said, "take Nana and Grandpa to a pew and save a place for me as close as you can to the aisle. I'll be right in."

Heather drew her, with a firmer grip and somewhat more strength than Hannah expected of a woman so slightly built, to a hallway where the everyday choir robes were stored on a moveable rack. "Mrs. Murrow. Hannah," Heather began. After a moment she burst out, "I knew it, I just knew it!"

"I'm sorry, Heather, I don't understand."

"That day you called Father Aloysius and left that message. You know, *1 Samuel 1:19*. No one ever quotes that passage. Believe me, after six years of taking messages for Father I've heard pretty much everything. Most people who cite the Old Testament go right to the big stories, you know, Adam and Eve, or the Ten Commandments, or Noah. Maybe Leviticus when they're feeling cranky about running across a 'lifestyle' they disagree with." She rolled her eyes. "But *Samuel*? I actually had to look that one up. And when I did, wow, it hit me like a bolt of lightning. I KNEW." Heather grasped Hannah's hand and looked at her with unabashed adoration. Hannah took a step back.

"And then when Father came out of his study after speaking with you, he had that same look on his face as when he has been communing with the Lord. Sure enough, when I asked him if anything was wrong, he said not at all. He said a wonderful blessing had been bestowed on a parishioner who had suffered for a long time. I knew it could only mean one thing: that you were pregnant!'"

"And so I am." Hannah smiled tightly, uncomfortable and anxious to return to her little family. She kept glancing back toward the sanctuary, hoping Heather would take the hint.

"And so you are! I mean, I barely know you now, and I certainly didn't know you when you were going through your trials years ago. And I would never, ever, *ever* have invaded your privacy to ask you about it, much as I wanted to. But then you went public, and it's all over the news now and in *People* magazine! I want you to know I've read all the articles and I'm on the St. Hannah mailing list." She gave a coy smile. "I've even asked Santa for a St. Hannah beanie for Christmas."

"Wow, that's great," Hannah said. But her reply did nothing to stop Heather's hymn of praise, or even to slow it.

"It's truly a miracle!" Heather exclaimed, her look ecstatic. "Just like in *1 Samuel*: 'The Lord remembered her.' You've been blessed, Hannah."

"I certainly have been blessed." She tried to withdraw her hand from Heather's but found it held hers even more urgently. Hannah became alarmed. "Thank you, Heather, but I really should be getting back. Mass will be starting in a couple of minutes."

"Just one more thing, oh, please! Hannah, I ... I want the Lord to remember me, too. I want the Lord to bless me with children. My husband and I, we've been trying for five years. We've been to three different specialists and, well, you know all about that.

"I've been praying every day to the Holy Ghost and to the Virgin, but I'm still barren." Tears filled Heather's eyes as Hannah's grew wide.

"Bless me, Hannah!"

To Hannah's horror, Heather pulled her hand to her belly and held it pressed there. "Please, Hannah! Can we pray together? Won't you ask the Lord to bless me, like he blessed you? I want a baby, too!"

It was only when she broke into sobs that Hannah was able to pull her hand away, and for long seconds she stood by Heather, not knowing what to do. She was so shocked by Heather's behavior that she felt an undeniable urge to flee the scene entirely. On the other hand, she wished she could comfort the young woman in some way; after all, she had been on the receiving end of the same bad news for so very long and knew its heartache.

In the end, Hannah produced a clean tissue from her purse, taking the same hands that had moments before held hers captive and closing them around it. Hannah cast around for something, anything, appropriate to say. Finally, she murmured, "Don't give up hope, Heather. Have faith." And she left the figure in green weeping against the backdrop of red and white choir robes, a melancholy Christmas tableau.

The organ music had already started by the time Hannah returned to the pew, her late arrival raising the few eyebrows that had not risen on her entrance to the church. "Where have you been?" Dolores hissed. "You're late! People are staring."

Still slightly shaken by her encounter with Heather, Hannah was not inclined to remind her mother that people had been staring at her from the moment she came in.

Soon, though, Hannah lost herself in the familiar liturgy and the music she loved. When it came time for Communion, Hannah took her place in the long line of her fellow parishioners.

As she received the Eucharist from Father Aloysius, Hannah closed her eyes and crossed herself, feeling the significance of the Sacrament more deeply than she ever had in the past. Her head felt light with the joy of returning to a cherished tradition, a generational memory in her family that reached back hundreds of years.

Though Hannah had never missed Christmas services, it had been many years since she had participated in Communion, the gaps in her beliefs and her reluctance to submit to Confession standing in her way. This year, though, despite lingering doubts about the usefulness or relevance of doing so—and the discomfort of having to confront her failings—she had gone to the church for Reconciliation a couple of days prior, confessing her sins sitting directly across from Father Michael.

"Bless me, Father, for I have sinned," Hannah had begun easily out of long custom, making the Sign of the Cross. "It has been … um …" And here she had paused, embarrassed, because she no longer remembered when she had last done this—probably not since Natty was a child. "Um, it has been many years since my last Confession."

Knowing where she had erred came more easily. Father Michael listened with patience and a serene face as she enumerated: "I've been proud. Frequently. Kind of comes with the territory of being a minor celebrity, I guess." She laughed nervously and cleared her throat.

"And, um, vain. That too, a lot. I want to look good. I want people to like me. Maybe too much.

"My marriage is ending. I guess you know that. I suppose I could have tried harder to save it. But I haven't broken my vows at all; I've been completely loyal to Ryan."

Father Michael nodded and remained mute, his fingers tapping silently against his knees, and Hannah with a resigned sigh finally admitted: "I've, um, put myself above others. Since I got pregnant, that is. I've acted as if I'm something special, allowed others to believe I'm something special. All right: *encouraged* others to believe I'm something special. And I'm just a woman. A really, really lucky woman."

Hannah had been under no illusion that any number of repetitions of "Hail Mary" or "Our Father" was going to change her conduct; she frankly admitted to herself that she was enjoying her role as St. Hannah too much. In fact, she knew she would be going directly from her Reconciliation to a scheduled personal appearance with The Knit-Wits of Temple Beth Shalom, where she would smile and joke and accept the admiration of a group of bespectacled grandmothers only a few years older than herself, as well as the pretty pastel sweaters and booties they had crafted for her child.

But when she reflected on what people considered laudable behavior, she also knew to reject certain supposed role models like Missy. The things that made her sister-in-law what many outsiders considered the "perfect mother" were actually a product of snobbishness and exclusion. The people in Missy's circle admired it; they were all much the same. Hannah had made many of her own mistakes, especially with Natty, but she hoped she was a better person than that.

She would work at being a better person than that.

"For these sins and all my sins, I am truly sorry."

HANNAH 2:11

"I understand you'll be hitting a milestone next month, Hannah," Dr. Felcher said toward the end of Hannah's five-month checkup. Hannah pulled her feet from the stirrups and pushed herself upright as the doctor tossed her surgical gloves in the bin. Midway through the second trimester, the baby was putting on the right amount of weight; Hannah, putting on slightly more than necessary. Robin, Kelsey, and their cameraman stood, quietly recording the entire exam, and Hannah no longer paid much attention to them; they were as much a part of the environment as were the exam table, the equipment, the wall decor.

"That's right: fifty-five," Hannah replied cheerfully. The usual post-Christmas letdown and midwinter depression Hannah had experienced since her late forties had been replaced by the delightful thought that her fifty-fifth year would bring the greatest gift of her life. Despite the persistent sciatica for which she was seeing a chiropractor and a few minor aches and pains, she was feeling good, energized—the fatigue and nausea she'd had in her first trimester long gone. Their brand had enjoyed a profitable Christmas and Natty, who seemed to have forgotten she had ever been angry with Hannah, had started giving her a peck on the forehead every time they met.

"Our little team has an early present for you." Dr. Felcher said as she gestured toward Kelsey and Robin, who removed a small, wrapped rectangle from her oversized Coach purse and handed it to Hannah. The camera zoomed in as Hannah opened the gift.

"Wow," she said, "this is amazing."

And it was: a hard-cover book of photos of Hannah's pregnancy to date, starting with that first, earth-shattering ultrasound (taken at Dr. A's office, Hannah reminded herself with a pang) and progressing through the images Dr. Felcher's sonographer had taken. Interspersed were color and black-and-white shots of Hannah and Dr. Felcher during the exams; candids of Hannah from her public appearances; and stills from the documentary in progress. The paper was glossy and substantial; the photos, both flattering and meaningful. Everything about it was professional, down to the gold logo with "St. Hannah 55" embossed on an otherwise blank, smooth white cover. After leafing through the book, Hannah turned it to the camera and smiled an honest, jubilant smile.

"Thank you all! I don't know if I've ever been given something so wonderful."

"We're so glad you like it." Dr. Felcher nodded in satisfaction as Robin and Kelsey beamed. "I thought we could offer it on the St. Hannah website as an exclusive, numbered limited edition for $24.95 each, and a signed copy for $34.95. The premium should cut down on the number of books you'll actually have to sign. We wouldn't want you getting carpal tunnel syndrome!"

"Oh." The smile faded and Hannah set the book down onto her lap. "I thought that, you know, it was a one-of-a-kind sort of thing. Um, just for me."

"Oh, that copy is yours to keep, of course," Dr. Felcher said, missing the point entirely. "We have a limited run of 500 to provide for the website. Have your Natasha contact Kelsey's people, and we'll set it all up and figure out how to split the proceeds.

"Before I forget …" she continued briskly. She handed Hannah a couple of brochures. "You might be familiar with Lamaze, as it's the one most people talk about, but the Bradley method has been around for decades and has its own passionate adherents."

"What's the difference?"

"Well, both of them do a good job educating parents on what to expect in labor and birth, and both teach skills to help the laboring mother deal with the pain.

"Lamaze teaches the mother breathing techniques and how to relax and focus outwardly through her contractions. Bradley takes a more holistic approach, giving recommendations on diet and exercise in the months leading up to labor, and making the mother aware of the control she has over her own muscles during contractions. More inwardly focused, if you will."

"That sounds interesting." *Though a lot more work*, Hannah thought. *But maybe doing the work beforehand would be worth it in the long run.* She was all for anything that alleviated the pain of childbirth, which by all accounts was of legendary and therefore terrifying proportions.

"Oh, I've had patients who've enjoyed a great deal of success with Bradley; by some metrics, it can be more successful than using Lamaze, if you consider 'success' to mean not having to rely on pharmaceuticals for pain relief. But it may not be right for you."

"Why not?"

Dr. Felcher turned away from Hannah and busied herself with her tablet before answering. "While both programs make use of a supportive partner during labor and delivery," she said casually, "Bradley is also somewhat archaically known as 'husband-coached' childbirth. It relies more heavily on the presence and coaching of a second individual. So, you see, it's far easier to commit to the Bradley method if you have a live-in partner, someone you can depend on, who can work with you, practice with you, and support you right up to the moment of delivery. So all things considered, I'd advise you to find a good Lamaze class."

Sounds like a challenge to me, Hannah thought, raising her chin slightly. Dr. Felcher was a pro, no doubt about it; she certainly knew her medicine. But she didn't seem to know much about her patient.

It was in that very moment that Hannah decided to do Bradley—Dr. Felcher and Ryan be damned.

A QUICK ONLINE SEARCH at home revealed there was only one local instructor team teaching a Bradley method course falling at the beginning of Hannah's third trimester. The timing would be perfect: if it hadn't already reached capacity, the twelve-week class would carry her straight through her due date.

Holding her breath, Hannah called the number. No answer. She left a message and paced nervously, nearly tripping over Sadie twice in the process. She knew she could do Lamaze as an alternative, and there were plenty of classes available, but she wanted to prove Dr. Felcher wrong, to show her she didn't need Ryan to have a "successful" birth experience.

Barely five minutes later, before she could even get started folding her laundry to burn off her nervous energy, her phone rang. "Is this Hannah Murrow?"

"It is," Hannah replied.

"This is Lark Williamson, the Bradley method instructor, returning your call."

"Yes, thank you for getting back to me so quickly."

"Oh, I'm a big fan of yours," Lark chirped. "What an inspirational story! I started following St. Hannah the minute I saw the report on the local news back when you first came into the public eye. I was so hoping you'd call us! What can I do for you?"

"Well, I was looking at your Tuesday night class, starting March 3. Is it too late to get in?"

"To be completely honest, Hannah, we do have a full class for that series."

"Oh." Hannah didn't know why she'd thought she could waltz right in six weeks before a class was set to begin. Dr. Felcher had warned her that spots filled up quickly because the classes were kept small, around half-a-dozen couples per. She cast around for a way to persuade Lark to take her anyway.

"But," Lark continued, "we would be delighted to make an exception for you."

"Really?"

"Oh, absolutely!"

Hannah smiled in relief. "Well, that's great. Three hundred dollars, right? Do I pay through the website when I register?"

"*You* don't pay. Not St. Hannah! It would be our honor to have you in the class. I can't wait to tell my husband, Patrick! He's as big a fan as I am."

"I'm so flattered. But listen, there is one thing." Biting her lip, Hannah plunged ahead; there was no getting around it. "Um, I have a contract with a documentary filmmaker and an author, and they kind of follow me around. They're going to expect to be able to come to the classes, too. The other parents are going to have to sign releases to appear in the film. If they choose not to, we can blur their faces. But it might become an issue."

"That will be no problem at all!" Lark said before Hannah had even finished her sentence. Hannah had been discovering for a while now that many people she encountered were willing to do almost anything for a brush with fame, minor as it might be. It was easy to forget that, prior to taking on the persona of St. Hannah, she had been just like that. And it was unsettling.

"Give me your email address and I'll send you all the information, the reading, and the exercises. Then all you have to do is bring your partner and enjoy the beautiful experience of getting ready for your baby!"

Ah, the partner. Because Hannah hadn't thought at all about childbirth classes until Dr. Felcher mentioned them, it had never occurred to her that her separation from Ryan would leave her in this awkward position. Now that she'd been all but challenged to find one, she knew who would be the best influence on her, the most calming and positive presence in labor and delivery.

"Hi, Amibeth! It's Hannah."

Once there had been a time when Hannah wouldn't have had to declare who it was, her voice familiar enough on its own to identify her. And once she could have asked anything of Amibeth or of Marla and her wish would have been granted. There had been a stated understanding among the three of them that, should one be fortunate enough to become pregnant during their fertility treatments, the others would make middle-of-the-night deliveries of Ben & Jerry's or anything else the lucky mom required. Even when that became increasingly unlikely, they still maintained their commitment to each other.

Well, until recently.

Now, after exchanging pleasantries, Hannah felt strangely tongue-tied. After the conversation in which Amibeth had given Hannah the name of her divorce attorney, they had only spoken once more, when Hannah had told Amibeth about their decision to use mediation. Even then she had felt the distance opening between them.

"So, what's going on? I hope everything's going well with the pregnancy."

"Oh, I'm fine, the baby's fine. That's actually why I'm calling. Without Ryan around and all ... well, it would mean a lot to me if you'd be my partner in my Bradley childbirth class."

"Oh." This syllable was followed by an extended period of silence, not the answer Hannah was expecting.

"Amibeth?"

"I'm sorry, Hannah," Amibeth said. "I'm honored that you asked, I really am, but I can't manage it right now."

Expecting this kind of reluctance, Hannah launched into a prepared speech: "I realize it's kind of a lengthy commitment, and it does require preparation and coordination between us. But the session doesn't start until March 3; maybe by then you'll … "

"That's not what I meant." She sighed. "I'll be honest: when I say I can't manage it, I mean that I won't. I'm going through a lot right now and don't want to subject myself to that kind of stress."

"I'll be doing most of the work, you know," Hannah half-joked. "The stress is all mine." But it came out sounding petulant. Though she was aware from Marla that Amibeth's divorce from Dorian had turned acrimonious over money, she'd hoped that the Bradley classes would provide a welcome distraction and perhaps even serve to bring the Witches closer together again.

"You misunderstand me," Amibeth replied in a voice colder than Hannah had ever heard from her, and she felt her stomach drop the way it does when a plane loses altitude. "Come on, Hannah, you're not that dense. I know all about Bradley; I did my share of reading when I thought there'd be a chance that … that I … It's not just the class and the time commitment and you know it. Bradley is a very intimate experience. Your partner in class is your *coach*, the same person who's going to be there guiding you through every minute of labor and delivery." Her tone turned bitter. "Cheering you on through the beautiful and natural experience of *childbirth*."

Hannah suddenly knew where this conversation was going and deeply regretted having made the call. Why hadn't she stopped for a moment to consider Amibeth's point of view; how it might hurt her by rubbing her nose in her own perceived failure? But there was no graceful way out of it now.

"I think it's more than a little *selfish* of you to ask me to join you for the successful end to a successful pregnancy *after all I've been through*," she added, her emphasis the Amibeth equivalent of a raised voice, a stomped foot, and a thrown vase. "I wish you all the best, Hannah, I really do. I hope your child is healthy, and your labor and delivery are easy. But I can't be a part of them.

"Good luck to you."

When Hannah hung up, she mentally slapped herself for how badly she had misjudged the situation, for not thinking it through. Hannah mentally ran through the local friends she might ask; it didn't take long. Although she was self-aware enough to know she wasn't a particularly warm and gregarious person, Hannah never before considered how few and how superficial her friendships really were. They were good for a glass of wine or a brunch date, a weekend at an out-of-town spa—not so much for a crisis. Two of them, those whose husbands were friends with Ryan, even blamed her for the breakup of her marriage and refused to speak with her. When it came to the people she could confidently call at 2 a.m. without judgment, only the Witches had ever passed muster. And now she didn't even have them.

"So, I seem to be stuck without a childbirth partner," she complained as Jonathan and Natty sat at the dining room table, returning St. Hannah emails. Hannah was knitting a lightweight spring blanket for the baby, the wool as soft as Sadie's fur when she was a pup. "I never thought it would be so difficult."

"You mean to find someone who's willing to commit to twelve weeks of two-hour classes and listen to you huff and puff? With the promise of another, I don't know, twelve hours of labor?" Natty said with mock incredulity. "Gee, I can't imagine why ever not. Sounds like a fabulous time."

"First of all, you're describing Lamaze, not Bradley. Either way, I get it, it's a big commitment. But you'd think there'd be at least one person who'd want to support me at a critical time like this."

"Maybe you've been asking the wrong people."

Hannah narrowed her eyes. "I don't hear you volunteering."

With a shrug, Natty replied, "I don't hear you asking."

"You mean, you'd want to be my birthing partner?" Hannah asked skeptically. Natty shrugged again. Jonathan leaned back in his chair, his arms folded over his chest, enjoying the exchange.

"As my coach, you'll have to tell me how wonderful I am and how great I'm doing. Constantly."

Natty rolled her eyes.

"And if I need it, you'll have to massage my back and rub my shoulders."

At this, Natty frowned and wrinkled her nose in exaggerated disgust. She looked at Jonathan, who laughed.

"Think you can handle it?" he goaded her. "Are you ready to step out of your comfort zone?"

"What do you say, Natasha?" Hannah asked, with the gravity of a marriage proposal. "Will you be my birthing partner?"

Natty made a show of thinking it over, and then said simply, "Yes."

HANNAH 2:12

*F*ifty-five.

Hannah opened her eyes and said it aloud: "I'm fifty-five." Sadie cocked her head, curious.

It didn't feel momentous. Certainly not like her 50th— everyone gets excited about big, round numbers. As far as Sadie was concerned, of course, this was a day like any other, with the same requirements of food and exercise. She was patient, but she had her limits, and had started to protest by poking her nose into Hannah's side. So Hannah hauled herself out of bed.

The first phone call of any birthday was usually from Dolores, who would take the opportunity to remind Hannah that she was the result of sixteen hours of "hard labor," during which Frank was at home, shoveling five inches of snow from the walk while Dolores languished in the hospital alone. Hannah wasn't sure she was ready for that particular conversation this year, as it would be a reminder of the difficulties that lay ahead for her; she didn't want to think about the horrors of labor.

This time, though, it was Natty who phoned, shortly before 9:00.

"Morning, Mom; happy birthday!" Natty warbled. Hannah was still getting accustomed to this new, cheerful Natty. It was at odds with everything Hannah thought she knew about her daughter's personality, particularly in the morning. Getting her to school, especially when she hit her teen years, had been a nightmare. Even her first months in college had been a trial, and Hannah had fretted she was in danger of flunking out. Thank God she was almost done! "How are you feeling today?"

"Not bad for an old lady. Pretty good for an old, pregnant lady."

"Great, great. Wanted to let you know we have an appointment at B. Fruitful at two."

"B. Fruitful?" She frowned down at her tablet, confused. "I don't have anything with Ke'isha on my calendar."

"I know. She called me and asked if we were available. I didn't see why not; we have nothing special going on today."

"Really? Nothing?" Hannah grinned. There'd been years when Natty insisted she hadn't known what day it was, or had earnestly sworn that she had planned to do something to celebrate but had gotten too busy and forgotten. During her most belligerent periods, she had deliberately gone out of her way to ignore Hannah's birthday out of spite. But those days had passed, and this birthday was so consequential—not just to the St. Hannah brand that had helped Natty bloom but also to the closeness that had been re-established between them. How could there be nothing special?

It had to be a surprise party. Well, she would play along.

"Do I have to call Kelsey & Company?" Hannah had already told the documentary team that there were no personal appearances planned for today, no plans to commemorate the occasion.

"I'll take care of that. Pick you up at 1:30?"

Out in the front yard, Hannah found an upsurge in St. Hannah gifts and resigned herself to devoting extra time to retrieving, sorting, cataloging, and deciding which were suitable for donation to the shelter and which had to go elsewhere. While most days the gifts were a combination of religious tokens and baby goods, today the focus was squarely on her. As Hannah's sweet tooth was well documented on the website and in fact a notorious in-joke among fans, among the presents were six birthday cakes—two store-bought, four homemade; three tins of home-baked cookies and two of her favorite local bakery's macarons; a deluxe Godiva gift box; and a small crate filled with Lindt truffles. No matter how tempting the homemade goods looked, though—and they did look delicious, she thought with regret—they were destined for the trash. There was no knowing what was baked inside, and there could be any number of ingredients, legitimate or not, that were detrimental to the baby's well-being. And to Hannah's, as well. Her sole indulgence (it *was* her birthday after all) would be keeping the macarons.

By the time Hannah had brought all the usable items upstairs to Natty's room and added the day's presents to the spreadsheet the company used to keep track of such things, her parents had phoned—and Marla, as well. (She wondered with a pang if she would hear from Amibeth, and concluded that she wouldn't.) Jason and Missy would call in the evening, as they did every year, insisting—quite unnecessarily, in Hannah's opinion—that their children each take a turn wishing Aunt Hannah a happy birthday. Far-flung friends—her college roommates, neighbors who had moved away years ago—also made their annual calls or posted their greetings on Facebook.

By the time Ryan's grandfather clock struck 1:00, Hannah had answered the door five times for the delivery of floral arrangements and one fruit basket. Though the bouquets were beautiful—the rich yellows, deep reds, and vivid purple blooms an appreciated bright spot in the depths of this perpetually gray and bleak February—she found the combined scent of them intolerable: overwhelming and reminiscent of the sickly sweetness engulfing mourners at a wake. She determined that Natty and Jonathan could take all but one particularly exotic bouquet to Mercy Hospital to brighten someone else's day.

Selecting a pistachio macaron to enjoy with her after-lunch decaf, Hannah leaned back in her kitchen chair with a contented sigh and reflected that her fifty-fifth had already far surpassed her fifieth, and there was still the surprise party to look forward to.

When they arrived at B. Fruitful, however, there were but a few clients milling about the store as Kelsey and the crew checked the lighting and ambient sound—nothing that would indicate a surprise party in the offing. Hannah felt a little let down and scolded herself for expecting too much. Nevertheless, she entered with a bright smile, waving with professional composure at the customers who were first confused, then delighted when they realized who had joined them. Cell phones came out; snapshots were taken and immediately posted to Instagram and Facebook.

Once the documentary crew indicated they were ready to go, Ke'isha seated Hannah in one of the floral chairs that had accommodated her on many previous visits. "We have something very special to show you," she said. Hannah looked to Natty questioningly, but she shrugged, indicating she was equally in the dark. Since Natty had always lacked a poker face, Hannah declined to believe her.

"Cheyenne!" Ke'isha called out. A tall young woman in her late twenties or early thirties, plainly in her third trimester of pregnancy, walked out from the try-on rooms. "Eric's cousin," Ke'isha murmured in an aside to Hannah. Cheyenne was wearing a lovely lightweight dress with half sleeves, in grass-green linen sprigged with white flowers, a thin white band riding high over the curve of her belly. It was youthful without being precious, and even more than the flowers she had received in the morning, it made Hannah long for spring.

"Oh, that's beautiful," she said sincerely, meaning both the dress and Cheyenne, who strode and whirled across the shop in her strappy sandals with the same easy grace as Natty, despite the burden of her pregnancy. If Cheyenne wasn't a model, she should probably consider it as a profession, her sculpted face and uncommon amber eyes making her all the more striking under a scarcely there closely cropped Afro.

"I'm glad you like it," Ke'isha said with barely contained excitement, "because it's the very first item in my brand-new St. Hannah clothing line!"

Cheyenne walked over to Hannah and showed her the embroidered logo subtly incorporated into the design over the left breast.

"I'm overwhelmed!" Hannah said, and meant it.

"It was Eric's idea," Ke'isha said, reaching for his hand as he stood behind her. "He said it was high time for me to design my own line, and that I'd be crazy if I didn't take advantage of this opportunity to do something unique.

"I've already designed a half-dozen more dresses and a handful of blouses. But you have to give it your blessing, Hannah. I can't do it if you don't approve."

"Of course I approve! But wait; let me talk to my management team." Turning to Natty and Jonathan with barely controlled glee, she asked, "What do you think, management team? Should we approve this use of the St. Hannah name and logo?"

"I vote yes," Natty said with a grin, holding up her hand.

"I second that," Jonathan agreed.

At that moment, the baby stirred, and Hannah nodded in satisfaction, her hand spanning her abdomen. "It seems to be unanimous, Ke'isha. Congratulations!"

The little audience of customers applauded and hooted.

Ever the practical one, Eric said, "I've written up a draft with some numbers for you all to take a look at. We'll have to come to an agreement about advertising, licensing fees, and …"

"I'll take care of it," Natty interrupted. "Meanwhile, let's have some cake!"

On cue, Ke'isha reached down to a low shelf and brought out a small, round cake frosted with chocolate buttercream. The St. Hannah logo was reproduced in color on an edible icing sheet, and someone had arranged two numeral "5" candles atop it.

"We couldn't put all fifty-five candles on it," Ke'isha explained as Jonathan lit the candles. "Fire hazard, you know."

"Very funny," Hannah said, but she wasn't offended in the least. "These will be easier for my ancient lungs to blow out anyway."

Eric carried the cake over to Hannah and held it before her as they all sang "Happy Birthday." When it came time to blow out the candles, Natty leaned close and said, "Make a wish, Mom."

In her callow, ignorant teen years, she had aspired to fame —a pipe dream of adulation from a starry-eyed public that would give her the attention and appreciation her mother had denied her.

As a young bride, her wishes and her prayers focused entirely on becoming pregnant, nurturing life within herself, becoming a mother.

And later, all she had wanted was Natty's respect and affection.

Now, in that frozen moment between taking a breath and releasing it, Hannah realized that wish was to have exactly what she had right now.

Life wasn't perfect, and she was aware that there was still an entire trimester looming ahead of her, full of its own perils. But right now, other than the healthy birth of her child, Hannah could think of nothing else to wish for.

A split-second later, the candles were blown out, but their glow remained.

TRIMESTER 3

HANNAH 3:1

"Welcome to the Bradley method of childbirth," Lark said, looking around the room. "Over the course of the next twelve weeks, my husband Patrick and I are going to help you develop the skills you need to bring your baby into this world in the most natural, healthiest way possible."

As she talked, Hannah, too, looked around the room, a large, fluorescent-lit classroom in a church annex. While she had fretted that she and Natty would be the only non-traditional team in the class, she was pleased that there were two others: a lesbian couple and another mother/daughter team … though in the case of the latter two, it was the daughter who was pregnant, and she looked to be about seventeen and profoundly bored. All five other pairs had signed St. Hannah releases and were now sitting in metal folding chairs, clutching their Bradley method workbooks and pretending to ignore the camera crew and still photographer who stole silently from corner to corner, seeking out the best angles. If the women were wearing slightly more makeup than they might ordinarily for a nighttime class; if the men appeared to have taken a shave and put on a fresh shirt shortly before arriving, well, Hannah and Natty might exchange a knowing look but neither was going to say anything.

Before the start of class, Hannah and Natty handed out the St. Hannah merch they'd brought with them, distributing St. Hannah XL sleep shirts, pins, stickers, and mini photo albums to the delighted participants. One couple who had originally signed on for the course had dropped out, Lark told Hannah in confidence while the couples showed off their gifts for the cameras.

"The husband said, and I quote, 'It would trivialize and commercialize the sacred birth process and make a mockery of the beauty of God's creation.' So I refunded their deposit and helped them find another class." Lark shrugged. "I'm glad they said something. It's vital that everyone in our classes be 100% comfortable with the experience."

From their single phone conversation and Lark's profile photo—natural-looking golden blond hair tumbling in carefully arranged waves over her shoulders, bright blue eyes ringed with several coats of mascara—Hannah guessed Lark to be either a bit of a cheerleader-style lightweight or a driven perfectionist in the mold of her sister-in-law, Missy. She was neither. Beautiful and confident, yes; she was also naturally curvy—substantially so—and unapologetic about it. At the session, despite the presence of the cameras, she wore next to no makeup. Hannah warmed to Lark immediately, finding her professional, empathetic, and forgiving. Lark's husband, Patrick, leaning against a wide metal desk, was somewhat less memorable: he was of a build that was once known as "portly," with the pleasant but bland looks that belonged on an alderman or city councilman.

During that first two-hour class, Lark led the instruction, with Patrick participating only when a demonstration called for a partner. Hannah imagined he would have more to say when the focus turned toward the duties of the coach, but she admired the way Lark wielded the power in that relationship. The expectant pairs were told what to anticipate from the rest of the course, instructed on the importance of communication between the mother and her coach and, after dragging yoga mats to the center of the room, shown the all-important exercises that would help the baby progress through the birth canal. Hannah, having received the workbook early from Lark and having already read the entire thing through, had already started practicing the exercises: tailor-sitting, squatting, pelvic rocking, butterfly, Kegels.

Despite her relative fitness for a woman of fifty-five, Hannah knew her age was working against her. Simply getting down on all fours was far more of an effort for her than it was for any of the other students. Her lower back complained, her knees groaned, her muscles squawked. But, aware the cameras were on her, Hannah kept mum. She was determined to show the class, and whoever might watch her documentary in the future, that "St. Hannah" wasn't a quitter.

When class was declared over, Hannah sat on a folding chair to catch her breath. She watched as the other woman her age, Gloria, reached into her handbag and handed her teen daughter Kayla a cell phone. The girl snatched it away greedily and sat down in a corner to text, apparently trying to make up for the two hours during which her mother had confiscated the device.

Gloria caught the sympathetic smile Hannah sent her way and walked over to sit beside her.

"I love your sweater," Hannah said, because she did. The sweater was obviously hand-knit with some skill, using a lacy "double vine" stitch in a flattering shade of light pink. "Did you make it?"

Blushing at the compliment, Gloria ran her hands lovingly over the strands. A heavyset woman with thinning brown hair, she had the kind of open, guileless face that somehow made Hannah feel she would be a good friend … something that was in short supply these days. "Thanks. Yeah, I did. I took up knitting when I gave up smoking, a few years back," Gloria said. "Gives me something to do with my hands.

"To be honest, though," she added under her breath, with an incline of her head toward the sullen Kayla, whose fingers hadn't ceased their motion and whose forehead had not unpuckered, "there have been times lately when I'd kill for a smoke."

"Well, you're very good." Hannah could appreciate the degree of difficulty involved in the pattern and the practically mechanical uniformity of the stitches. If knitting were an Olympic sport, this sweater would be in gold-medal territory. "I love to knit, myself."

"Oh, it's my greatest pleasure. But I'm getting in as much as I can now, because I know there's not going to be a whole lot of time for it once the baby's born. I want Kayla to finish high school, and I'm all she has. The father is out of the picture."

"Oh, I'm sorry."

"Don't be. I'm relieved. It's the most useful thing that jackass has ever done." She blew out a breath. "But I don't know how I'm gonna do it. Taking care of a baby again, at my age. You have no idea how terrifying that is."

"I think I do."

Gloria laughed in embarrassment and waved her hands in denial. "Oh, I didn't mean it like that! Of course, you of all people would know! I just mean you're not gonna have to go it all alone like me. You don't know how lucky you are."

"Excuse me?"

"I mean your daughter. Natasha. She's really got it together. Look at her." Gloria gestured at Natty, who was making notes on her tablet as she nodded at something Kelsey was saying. "So mature for her age! I hope one of these days Kayla will grow up a little, be more like her."

Looking at Natty through Gloria's eyes, Hannah was filled with pride. Natty, *this* Natty—Natasha—had been a huge comfort and an even bigger help. And knowing, as Gloria didn't, that Natty hadn't always been like that, Hannah suspected that it might benefit Gloria to talk to someone who'd been where she was right now. On impulse, she took a St. Hannah card out of her handbag and wrote her number on it.

"This is my cell," she told Gloria. "Call me and we'll talk. I know a few things about difficult daughters."

HANNAH WAS SATISFIED that her classes would prepare her well for labor and birth. But like any other expectant mother, she soon found that good preparation alone couldn't eliminate all unexpected complications. It was at the end of the second class that Lark approached Hannah and Natty.

"Hannah, when is your next appointment with your OB?"

As if the question were addressed to her, Natty took out her tablet and checked the calendar. "A week from Tuesday. Why?"

"I don't mean to alarm you, but have you noticed much unusual swelling in your extremities?" She rested two fingers on Hannah's wrist. "It's normal to have some swelling, of course, but I've seen a change in you since last week's class, and I think you should have your OB check your blood pressure and your urine. I'm sure you already know that at your age, you're at greater than usual risk for preeclampsia."

Hannah nodded. She had noticed some swelling in her second trimester, giving her an overall more "filled-out" look that her reading had told her to expect, and she had long ago abandoned wearing any rings. But recently her shoes had felt tighter and her Fitbit had become unbearable. Wordlessly, Natty passed Hannah her phone, and she dialed Dr. Felcher.

⁓

"'GESTATIONAL HYPERTENSION?'"

"It means elevated blood pressure due to pregnancy," Dr. Felcher explained crisply, not just for Hannah and Natty's benefit but also for the camera's.

"As we've already determined, you have edema, an accumulation of fluid in your extremities. Perfectly normal. Your edema has increased somewhat since your last visit and it was appropriate of your childbirth educator to point it out, but I don't find it as severe as she does, at least not in and of itself. Fortunately, your urinalysis doesn't show the presence of excess protein, which would be a sign of preeclampsia.

"I am grateful, however, that her concern brought you in here. According to the records I received from Dr.

Anandanarayan, your pre-pregnancy blood pressure was a textbook 115 over 80 and it had risen only a little over the course of your pregnancy. Right now it's at 150 over 100. That's past 'high' and heading into 'dangerous.'

"I'm going to send you home with a blood pressure monitor, and I want you to take your pressure every day at the same time. I'm also going to recommend some changes to your diet: I want you to drink more water, and cut down on salt and processed sugar." Hannah looked at her in horror. With all the sacrifices demanded by her pregnancy, how could Dr. Felcher take away her sweets?

"And I'm going to advise that, other than your childbirth classes and your visits here, you do your best to stay off your feet for the remainder of your pregnancy. That means no errands, no trips to the mall, no long walks in the park."

Dr. Felcher held up a hand to stave off the protest Hannah was about to make. "This is never a popular decision, Hannah. But it's a necessary one. I don't need to tell you that your advanced age exacerbates this problem."

"But I have personal appearances scheduled clear through April," Hannah said, still stinging from the loss of her desserts.

"I understand," Dr. Felcher replied. *Indeed; married to a TV producer, she probably did understand better than another obstetrician might.* "You'll be able to keep those commitments if—and I'm serious about this—*if* you have someone transport you there, if you keep the walking and standing to a minimum, if you don't cross your legs or ankles, and if you keep your feet elevated throughout.

"I'm not talking about mandated bed rest here, Hannah, or hospitalization, but that's the path you'd be on if you're not careful about this.

"It's really a small price to pay to protect yourself and your baby."

Hannah reluctantly agreed. Of course, she would do everything in her power to keep her baby healthy, but this was no small inconvenience. She had only recently become accustomed to being without Ryan in the house; there was already no one to give her a hand with housework and chores; no one to help lift and carry.

And she was going to miss her walks with Sadie. Come to think of it, she would have to hire a dog-walker. Maybe she could have more St. Hannah events set up, get Natty and Jonathan to deliver her there and make sure she followed Dr. Felcher's orders. But how could they do that when they already seemed to be working full time on St. Hannah?

She suspected she was going to get a serious case of cabin fever.

HANNAH 3:2

"Sadie! What is your PROBLEM?"

It was—Hannah picked up her cell phone and squinted blearily at it—2:18 a.m., and Sadie was barking at the front door, an urgent, incessant racket, yips alternating with whines that were distinct from her "go outside" bark or her "thank God you're home" bark. She had long since grown comfortable with the arrival of Harvey the UPS driver and Olivia the FedEx delivery woman and would give two short barks in greeting to them. It wasn't even the kind of intense noise that she made when total strangers came to the door. There had been no doorbell rung, or so Hannah thought, but she had been in a deep sleep and couldn't say for sure.

Out of reflex, Hannah looked over at Ryan's side of the bed and sighed when she remembered once again that, while she had moved back to the master bedroom from the guest room, he hadn't been in his usual spot on the left for months. She'd have to handle this, whatever it was, on her own.

Grateful for the alarm system Ryan had insisted on installing some ten years prior during a rash of neighborhood burglaries, Hannah dragged herself out of bed with a pained groan and put her robe on over her nightgown. She waddled heavily to the bathroom. If there was going to be an intruder, she wasn't about to confront him with a full bladder. Sadie's barking continued.

Finally, Hannah made her way carefully down the stairs and disarmed the alarm. Glad to have finally attracted her attention, Sadie circled around her feet, trying urgently to communicate the only way she knew how. Keeping one hand on the panic button of the keypad, Hannah looked through the peephole. Seeing nothing, she cracked open the door.

She opened it wider when she realized there was nothing on the front porch but a large, battered, unsealed cardboard box. "Hello?" she called uneasily into the hazy darkness beyond the porch light. But whoever had dropped it there was long gone.

Sadie immediately wriggled out the door and lunged for the box, sticking her snout in the opening, her body tense with excitement. A thin, high, unmistakably canine whine came from within.

Dear God.

Hannah stepped out onto the porch in the cold, damp air, her slippers slapping against the wood slats, and pressed the top flaps of the box open. Inside, there was a small dog: an oddly winsome mixed breed with spiky white hair and black button eyes and nose; hugely pregnant; and maybe—yes, certainly—in labor.

Ah, shit shit shit! Her robe gripped tightly around her, Hannah bounced in agitation on the balls of her feet. As both a dog lover and an expectant mother, she couldn't bear to leave the poor thing out here alone to fend for itself, particularly when the puppies could arrive at any moment.

And yet she felt unequal to handling the situation on her own. For the second time that night, Hannah was selfishly sorry for Ryan's absence.

Hannah eyed the panting dog. Based on the difference in size with Sadie, who weighed forty-six pounds at her last vet visit, she figured the dog couldn't be more than fifteen pounds, tops. Surely she could manage *that*, if she was careful. With Sadie pacing back and forth in a mixture of anxiety and keen interest, Hannah took a deep breath in, turned out her toes, and, exhaling, did her best Bradley method squat.

Grabbing two corners of the box, she pulled it toward herself and walked slowly backward, dragging it up the doorstep.

"Sorry, girl," she apologized as the carton bumped over the threshold.

The dog yelped. Sadie barked. Hannah cursed.

Wheezing as much as the whelping dog, Hannah finally stood in the foyer, undecided. Mindful of the strictures of her hypertension diagnosis, she knew she wasn't supposed to be engaging in this sort of activity. As much as she hated to do it, she had to call for help. How very strange it was, too: someone had found a pregnant dog, kept an eye on it until it was in active labor, loaded it into some kind of vehicle, and deposited it on her doorstep in the middle of the night. This time it wasn't a gift, like the candles or cookies or baby clothes. It felt like a threat.

She called the police on the non-emergency line, trying to keep her voice from shaking as she gave her address, and then speed-dialed Jonathan.

Jonathan arrived, and Natty with him, just as the officer was taking Hannah's statement. Hannah couldn't imagine what Natty was seeing, the sight she must make, in her maternity gown and robe, her hair unbrushed, her face sleep-weary and perhaps even bearing the impression of the wrinkled pillowcase. Natty, too, was unkempt, in a dirty sweatshirt and pajama bottoms under the same winter coat she'd worn for four years, yet she somehow still managed to look like a Calvin Klein model. *The gift of youth*, Hannah thought.

"Mom!" Natty's usually cool demeanor was gone, and she threw herself into Hannah's arms. Hannah reveled in the warm weight of her daughter, the silken hair pressed against her cheek. The years peeled away, and for a brief moment Natty was the preschooler Hannah could still comfort with a stuffed animal and a fresh cookie.

"I'm fine, really, I am," she said at last, reluctant to lose her armful of daughter. She pressed a kiss to the top of Natty's head while she could. When Natty pulled away, Hannah was still warm from their embrace.

Jonathan was already kneeling beside the box, examining it and its contents, smiling stupidly as one does at the wonder of life renewing itself, at the eternal struggles of mothers, at …

"Puppies!"

And sure enough, here they came, or at least the first one. Fascinated, Hannah watched as the newborn began to squirm and wriggle its way out of the mother. Hannah had never actually been present for any sort of birth before and was deeply moved as the first puppy made an appearance, still surrounded by what she presumed was the placenta, blood-red and glossy. The attentive mother licked, bit at, and swallowed the placenta until the puppy, only a couple of inches long, was left damp and mewling on the stained blanket.

They all looked on in awe. Even the police officer—a tall and absurdly young man with light-brown hair and a mild case of acne, who looked to Hannah to be about eighteen—was smiling.

"Any idea who might have done this?" the officer, by the name of Halpern, asked, finally tearing his eyes away from the dogs.

Hannah had been thinking about this very question while she and the mother dog (which she was privately referring to as Pookie, though she did not say this aloud) waited for him to arrive. "Well, a couple of Right-to-Lifers visited me a while back, right after Thanksgiving. Wanted me to be the face of their campaign. When I wouldn't agree to be part of it, they left unhappy."

"Uh-huh. 'Unhappy.'" Halpern made a note. "Did they threaten you in any way?"

"Not at all. And I never heard from them again after that. But they're the only people I could think of."

"Oh, I have a few," Jonathan piped up, getting to his feet and reaching for his backpack. Although she'd seen him take it and his laptop with him everywhere except church, Hannah couldn't imagine why he would have brought it with him in the middle of the night.

He drew out a manila folder. "I've been keeping a file, screenshots of messages on the St. Hannah Facebook page that don't, um, fall within accepted behavioral standards."

That was certainly odd. Hannah had never seen anything on the site that was even remotely disturbing.

Natty caught on immediately to her confusion and explained, "Jonathan and I monitor the comments and remove anything offensive. Keeps us busy."

"There are offensive comments on our Facebook page?"

"There are offensive comments *everywhere* online, Mom," Natty said gently. "You don't spend all that much time on Facebook, do you?"

Hannah shrugged. "I'm on there enough."

"To share cat videos and knitting patterns, right? You don't get involved with, say, political discussions?"

"It's been a while," she answered. "No one seems to want to have a civil conversation anymore."

"Well, Mom, let's just say you'd be rudely awakened by the sort of thing that goes on online, including in the public comments areas of the St. Hannah page. And in our emails." Natty considered for a moment, then added, "Let me give you some advice: stay off Twitter entirely."

"This one in particular ..." But before Jonathan could offer the piece of paper to Officer Halpern, Hannah grabbed it out of his hand.

"'*You pregnant bitch*'," she quoted incredulously. Feeling deeply wounded and slightly sick, she shoved the paper at the officer as if she couldn't release it quickly enough. She felt as if she should wash her hands, maybe take a shower. "Who would say such an awful thing?"

"We've had a few posts from this man before, Hannah," Jonathan said. "Fortunately, he isn't smart enough to pretend to be someone else or even hide his tracks. He seems to be angry with you."

"With me?" Hannah, exhausted, stressed, and hormonal, felt the tears rush to her eyes. "What for? What could I have possibly done to him?"

"From what I gather, his wife met you several months ago at an event, maybe at Ke'isha's place, I'm not sure. She thought that you could, um, bless her womb so that she could have children." Jonathan grimaced. "Apparently, they're still disappointed in the results."

"Bless her? Oh, please! Why would anyone think I can ... oh."

"'Oh,' what, Mrs. Murrow?" Halpern sensed an opening.

"It was Christmas, Midnight Mass. Remember, Natty, when I sat down late, and Nana was annoyed with me? It was because I'd been cornered by Father Aloysius's secretary, what was her name? Uh." Hannah tapped her forehead as if she could jostle free a reluctant memory. "H-E something. Heidi? Helen? No, Heather. Heather. She said she wanted to be blessed with a child like I'd been, and she wanted me to lay hands on her womb or something. I thought it was weird and, um, declined politely."

"Seriously?" Natty, wide-eyed, asked from the floor, where she was now seated on her coat, taking close-up video of the newborn puppy on her cell phone.

"Is this her last name?" asked the officer, showing Hannah the Facebook profile of Jonathan's primary suspect.

"I don't recall. I haven't been back to the church since Christmas, though I was hoping to go for Easter. I'm sure Father Aloysius at St. Agnes will have her information."

"I'll take the rest of those printouts, if you don't mind."

Jonathan handed the folder to the officer, who continued, "We'll question the husband. If he dropped off the dog as a threat to you, we could probably get him on harassment."

Hannah shook her head slowly. "I don't know about harassment. ... There's really no harm done. I mean, I've been there, and I know how angry and frustrated infertility can make you." She ran her hand over her belly. "Poor Heather. She was so desperate."

"That's up to you, Mrs. Murrow. But I think we're also looking at animal cruelty. No one should be uprooting a mother in labor."

"I'd have to agree with you there."

"We're going to look into it anyhow," Halpern said, heading toward the door. "We don't know for sure if it was your guy or not, and we need to have this on record, in case … well, in case the situation escalates. I'm a little surprised it's taken this long for something to happen, given the level of your celebrity and the easy access to your house."

Hannah shuddered, gathering the neck of her robe closer.

The officer caught her movement. "Do you want police protection, Mrs. Murrow?" he asked with his hand on the doorknob. "We can do that, if you like."

Shaking her head, Hannah said, "I don't think that will be necessary."

Halpern looked doubtful, but he shrugged. Hannah hoped he wouldn't ask her again, because she might very well change her mind. "So what are we supposed to do with the dog?" she asked.

"Dogs, Mom," Natty corrected. "There's only one puppy now, but I doubt she's done."

"There's not much we can do about it at this hour, I'm afraid," Halpern said. "I suppose you could move them into the garage, give 'em a few blankets to keep 'em warm. In the morning, you can call Animal Control. Good night, Mrs. Murrow," Halpern said as he walked out. "I'll give you a call when we have any new information."

Hannah locked the door behind him.

They all watched the new mother lave the puppy, jelly-bean shaped and cream-colored, with her tongue and nudge it with her nose despite her obvious discomfort. Hannah felt a flood of affection for the poor creatures and couldn't imagine moving them anywhere at the moment, least of all to the cold cement floor of the garage. But she was in no condition to give them the attention they needed.

"Don't worry, Mom," Natty said, as if reading her thoughts. "Jonathan and I already agreed we'll stay here for the rest of the night. He's looking into what to do for the dogs."

"Are you sure?" Hannah asked weakly. More than anything she wanted to turn the responsibility over to someone, anyone, and go back to bed, where she had been warm and safe and blithely unaware that there were people in the world who referred to her as a bitch or worse.

"We're sure. Go to sleep, Mom."

Grateful, Hannah pressed another kiss atop Natty's head, because who knew when Natty would permit her to do so again, and lurched slowly up the stairs to the master bedroom. Sadie, torn between her duty to Hannah and the excitement of new members of the pack, declined to follow.

Hannah lay down on the bed, listening to Natty and Jonathan murmuring over the dogs. From the change in the tone of their voices, she surmised a second puppy was making an appearance.

She tried to make herself comfortable, without success.

IT WAS AN ELBOW. Or maybe a heel. Hannah knew it could also be the top of a head. When the baby got restless, there was no telling what appendage would be poking out of the side, the top, or the bottom of Hannah's belly. The first time it happened, she was startled. While she knew, intellectually, that she was growing a tiny human inside her, on nights like this when something disturbed her, she couldn't shake the *Alien* imagery of a creature bursting out of some poor scientist's midsection. It compounded the stress that the unexpected package and its sinister message had caused. Despite her exhaustion, sleep eluded her.

Once asleep, though, she slept like the dead. By the time Hannah roused herself, it was late morning. Sadie was once again beside her, looking concerned at the late hour and no doubt anxious for breakfast. The house was unexpectedly quiet.

Hannah grabbed for her phone. A text from Natty confirmed that she and Jonathan had removed Pookie and her puppies—six in all, although only five had survived—to a rescue shelter when they opened at 9, and were catching up on their missed sleep. Relief seeped out of every pore. As much as she adored dogs, she was in no position to take responsibility for a half-dozen new lives when the one she was expecting would be challenge enough. She promised herself not to feel guilty about turning them over to the shelter, though of course that was a lost cause. Sadie would be the beneficiary of her guilty feelings: a larger than usual breakfast was in order.

Once Sadie had been taken care of, though, Hannah was at leisure to recall what had happened the night before and was newly disconcerted. Until now, she had considered her celebrity to be entirely benign. How naive she had been! She wondered what else she'd accepted at face value; what else she'd been wrong about.

And she thought perhaps it would be best if she stayed off of social media completely for the time being.

HANNAH 3:3

Hannah had started to calculate the time she could be safely in a car without needing to go to the bathroom, and decided that she could make the trip to her parents' apartment if she peed before she left and bypassed the usual barrage of questions from Dolores by heading straight for their powder room when she got there.

She knew Dr. Felcher wouldn't approve, but she was so lonely in the house that even a trip to see her parents was a welcome treat.

And what Dr. Felcher didn't know wouldn't hurt her.

"Hi, I'm on my way to Nana's," Hannah said once her car's Bluetooth connected her with Natty.

"I thought Dr. Felcher wanted you to limit your time on your feet for the rest of the pregnancy."

"She said she 'recommended' it, not that it was mandatory."

"I don't think it works that way, Mom. You're too close to your due date. You shouldn't be out alone."

"I'm not going to be alone, I'll be with Nana and Grandpa." As if on cue, her phone beeped, and 'MOM and DAD' showed up on the Caller ID screen. "See, they're calling me already. You know Wednesdays are my days to visit. Imagine what hell I'd catch if I missed a week. Your Uncle Jason would never let me hear the end of it. He'd be saying that Aunt Missy would have gotten there on a unicycle while she was *in labor*."

Natty laughed. Hyperbole or not, they both knew that Hannah wasn't far off the mark. "She probably could have, too."

"Probably."

"Call me when you're back home, okay? So I know you got back okay?"

"Okay." How their positions were reversed! Hannah remembered those days when Natty was making late-night drives to visit friends. And that summer when she went to Costa Rica. There would always be a phone call, just to assure Hannah that she had arrived safely. Whatever challenges she was facing after the baby was born, she felt comfortable in knowing she would have Natty, her parents, and now even Jonathan there to help.

Hannah's plans to pull straight into the first available handicapped parking spot were foiled by the presence of an ambulance idling, lights flashing red-blue-red, in the parking lot. She cursed aloud. The pressure was beginning to build in her bladder, and driving around the parking lot had not been in her schedule. She spotted a tiny, middle-aged woman of about Dr. A's size hauling herself up into a massive SUV and waited impatiently, shouting vitriol from the anonymity of the car until the woman finished touching up her lipstick in the mirror and pulled out of the spot.

"Thank God!" Having already removed her seat belt before even shutting off the car, Hannah grabbed her purse from the passenger seat and exited the car as fast as she could manage, maneuvering her belly around the steering wheel. She walked as briskly as her swollen feet would let her to the entrance, telling herself it was just the pressure from the baby, her bladder wasn't full, she wasn't in danger of embarrassing herself. Ignoring Opal at the front desk, who was calling to her, she hustled into the ladies' room just as her phone rang again. Well, there was no time for that now.

Sighing with relief, Hannah washed her hands and walked at a leisurely pace down the corridor toward her parents' room. A few residents hovered in the hallway but parted for her like the Red Sea as she lumbered toward them.

Odd. The door was already open.

"Mom?"

To her horror, Hannah could see the backs of two paramedics. A cold hand clutched her wrist.

"Hannah, thank God you're here! I tried to call you! I tried and tried."

Dolores's mascara was dripping in black streaks down her rouged cheeks.

"Mom? What happened?"

"Daddy had a stroke, or that's what they think anyway," Dolores said, her voice high and thin. "It could be a bad one. He said he wasn't feeling right and went to take a nap, but I tried to wake him up and I couldn't. They're taking him to the hospital. What am I going to do?"

Having already started Frank on oxygen and maneuvered him expertly onto a gurney, the paramedics rolled him out the door. Hannah and Dolores squeezed themselves into the kitchenette to let them pass.

Hannah never knew her mother was capable of moving as quickly as she did following her husband's gurney down the corridor. Her throat tight, her eyes stinging with tears, Hannah labored to keep pace with them as they headed to the elevator. The few remaining onlookers in the corridor stared solemnly.

"Daddy!" she shrieked. "Daddy, it's me, Hannah!" Her father gave not even a flicker of awareness.

The EMTs glanced at each other; no doubt they had seen pretty much everything and were surprised by nothing. They could hear the elevator starting its journey from the first floor.

"You can't do this, Daddy! Not now!" Hannah screamed at him as the elevator rumbled upward. She gripped his hand, lax against the coarse white sheet, and it was then she recognized the cardigan she'd knitted him for Christmas. Running her hand over the familiar stitches, already pilled from frequent wearing, she implored, "You'll want to meet your granddaughter, won't you, Daddy? She'll be here in just a few more weeks!" Hannah pressed her father's hand against her belly, and as she did, the baby somersaulted.

"Feel that, Daddy? It's your grandchild, your impossible miracle grandchild! She'll be here really soon." The elevator doors opened and the paramedics pushed Frank into it. Hannah, still clutching Frank's hand, was pulled along. Dolores followed behind, breathing heavily from her tears and exertion. "Can't you hang on that long? To meet the baby?" *One more miracle,* Hanna prayed, squeezing her father's hand.

Please, God, give us just one more miracle.

"How do you know?"

"What?"

She was four, and her father was singing that song, that old song about pennies raining down from the sky … .

Groggy, fuzzy-headed with stress, Hannah was drowsing on a hospital bed. The rain had started as a light tapping against the window shortly after they'd followed the ambulance in, and was now coming down in torrents of soothing white noise.

How did it go again? She'd always loved that song, the raining pennies song, because he only sang it for her. Why did he ever stop?

A nurse wearing an ID indicating her name was Jacqui had guided Hannah and Dolores into an unoccupied room and gently insisted on taking Hannah's blood pressure. It was elevated, but not dangerous. She invited Hannah to lie down for a while and put up her feet, which Hannah accepted gratefully. It had barely been forty-five minutes since Frank was brought in, but it already felt like hours. The baby, quiet since the height of the crisis, had started to stretch and roll. Hannah pressed her hands to her belly, glad for some normalcy in this horrific situation.

"How do I know what?"

Dolores leaned toward Hannah from her seat next to the bed. She had washed the makeup off her face. It had been years since Hannah had seen her in this natural state, and she thought she looked beautiful, exactly how a woman her age should look. "How do you know the baby's a girl? You said to Daddy, 'You'll want to meet your granddaughter.' I thought you said you didn't want to know, that Dr. Felcher promised not to tell you after the amnio."

Hannah thought for a moment. She barely recalled saying such a thing to her father as they spirited him away to the hospital. "I don't know. It's just a feeling I have. When I talk to the baby, I think of her as a girl." She smiled wanly. "Wishful thinking, maybe."

"You don't want a boy? You have Natty."

Yes, she had Natty, and all the fights, and tears, and struggles, and heartaches that had come with raising her. Hannah wondered if somewhere deep inside she was hoping for a second chance, if some part of her was thinking, "If I could only do it all again, I would do it so much better."

But she was too worried, too weary to ponder that now. "We'll find out soon enough, won't we?"

"I never thought I wanted a girl," Dolores said in a weak voice.

Hannah looked at her quizzically.

"I always thought girls were too much trouble," Dolores continued. "Too much drama, first with girlfriends and then with boyfriends. The fuss, the broken hearts! I had plenty of that when Connie and I were growing up. I was six years older than her, and to your grandmother that meant I was old enough to act as a second mother while she did her housework and helped in Papa's store. All the nights I couldn't go out with my own friends because I had to mind Connie! I resented her plenty; we didn't become close until she grew up and I didn't have to watch her any more.

"But somehow I knew from the moment the doctor told me I was pregnant that you were going to be a girl. And it was so different from what I expected that maybe I didn't really know how to give you what you needed. But your daddy sure did. He could never resist his little girl, with her big eyes and her red hair. He even wanted to name you Penny, did I ever tell you that? For your red hair. Beautiful red hair, just like Connie's."

"Mrs. Cavanaugh?" The doctor in the doorway looked drawn and somber, a deep frown elongating his handsome face. Hannah's heart sank. She struggled to sit upright, and Jacqui came in to stand beside the bed, assisting her with a light hand on her back. The warmth of Jacqui's hand bled through Hannah's blouse with the comfort of a hot water bottle.

"I'm Dr. DiBenedetto, Mrs. Cavanaugh, and I'm afraid I have some bad news. Mr. Cavanaugh had a hemorrhagic stroke, bleeding into the brain. An aneurysm. There was nothing we could do. I'm so very sorry for your loss."

"Oh, no!" Dolores wailed. "No, no, no, no!" She folded herself in half on the chair.

"Daddy," Hannah whimpered. Her eyes filled, then overflowed, then washed down her face and dripped off her chin. Jacqui handed her a box of tissues, then moved silently on white rubber-soled clogs to offer another to Dolores. "Daddy."

Hannah wanted to put her arms around her mother, needed to, but felt weighed down, immobilized not just by her pregnancy but by her grief. She struggled to shift her legs to the side of the bed.

"Hannah," said Jacqui in a melodious Jamaican accent. "Hannah, let me help you, honey." With an arm around her shoulders, Jacqui eased Hannah to her feet and walked her over to embrace Dolores.

Dr. DiBenedetto looked at Hannah, sympathy etched in every line of his face. "If you like, we'll take you to say your goodbyes. If you're feeling up to it, that is. Please take your time."

"I'll get them there, Doctor," Jacqui said. The doctor nodded and left them to their grief.

IT WAS SO STRANGE, and Hannah would be unable to explain it, but the body on the table no longer looked anything like her father. He'd only recently passed, and yet whatever spark of life that made Francis Cavanaugh the man so loved by his family was totally gone. He might as well have been made of wax.

With a knot in her throat, Hannah pressed a kiss to his forehead and murmured, "Goodbye, Daddy." It was all she could manage.

Jacqui was by her side in an instant with fresh tissues, and Hannah nodded her thanks as she walked away to give Dolores some time alone with Frank.

"I have to call Jason," Hannah said to herself, and then to Jacqui: "I have to call my brother." She chastised herself for not having called him sooner. She should have told him right when it happened; he deserved to know.

"And Natty. My daughter." It would not be the call Natty had been expecting, the one that said, "I'm home, I'm safe. Everything is all right."

"Let's get you and Mom back to your room, honey, and you can do whatever needs to be done."

Her eyes glazed and red, Hannah dialed Jason. She checked the time, realizing he'd still be at work, and was about to hang up when the phone rang for the fourth time and Jason answered.

"Hey, Hannah," he said, clearly preoccupied. She pictured her brother behind his desk, folders four or five deep on every available surface. "Wait—what?" he yelled at someone else who was apparently outside the room. "No, I don't have the Schopner file; you have it. I gave it to you yesterday, for God's sake!

"Hey, Hannah," he repeated, "what's going on?"

"It's Daddy," she choked out. "J, he's gone."

"What? Jesus, Hannah, what happened?"

"A stroke. Start to finish, it was only a couple of hours. And now he's gone!"

"Ah, shit. Ah, shit, that's awful. How's Mom?"

"Not great. We're still at the hospital. I'll have to, um, I've got to plan the funeral …" she said as she burst into sobs.

Jason let her cry for a minute, then tenderly said, "Hannah? Listen. Mom might not be thinking clearly about this right now, but we had the whole thing pre-planned when I updated their will: the wake, the Mass, the burial." He sighed, the sound heavy with sorrow. "I'll dig up the paperwork and get back to you. Missy and I will bring the kids out for a couple of days so we can all be together. All right?"

"Yeah, okay," Hannah sniffled. She realized how much she'd missed this Jason, the one who would shadow her on the playground and buy her milkshakes and dance "The Twist" with her at parties. She hadn't seen him in a long, long time and had very nearly forgotten him entirely. "I gotta go. Mom needs me."

"You go. I'll take care of things on this end. You can give that priest a call, the one they like: Father Aloysius."

HANNAH 3:4

Dr. Felcher hadn't even wanted her to attend the funeral. She had gently scolded Hannah for having gone to her parents' apartment in the first place, fretted over her blood pressure and her swollen ankles, practically forbade her from attending the wake, Mass, and interment. Hannah had to bite her tongue to remind herself that the doctor only had the baby's and her best interests in mind.

"The Lord giveth, the Lord taketh away," Father Aloysius intoned.

Ain't that the truth, Hannah thought with a lump in her throat. Dolores was seated between her and Jason, his reassuring arm wrapped around their mother's shoulders. Hannah found her unspoken longing for similar solace answered as she felt Natty's thin arm go around her. Hannah relaxed into it, resting her head on the bony shoulder. Jonathan was on Natty's other side, holding her hand, and Hannah felt the contentment of having a family even as she was saying goodbye to her father. She smiled sadly up at Natty, noting with approval that she had removed her nose stud (presumably out of respect for her grandfather, who had never liked it but had, unlike the rest of the family, never given her any grief over it). Her eyes flicked down to Natty's throat, and she sat up abruptly.

"Natasha! You're wearing your First Communion crucifix!" Hannah whispered.

"Yeah, I thought Grandpa would want me to," Natty whispered back.

Hannah, moved, felt her eyes fill again. "I thought it was … um, lost."

"Nah. I just kind of outgrew it."

It was true. The crucifix was indeed too small for an adult, its thin, too-short chain leaving the cross glimmering in the notch of Natty's throat. It was probably uncomfortable and it was definitely not Natty's style. Hannah had never even considered that Natty had had a good reason to stop wearing it. She felt ashamed of her assumptions and glad she had never voiced them to Natty.

"Dad's here, you know," Natty continued in a low voice.

"I know." Hannah had seen him come in and sit down in the back. "He always liked Grandpa."

"Well, props to him for coming."

Hannah wasn't sure that Ryan deserved props for anything, but she appreciated that he could set aside his own animosities and pay his respects. The divorce was still not final, the mediator having warned it might take months to iron out the details, particularly when there were issues of support involved. She wondered if he had also attended the wake and made a mental note to check the guest book. Her own time at the wake had been limited by her low tolerance for the overpowering smell of a roomful of flowers, which made her as nauseated as anything had during her first trimester. Hannah had stayed only long enough to accept the deep comfort of a visit from Marla, who had held her silently in her arms as she had done on so many sad occasions so long ago.

She wondered, too, what she would say to Ryan when he inevitably approached her. She could afford to be magnanimous: she was now mere weeks away from her baby's birth, and as she waited for that truly blessed event, Hannah was enjoying the blissful experience of creating life inside her, an experience she had thought she'd never have. And, she acknowledged, she had Ryan to thank for all of it.

After the Mass was over, Ryan detached himself from a circle of their mutual friends and came over to speak to her. "I'm sorry for your loss, Hannah," he said. "Frank was a good man. He loved his family, and he always made me feel part of it."

That was true. In many ways, Frank made up for Dolores's distance, doling out affection and compliments to all in his orbit. "Thank you. Dad would have been glad you're here."

"You look good."

Hannah coughed out an incredulous laugh. It was a charming lie. She hadn't owned any black maternity clothes, certainly nothing appropriate for a funeral, and hadn't considered a need for them. Ke'isha was kind enough to provide her with a suitable black-and-white pantsuit on short notice, a clearance item left over from the winter line. It fit well enough, and Hannah was grateful, but she found it unflattering.

"I think I look like an orca."

Ryan smiled kindly. Hannah felt a pain in her chest like an old wound reopening. She willed herself not to start crying, though she wasn't sure she had the strength left to do so.

"And I'm sorry about us, too," he said, "I really am. But I just can't start over at this point in my life, Hannah. I love you and Natty and all of it, but I want to retire and enjoy what's left of my life. My dad died too young and never got to enjoy the fruits of his labors. I can't ... I don't know how much time I have left, none of us do. Call me selfish: okay, I'm selfish. But believe it or not, what I really am is tired. Really tired. I can't expect you to understand."

Hannah, tired too, exhausted even before the baby arrived, thought perhaps she understood.

"And ... and if I'd like to see him once in a while, I mean the baby, maybe you'll be okay with that? You'll let him know his dad?" He tilted his head and gave her a long, earnest look. For a moment she remembered why she'd loved him in the first place, and her heart gave a painful heave.

"Sure, Ryan." Laying a hand on his arm, she kissed his cheek. And then she watched him walk away. "Sure."

HANNAH 3:5

Despite Dolores's complaints that she would be "all alone," the family agreed that for now at least she would remain at Best of Times, where she actually did have a social group and activities. Hannah was pleased at how the other residents rallied around her to keep her from getting lonely. Although dinner tables were assigned, several couples and other widows made plans to join her for lunch, card games, and what her generation referred to as "coffee-and," the cake or doughnuts being implicit.

In the lead-up to her due date, Hannah split her time between the ungainly but practical "zero gravity" lounge chair that Lark had recommended and her bed, rarely leaving the house for anything more than her visits with Dr. Felcher and her childbirth classes. So she was forced to consider whether she wanted her mother living with her. Dolores would be a big help, she knew, particularly when the baby arrived. But Hannah wasn't keen to introduce that kind of friction back into her life. She had begun to relish the quiet routine of Natty and Jonathan's arrival, their conversation as they conducted St. Hannah business at the dining room table, the sweet contentment of Sadie having a whole family in the house again (and young people exercising her).

Natty did promise to bring her grandmother over to Hannah's bedside, however, and a week after the funeral, Dolores arrived with a gift. "Dad wanted you to have this," she said, setting down a jar with a heavy thud in front of Hannah.

"Pennies?" The coins inside fairly glowed orange, like the warm remnants of a fire.

"All 1963 pennies, at least a few hundred of them. A couple hundred uncirculated, the rest pretty new or polished up. Dad started collecting them by the roll the year you were born. He did so love your hair."

Hannah twirled the jar around, fascinated, her eyes filling with tears. She fought them off by blinking rapidly, unwilling to start crying in front of her mother, who would either criticize her for her sentimentality or start crying herself. Neither was a good result.

"There's your inheritance, Hannah—worth about ten bucks. Twelve, if you're lucky."

"It's beautiful."

Dolores shrugged. "That's all there is, you know. Can you believe your sister-in-law came over to our apartment right after the funeral, asking about Dad's coin collection, the sneaky little vulture!" Hannah certainly could believe it. But it was rare for her mother to criticize the faultless Missy.

"With Daddy barely dead a week! I was happy to tell her that he'd sold it off years ago, and there was nothing left of it. Except this," she added, tapping the jar with a lacquered fingernail.

"Daddy did have a small life insurance policy, but I'll need that and Social Security to keep me afloat at Best of Times." She tried to look nonchalant. "Of course, if I moved in with you …"

"You'll be fine where you are, Mom, where your friends are."

"Those old people?" she snorted. "I wouldn't exactly call them *friends*."

But Dolores did have friends. Hannah was impressed that Best of Times had provided transportation to the Mass in the facility's van for eight or nine residents, many of whom Hannah recognized from her visits: the Zywiecs, the McKennas, 101-year-old Mr. Glenn. They had moved into the church and then out again afterward in a slow, painstaking ballet of walkers and canes, like sea creatures flowing with the tide. Regardless of what Dolores had to say, it was clear they cared about her and Frank.

Once Natty had taken Dolores home and Hannah could be alone with her thoughts, she picked up the jar again, tilting it back and forth. She regretted she didn't have a recording of Frank singing that "raining pennies" song, wished she could hear him sing it just once more. This time she let the tears fall.

Hannah kept the jar of pennies on her bedside table, and every now and then would take it up and turn it to watch the contents spill and change in the light: copper waves breaking on the beach, a shiny monochromatic kaleidoscope. She loved the heft of it in her hands, loved the rolling bass rainstorm sound of it, and especially loved the thought of her Dad going to bank after bank to request dollar bills broken into rolls of pennies—pennies that gleamed like his little girl's hair. She intended to keep the jar intact and pass it on to the baby.

If it was a boy, she would give him her father's name.

IT WAS THE FIRST WEEK IN MAY, Hannah's due date a mere two weeks away, and Natty was at the house as usual, helping her mother prepare the overnight case she'd need when she went to the hospital. Sitting up in the bed, Hannah was polishing off the last of a pint of "St. Hannah Banana," a limited-edition flavor (banana-flavored ice cream, fudge swirl, chocolate pieces, and both almonds and pecans—because, as the description read, "She must be at least a little nuts!") created by a clever local ice cream place in her honor. Hannah hadn't had so much as a vanilla wafer in three days and felt entitled to a reward.

As she scraped the bottom of the container to retrieve the last chocolate chunk, Hannah admired the efficiency with which Natty buzzed in and out of drawers and closets, checking items off her list, retrieving clothing, toiletries, books, a phone charger. She smiled in wonder. The Bradley classes had done a lot to bring out the caregiver in Natty, but when had she finally learned such responsibility, where had she developed such an intense work ethic? Were the community college courses the key that had turned her life around?

The smile faded, and Hannah slowly set the empty carton down on the bedside table. It was the first week in May, and Natty was at the house as usual. In fact, she had been at the house pretty much all day, every day, working on the St. Hannah blog and social media and overseeing the merchandise distribution, since Frank's death.

"Natasha," Hannah asked, "why aren't you in school?"

"What?"

"Why aren't you in school? You've been working on St. Hannah exclusively since the launch. I've never seen you open a book or work on a paper or say you had to get to class. You'd be in your last semester now, wouldn't you? Finals would be coming up, and then graduation. You haven't said anything about either. Yet you've been here every single day since Grandpa died." She thought for a moment. "And before that, you were either at your apartment, with vendors, or at Nana's.

"You haven't been to school at all, have you?" she said, amazed that she was just making the connection now.

Natty folded her arms in front of her chest and compressed her lips tightly. It was a mannerism she had picked up from Ryan.

"And what if I haven't?"

"I can't believe you!" Hannah exploded. "You took Dad's money; it was specifically for school! What have you been doing with it?"

"I invested it."

"You invested it? In *what*?"

The set of Natty's jaw told Hannah all she needed to know, even before the answer came: "My future."

Hannah threw up her hands. "*School* was supposed to be an investment in your future! *A degree* was supposed to be an investment in your future. Now you'll have to repeat the whole year, and where is that money going to come from?" Her head started to hurt. "We don't have it. Your father doesn't have it. He barely has enough to contribute to the support of his own child."

"His *own* child! I'm his child, too, or don't I matter? No, no, I never did, because I wasn't your 'real' child, was I? Your biological child. And now, you've got *the baby*, and it's all about your 'real' child, isn't it?!"

Hannah realized with dread that she had made a huge mistake. She backpedaled furiously. "Don't be ridiculous! It never mattered to your dad and me that you're not our biological child. Never! We love you just as much; we always have." The words were true, but damn, they sounded trite and scripted.

And way too late.

"Hah!" Natty was crying now, but her tears were born of rage, not sorrow. Hannah hadn't seen her this angry since her early teens, when she had shattered three entire place settings of stoneware on the ceramic tile of the kitchen floor, exploding blue, green, and white shards like a wave crashing on a beach, the detritus reaching clear into the living room.

"You don't see it, do you, Mom? You don't really want to be a *mother*, do you? You just want to be *pregnant*. There's a difference, you know. A pregnancy is only for nine months, but being a mother is *forever*.

"This *pregnancy*, it's been a blast, hasn't it, just like you always dreamed: you've had all the attention and the feeling of something with your precious DNA growing inside you. Well, guess what? The good part is almost over. And then there's nothing left for you for the rest of your life but the hard part, the part you suck at: being a *mother*. Putting your kid's needs first. Making that kid feel wanted. Even if that kid isn't easy, or what you had in mind, or what you thought you deserved."

There it was. The acrimony Natty must have been carrying around with her for her entire short life; the notion that she wasn't enough for Hannah. All this time Hannah had thought that Natty's problems were due to her traumatic first two years, while discounting the effects of her own attitudes and actions on the succeeding twenty-plus. *Had she really communicated that?* Hannah was horrified. She racked her brain for evidence that she had treated Natty with less than her full love and attention. But there were too many years, too many avenues to go down.

Maybe it was more subtle than that. If Natty didn't know how thankful Hannah was to have her, was that because Hannah hadn't spoken it aloud, made it clear enough? By the time Natty was old enough to fully comprehend and remember what was going on around her, she was already acting out at school, biting other children, throwing tantrums. There were constant, crippling attempts at discipline, at prevention, at intervention. Of course that's what she would remember. Natty would not have known the heartbreaking gratitude Hannah had experienced when she found out the sweet, dark-haired girl would be joining their family; could never know the nights Hannah spent gazing at her as she slept, thanking God and Christ and the Virgin for this blessing and praying for guidance.

"Natty, I ..."

"DON'T YOU FUCKING CALL ME THAT!" she raged. "You want to erase what came before I lived here because it means that I had a *real* mother somewhere, in Russia. My name is Natasha!"

Before Hannah could react, Natty grabbed the suitcase she had moments ago finished packing and hurled it with all her strength, sending the contents in a shower over the room and leaving a nasty hole in the drywall.

Barking at the commotion, Sadie jumped off the bed and made figure eights around the room, circling through and further dispersing the drifts of clothing. A small plastic baggie floated to the ground and landed at Natty's feet. She snatched it up and removed the contents, holding it up for Hannah to see.

"No, Natasha, don't … !"

But Natty held the paper up by the fingertips of both hands and tore it in two. For good measure, she layered the pieces and tore them again, and again. When the stack grew too thick to tear, she flung the ragged pieces in Hannah's direction. They wafted to the carpeting like dull, grim confetti.

Sadie yipping in her wake, Natty stormed down the stairs and slammed the front door behind her for good measure.

Stupid, stupid, stupid! How could I be so stupid? And why would I pick a fight when things were going so well? That she's not going to school is worrying, sure, but I certainly could have approached the issue better. Or rather, I couldn't have approached it worse.

Sadie padded back into the room and jumped onto the bed. Pressing herself to Hannah's side, concern obvious in her bright-blue eyes, she rested her head atop Hannah's huge belly. Her head comically rose and fell as the baby pushed and stretched.

Though Hannah desperately wanted to set things right, from experience she knew Natty wouldn't answer the phone now if she tried to call. So she did the next best thing: she called Jonathan.

There was no answer; her call went straight to voicemail. Hannah remembered him saying something about an interview with a potential client and realized he had turned his phone off. She decided to leave a message anyway:

"Jonathan, it's Hannah. I've done something really stupid; started a fight, a major one, with Nat ... Natasha, and now she's not speaking to me. I need to fix this. Call me. Please."

HANNAH 3:6

Hannah must have fallen asleep, because it was dusk when she heard someone open the front door. Sadie, who had been snoring softly next to Hannah, went from asleep to awake in an instant, flying downstairs, barking. Momentary panic set in, but then she remembered that Jonathan had a key.

"Hello?" he called from the foyer. "Hannah?"

"Up here!"

"Don't come down; I'll come up."

Hannah could hear Sadie panting with excitement and the sound of her claws as she ran circles around Jonathan, herding him upstairs to Hannah's room. She was embarrassed that he would see her and her room in such an unkempt state, but only a little. Nothing seemed to faze him.

He took in the dent in the wall, the broken suitcase, the personal effects scattered around.

"Oh, I see."

"Yeah." Hannah's discomfiture increased.

"Natasha has a fiery temper."

"Oh, does she? I hadn't noticed." Being flip did nothing to help the problem, so Hannah shook her head at her own foolishness. "I set her off, and then she said some despicable things that I absolutely deserved."

"What did you say to set her off?"

"I asked why she hasn't been going to school."

"Ah."

"I basically accused her of wasting her father's money, or taking it under false pretenses. Whichever is more offensive, I guess. She said she invested the money, but didn't explain how, and I hit the roof." She bit her lip. "It's, um, a bit of a hot-button issue for me. Maybe Natasha has told you about her father and the reasons why we split up."

"Yes, she did. But I think she does owe you a bit more of an explanation and probably would have given it to you, had she been in a better frame of mind." Jonathan looked around for a suitable spot and finally settled himself into Hannah's reading chair, dropping his backpack next to it. "So I'll do it for her."

Hannah's eyebrows shot up.

"When Natasha and I started getting serious and decided to live together, we agreed that in order to make it work, we'd be equal partners in everything. We would share the housework, the expenses, the responsibilities.

"We started this relationship around a year after I helped launch 'sriusly.com.' Ever heard of it?"

"Uhh, I think so. Sounds familiar, but I couldn't tell you what it is."

"It's a lifestyle site. Fashion, music, food for … ah, younger people. You know: Millennials, and whatever they're calling the next set. Gen Z, or whatever. It went very big, very quickly.

The partners didn't have enough money to pay me outright when I designed the site, so they gave me stock. When they sold it to one of the big entertainment corporations, it made me quite a lot of money." He paused for effect, drumming his fingers on his knees. "A lot."

"Oh." So much for his little "nest egg." She blushed at her assumptions of his destitution.

"I wanted us to live comfortably because I certainly could afford it, but Natasha didn't want to be 'kept'—her word, not mine. Who knew she was so old-fashioned?"

"Not old-fashioned, Jonathan," Hannah sighed. "Just *relentlessly* independent."

"Anyway, she insisted on contributing equally to the household and couldn't afford a lot, which is why we're living in that tiny studio apartment. I want you to know that I argued with her about the tuition money, said it wasn't fair to you and her dad, but she said, 'Dad gave me money for my *education*, and I've learned more from you in two months than I learned from a year at college.' So we put the money toward our start-up fund.

"And then we found our start-up. Or rather," he said, grinning at Hannah, "our start-up found us."

"Well, that certainly explains a lot. Why didn't she just tell me?"

"Is that really what you wanted to hear?"

Hannah thought for a moment. "I guess not. But I feel particularly bad that I caused this huge kerfuffle when we were finally getting along. It's been years since we've had this kind of amicable relationship, any kind of relationship. I have to tell you, Jonathan, when you brought the idea of St. Hannah to me, I was shocked that Natasha would want to spend this much of her time and energy on me. It's partly why I agreed to do it. I was really touched."

Jonathan looked a little sheepish. "Well, to be honest, when it all first started, she was only really interested in the business side of things and the opportunity the pregnancy presented."

"Oh." That hurt.

"But that was only for the first few weeks," he added hastily. "Once we really got rolling, she saw that the reason she was enjoying herself so much, beyond the satisfaction of the work and seeing a return on her investment and her time, was that she could see how much you appreciated her and how impressed you were with what she could accomplish. She's proud of herself."

"And I'm so proud of her." It came out as little more than a whisper.

"Plus, being your Bradley partner has put her in touch with a lot of her feelings about you. No doubt dragged a bunch of stuff to the surface that she has to deal with."

"Apparently," Hannah said wryly as she surveyed the damage in the room. "So now what?"

"Don't worry; she'll come around."

"I'm not so sure. I've known her a lot longer than you have."

"We'll see," Jonathan said as he started cleaning up the wreckage of the room over Hannah's objections. She was red-faced over the idea he'd be handling her personal effects, but he was unperturbed as he carried the mass of clothing to the bed. Then, scooping up the handful of torn-up papers, he spotted the plastic bag and put two and two together.

"Hannah ... Did Natasha really tear up your first ultrasound?"

"Yes."

"Oh, shit."

"It's okay, Jonathan," Hannah said with a shake of her head. "It really is. I scanned that image into the computer the day after I got it from Dr. A. The picture was more symbolic than anything else: a … a little totem I could hold and stare at that represented this new chapter of my life. I guess Natasha wanted me to stop looking at *it* so much and see *her*, as well. Message received."

By the time Jonathan was ready to leave, offering to take Sadie on a quick dash around the block before he went home, Hannah was feeling much better. Natty would be back soon, he promised, and Hannah could relax and enjoy the waning days of her pregnancy, saving her energy for the labor. Hannah gave him an awkward hug.

"If Natasha doesn't marry you, Jonathan," she said, "I just might."

⁓

"MOM, OH, MOM, I'M SO SORRY …"

"No, I'm the one who should be apologizing, Natasha," Hannah interrupted, carefully making sure she called Natty by her preferred name. Closing her eyes with the force of her gratitude, she gripped her cell phone tightly and recited the script she had prepared, hoping Natty would give her the chance to make amends. "I shouldn't have jumped down your throat. I should have let you explain …"

Now Natty interrupted. "No, Mom, that's not what I'm calling about. I *am* sorry about our fight, and particularly about the ultrasound; that was awful of me. But we're good. And we have more important things to deal with right now."

"Why? What's happened? Is it Nana?" *Please, God, not so soon after Daddy!*

"Nana? No, as far as I know, Nana is fine. It's ... well, I just got a call asking for comment, and I was as surprised as anyone."

"Natasha, please don't drag it out. Just tell me what it is."

"Do you have your tablet with you?"

Hannah couldn't survive alone in the house without it. "Yes."

"I'm sending you a link, and I'm going to stay on the phone with you while you read it."

Full of trepidation, Hannah opened the email and clicked on the link for an article from an online gossip mag called *CelebSlice*. The headline said it all:

"SCOOP! St. Hannah's Baby: It's a Girl!"

"What?" Hannah wailed. "How could they know? How could *anyone* know? *I* didn't even know! Read it to me, will you? I can't do it."

Natty began: "In a conversation yesterday with obstetrics superstar Dr. Suzanne Felcher, our source reports that Hannah Murrow's own perinatal specialist unexpectedly let an important detail slip. Dr. Felcher, questioned about St. Hannah's amniocentesis performed 16 weeks into the pregnancy, said, 'At the time, of course, we were all very nervous for the well-being of Hannah's child. But to everyone's great relief, we found the baby to be genetically sound, with all her developmental milestones conforming to schedule.'"

"Shit!"

"The cat's out of the bag. Sorry, Mom. I hope you're not disappointed."

Hannah tried not to be. "I ... I'm certainly not disappointed it's a girl. I've kind of always felt that it was. That she was. I even blurted it out to Grandpa on the way to the hospital. But I did want it to be a surprise." Tears of frustration, sadness, and anger started to fall. "And I wanted it to be in the delivery room, where I would see the baby for the first time and the doctor would say, 'Congratulations, Hannah, you have a little boy' or, 'Say hello to your little girl.'"

"I know. I feel bad about that. I guess you'll have a few choice words for Dr. Felcher. Listen, my phone is already blowing up with calls and emails from my media contacts, wanting to know why they weren't clued in first, and I'm going to have to go manage them now."

"One more thing, Natasha: Did the article say who their source is?"

"Um, let's see. No. Any ideas?"

"None at all, but I'm about to find out." Hannah's phone was beeping, indicating an incoming call. "Dr. Felcher is calling me. I'll talk to you later. Thank you, Natasha. I ... I love you." Maybe it was time to start saying this more often.

"Talk to you later, Mom. Hang in there."

Hannah touched the screen to accept the call and heard the familiar, schooled voice say, "Hannah, it's Dr. Felcher. It's come to my attention that some sensitive information has been leaked to a small online news source."

"Yes, I know," Hannah responded with barely contained rage. "Care to elaborate?"

There was a brief silence on the other end. Clearly Dr. Felcher had not expected Hannah to be already aware of the breach. "To be clear," she said in her precise way, "this was not an interview. Per the terms of our agreement, which allows me to freely discuss your case with others in any circumstance without being in violation of HIPAA standards, I was having a casual conversation at dinner with my husband and one of his colleagues and her husband. She asked how we could be comfortable that the baby was likely to be free of the most common complications despite your advanced age. So I described how the amniocentesis went, concluding with a very positive comment about the encouraging results."

"Yeah, a very positive comment that happened to contain a very specific pronoun," Hannah fumed. "How could you be so careless?"

Unfazed by Hannah's anger, Dr. Felcher continued in her usual measured tone, "It was an honest mistake, Hannah, a slip of the tongue. In other circumstances it would have gone completely unnoticed, but this particular colleague does some work with the broadcast arm of CelebSlice, and unfortunately she was not as circumspect as the situation warranted." She added primly, "My husband and I have communicated our severe disappointment to her, and she has apologized."

Hannah waited for Dr. Felcher to say more, but it seemed she had said her piece. "That's it? She apologized and everything's fine?"

"Of course."

"Nope."

"I don't understand."

"You sure as hell don't! Everything is *not* fine, Doctor. This was a sensitive piece of information—in fact, the only piece of information that I specifically embargoed. You knew I wanted to be surprised in the delivery room. It was one of the few things I asked of you specifically in return for being filmed and photographed during my most personal moments.

I sat through countless interviews with Robin and Kelsey and answered difficult questions about my marriage and our sex life for the record. To be fair, *they* managed to keep any information they took from their visits to themselves. Yet somehow, you didn't."

"You're blowing this way out of proportion, Hannah," Dr. Felcher said, her voice showing an edge for the first time in the conversation. "An insignificant little gossip website is hardly *The New York Times*. The audience for that site couldn't be more than. ..."

"You have no idea, do you? The article in that 'insignificant little gossip website' is triggering phone calls and emails from legitimate news sources. And thanks to you, I now know that the insignificant gossip website also has a broadcast arm, no doubt on some sort of lifestyle cable TV network watched by exactly the sort of people who are emotionally and sometimes financially invested in St. Hannah.

"So by the end of the day, the whole world will know what only one individual knew—what only one individual was supposed to know—as late as yesterday afternoon!"

"Well," Dr. Felcher said, in the voice of someone who was not accustomed to apologizing and was moving forward with the words as stiffly as someone walking in a new pair of shoes, "I am very sorry to have disappointed you. I assure you it will have no effect on the quality of your treatment going forward."

There was no doubt that Dr. Felcher was an exceptional physician, and up to this point her care had been exemplary. Any other woman would clamor to be her patient, particularly in Hannah's unusual situation. But she had crossed the one line that Hannah could not forgive: she had thoughtlessly marred Hannah's otherwise perfect once-in-a-lifetime event, and no amount of apology was going to undo it.

"Not good enough. You're fired."

"I'm what?"

Hannah had the satisfaction of hearing Dr. Felcher begin to lose her composure and along with it, her carefully cultivated accent. There was unmistakably some New Jersey or Long Island in there, and it wasn't pretty. "Hannah, don't be ridiculous. You're too close to your due date to find a new perinatal specialist—you could give birth at any minute—and besides, you need someone who knows your case."

"I know," Hannah said decisively. "That's why I'm going back to Dr. A. She knows me better than anyone, and has for about thirty years. I'll call your office tomorrow to have the records transferred."

"What about the book and the documentary?" *And my reputation* was the unspoken corollary. Hannah had always known that Dr. Felcher had ambitions beyond her practice. The careful articulation, the wardrobe, the hair and makeup: she wanted to be widely known outside of the medical community; had her sights set on being the expert called by cable TV news shows. Maybe even on becoming the next "Dr. Oz" and having her own daytime show.

But Kelsey and Robin were blameless and deserved some consideration. And they did, after all, have a separate contract. "I'll think about it. About all of it."

"Well, you know, if you do think better of this hasty move and decide to do what's best for the baby, it will be my honor to see you through delivery as we always intended." Although she was trying to maintain her dignity, Dr. Felcher was beginning to sound desperate.

Good.

"Thank you for the offer. Now if you'll excuse me, I have to check in with my daughter and find out which Vegas betting pools you've screwed up."

Poking at her phone more aggressively than necessary, Hannah disconnected the call. She had to admit to herself that she had no regrets about firing Dr. Felcher, whose obvious ambition was off-putting and whose artificial compassion had never really fooled Hannah. Lately, she recalled, even Dr. Felcher's voice had begun to set her teeth on edge. And Hannah had missed Dr. A so much, wondering what she would say at each of the baby's milestones and secretly longing that she would have a reason to go back. Was this crisis a blessing in disguise? Hannah decided it was, in more ways than one—and not the least of which was because Natty was talking to her again.

The baby took that opportunity to perform her daily stretches. "Hello, little girl." Hannah watched, marveling as her entire midsection shifted, the baby rolling restlessly from one side to the other. It was good to have her gut feeling confirmed. Now she could concentrate on one group of names.

And so could the betting pools.

HANNAH 3:7

Without being asked, Natty showed up the next day and set herself up to work in the living room so that Hannah could sit comfortably in the recliner and have company while she relaxed with her knitting. Hannah vowed not to make a fuss about Natty's return to the house, but when Natty wasn't looking, she would smile at her with incredulous joy—ecstatic to have her back with so little friction. And just in time for their next birthing class, too.

Hannah put off calling Dr. A for as long as she could, ashamed at having to come crawling back. But crawl she would, if necessary. She brought up the Contacts list on her phone and sighed as the call connected.

"Dr. Anandanarayan's office," a familiar voice said expertly. Hannah knew every employee of Dr. A's practice, from the nurses to the phlebotomist to the receptionists and even the cleaning crew, down to their office shifts. Jeanine—funny, warm, sympathetic—was one of Hannah's favorites, and she had waited specifically to call at this hour.

"Hi, Jeanine, it's Hannah Murrow."

"Oh, Hannah! How are you? We've all missed you, you know."

Hannah felt her chest constrict. "I've missed you, too. So much."

"I have to tell you ..." There was a small pause, and Hannah had the sense Jeanine was looking around to make sure she wasn't overheard. "We're all big St. Hannah fans here, and we've been following the pregnancy online. So excited that you're having a girl!"

Rolling her eyes, Hannah covered up the irritation she still felt about that piece of news getting out and spreading so quickly. "Thanks; I am too. Listen, could I leave a message for Dr. A? I'd really like to talk to her. It's kind of important."

"Sure, but you don't have to leave a message. She's in between appointments right now. I'll get her."

"Really? Oh, thanks, Jeanine."

"Sure thing. Hang on a sec."

While she was waiting, Hannah pictured Dr. A at her desk, her tiny brow wrinkled in concentration as she worried over a patient's chart.

"Dr. Anandanarayan here. Hello, Hannah."

Her heart broke at the voice. She fought to keep her own steady. "Hi, Dr. A. How are you?"

"Well, very well, thank you. More importantly, how are you?"

Hannah suspected Dr. A knew exactly how she was. If she didn't follow the website herself or keep track of the "Eye on St. Hannah" column in the local weekly newspaper, the rest of her office could clue her in.

"I'm doing wonderfully well, Dr. A. Everything is normal, thank God. With the baby, with me. The thing is, though," she gathered up her courage, "I want to come back. To your practice. Please, will you let me come back? Will you be my doctor again and deliver my little girl? I promise I won't push you to do anything you don't agree with. You'll completely run the show."

"Interesting choice of words, Hannah." *Run the show.* Hannah silently cursed herself for the gaffe; the last thing she wanted to do was to remind Dr. A of the "show biz" aspect of her pregnancy that so offended her. "I don't know, don't you think Dr. Felcher ..."

"I won't work with Dr. Felcher anymore, Dr. A. She betrayed my trust—she's the reason everyone found out about the sex of my baby before I did."

There was silence from the doctor.

"You're not saying it, Dr. A, but I know you. I can hear you thinking, 'I told you so,' as clearly as if you'd said it out loud," Hannah said. "Will you take me back? I'm only two weeks away from my due date, and Ryan and I are no longer together. I could really use a steady hand and a familiar face right now." Close to tears, aware her voice was starting to shake, she added, "Please."

"Of course, Hannah. I only want what's best for you and your baby. I'd like to have you come in next week. I'll put Jeanine on to schedule you for an appointment. In the meantime, you should get in touch with Dr. Felcher's office to have your records transferred."

"Thank you, Dr. A. I can't tell you how much it means to me."

When Hannah finally hung up after making her next appointment, she felt wrapped in the warm feeling of coming home.

⌒⌒

"I'LL BET DR. FELCHER IS SORRY she's missing this," Ke'isha said, putting another slice of cake onto a plate.

"No doubt," Hannah agreed. The baby shower had been Natty's idea, and Hannah admitted it was brilliant. They had held a contest for fans on the St. Hannah website, with two dozen lucky winners chosen at random invited to enjoy hors d'oeuvres, cake, wine, collectible T-shirts, party favors, and selfies with Hannah for the promise of a donation of goods or money to Hannah's favorite women's shelter. One of the winners and her twenty-something daughter had driven five hours to attend; an incredulous Jonathan decided to put them up for the night at a nearby Hyatt so they could safely enjoy a glass or two of pinot noir. A stack of diapers, formula, and baby clothes nearly as tall as Eric in one corner of Ke'isha's shop attested to the generosity of the St. Hannah winners and the runners-up.

Ke'isha had offered the use of B. Fruitful on a Monday, when it was ordinarily closed. It was, in fact, the Monday after Mother's Day, and Hannah couldn't think of a more felicitous date to celebrate. She and Natty had spent a sedate Mother's Day at the house with Dolores, eating low-sodium take-out and showing off the nursery and layette to the grandmother-to-be. The "three generations" photo that Jonathan popped in to take would, he assured Dolores, arrive on canvas in three weeks, and he promised to hang it in her apartment himself. Hannah hoped there would be an opportunity to take an updated picture, with her mother proudly holding the new addition, very soon. If all went well.

Jonathan and Eric spent the morning rearranging the store's racks to make room for tables and chairs. At Ke'isha's urging, Hannah declined to festoon the whole place in pink and settled instead on a more diverse spring floral color palette that included yellows, lavenders, and greens as well as pinks and blues.

After a brief discussion with Natty, Jonathan, Eric, and Ke'isha, Hannah had invited Kelsey and Robin to the festivities and agreed they would be allowed to follow through with their original plans. Although Dr. A had been invited as a courtesy, Hannah knew that this was exactly the type of thing she disapproved of and correctly assumed she would not come. Dr. Felcher had been pointedly advised that she was unwelcome. (Nevertheless, when the day arrived, Hannah kept both of her doctors in mind and stayed seated with her feet elevated during the bulk of the party, struggling to stand with the help of Jonathan or Eric for her frequent trips to the bathroom.)

"It's too soon," Dolores had demurred when Hannah had asked her to come. "I can't go to a big party so soon after Daddy's passing. I'll get all weepy and ruin the whole thing. You go and have a good time." So Hannah promised, "We'll take plenty of pictures for you, Mom. And the camera crew won't miss a thing. It'll be just like you're there with us." In the end, the team had hired a dedicated camera for a streaming live feed, and Jonathan had set up the flat-screen TV in the Best of Times activity room so that Dolores and her friends could watch. Hannah had no doubt that Dolores was eating up the attention.

When Natty asked who else she wanted at the shower, Hannah immediately added Gloria and Kayla. Kayla was only days away from her own due date, but with the benefit of good health and youth, she carried the extra weight with enviable ease. Though Natty was uneasy, knowing the two had a prickly, even combative, relationship that occasionally flared in class in the form of tantrums and tears, Hannah countered that they might benefit from doing something fun together, something Kayla could brag about to her peers.

Watching the mother and daughter now, Hannah thought with some satisfaction that she might have been right. While Kayla was still on her phone, she was smiling and taking plenty of pictures, and Gloria looked more relaxed than usual as she showed off another of her expertly knit sweaters to Ke'isha, who was examining it with an appreciative eye toward, perhaps, another B. Fruitful exclusive.

If she had been able to leap to her feet, Hannah would have done so when Marla and Amibeth arrived together, bearing a case of infant formula and a large box of organic baby food. Amibeth, who had been on a tour of Scandinavia when Frank died (or so Marla said), hadn't seen Hannah in months, and she gaped at Hannah's expanded waistline.

"Well, would you look at you!" Amibeth said when she returned from stacking their contributions along with the others. "I'm having trouble wrapping my mind around it."

"I know how you feel. I'm as big as a house, and at this point there's no wrapping anything around it."

For a moment the three friends laughed heartily, the way they used to. But then Amibeth said: "Hannah, I'm so glad to see you so healthy and beautiful. But we can't stay."

Hannah's face fell.

As Kelsey and the cameraman approached, Marla waved them off. They retreated without argument.

"Why can't you stay?" Hannah asked, hurt.

Looking uncomfortable, Amibeth shrugged. Marla, given her cue, said, "C'mon, Hannah. We don't really belong here, and you know it. This is for your fans, for the media. Amibeth and I would prefer a celebration that's a little more intimate, for 'The Three Witches' alone. Wouldn't that be better? Maybe sometime after the baby is born, okay? So you can show her off?"

"Of course," she responded, summoning a smile that she didn't mean. Yet no one made a move to take out a cell phone or a datebook, and without a firm date among the three of them, Hannah suspected it would never happen. Still, it meant something that they had made the effort to show up. Hannah was grateful that Amibeth, in particular, cared enough about her to forgive her thoughtlessness. She would have said something to that effect but realized that bringing the subject up again would only make matters worse. So she craned her head up to receive the kisses the two Witches each dropped on her cheek and watched glumly as they left.

There was little time for Hannah to feel down, however, as Jonathan began to lead the guests, one by one, up to her for their promised personal conversations and selfies, plus a professional photo they would be emailed later. Although at first Hannah felt like a department-store Santa, certainly having the belly for it if not the beard, she soon got into the spirit of the occasion, welcoming hugs from perfumed grandmothers and inarticulate giggles from star-struck young mothers and mothers-to-be with equal good humor. She smiled, made funny faces on cue, and sympathized with the occasional story of infertility heartbreak. When all the personal interviews were done, the guests swarmed around the refreshments table to be served their second (or third) glass of wine while the pregnant and underage invitees enjoyed a glass of Ke'isha's tasty non-alcoholic sangria.

As Natty went to fetch Hannah something to eat, Ke'isha took her place at Hannah's side. "Did I ever tell you what the 'B' in B. Fruitful stands for?" she asked.

"No." *Did it stand for something?* Hannah had assumed it was a cute play on the biblical phrase about fertility. She was intrigued; it had never occurred to her to ask.

"It's for my mom, Beatriz. My dad died young—at thirty-four—from an accident on a building site, and Mom raised my sister, Alice, and me by herself. She was a nurse, and she worked soul-crushing hours so that Sis and I could have everything we needed. My Nana helped," she added, her eyes filled with affection, "but it really was all Mom."

"That's wonderful. Where is she now?"

"In Atlanta, with Alice. Sis is a pharmacist and has a husband and a toddler. Mom is supposed to be retired, but it's not her way, so she's taking care of my nephew while Alice and Brian are at work. Mom had great plans for me. She told me she was working double shifts so I could be anything I wanted."

"She must be very proud of you."

"Oh, she is now. But she wasn't at first. See, she figured I'd go into law or medicine or some other high-paying field— that's what she thought all her hard work was paying for— and I didn't want to. Didn't like it one bit. So I dropped out of college."

Ke'isha gave Hannah a significant look, and though she had no idea who had told Ke'isha about her recent altercation with Natty, Hannah got the message immediately.

"I knew I wanted fashion design and retail and that it would make her angry. And she was at first, believe me. We had some real knock-down, drag-outs over it. At one point we didn't talk for three weeks. But then one day she finally came around, and I could tell that decision took a lot out of her.

"She said to me, 'Ke'isha, if you can find your way in this, if you promise to work your hardest and live your passion, I'll support you in it.' And she did. Helped me get through design school. Helped me open this store.

"When I told her about the St. Hannah line, designs I had created on my own, she said, 'Congratulations, baby, you've made it.'"

Natty was heading back with a full plate, and Ke'isha leaned down to Hannah. "Let Natasha find her way. It might not be what you had in mind, but you can bet you did a good job. She'll be all right."

Her heart full, Hannah nodded. She took Ke'isha's hand and squeezed it in gratitude and admiration. It certainly had been Hannah's good fortune to have happened into her store that day last year.

Letting Jonathan, Eric, and Ke'isha see to the guests, Natty stationed herself once again at Hannah's side to make sure that she had everything she needed and wasn't becoming overwhelmed with the attention or enthusiasm of any particular invitee. Though she would have preferred a piece of the layer cake laid out for the guests, Hannah obediently dug into the carrots, celery, cheese, and crackers that Natty, taking her role as childbirth partner very seriously, had selected for her.

Hannah beamed. She was sure this was the highlight of her life thus far: she had never been showered with so much attention and affection, and Natty ... well, Natty hadn't been this warm and happy and cooperative since a brief period in her pre-teens, before puberty had kicked in.

Naturally, it couldn't last.

HANNAH 3:8

"Natasha," Hannah said abruptly.

"Yeah, Mom?"

"Would you excuse us for a minute?" Hannah said sweetly to a stout, gray-haired guest sporting her new St. Hannah T-shirt over a pink long-sleeved oxford with a Peter Pan collar. Clicking off one more photo of Hannah and Natty on her cell phone, the woman waved gaily and moved off to the snack table.

Hannah stuck out a hand and grabbed Jonathan by the wrist as he happened by on her other side. She handed off her glass of orange-infused water to him and said to the both of them, "I could be wrong, but I think my water just broke."

"Oh, shit."

Hannah heard that in stereo. "Yeah, it's that or I just wet myself. Not a good look either way."

Jonathan glanced over his shoulder at Kelsey and the cameraman, who were taking a break by a rack of pretty spring dresses with the reporter from the local news. They had all downed a few glasses of wine and seemed to be relaxed and having a good time. "Do you want me to run interference with the media?"

Hannah had barely said, "Yes," when Jonathan grabbed the closest bottle of wine and crossed the room in long strides. *That man is certainly quick on the uptake,* she thought.

"Natasha, please bring Ke'isha and Eric to me right away with as much subtlety as you can muster, and then go off to join Jonathan so you don't attract any attention."

"Got it. Sit tight."

"I guarantee that's the only way I can possibly sit at the moment."

Her heart beating wildly, Hannah focused entirely on the lower half of her body. She had read about water breaking and imagined it as more of a gush than its current trickle. Which meant it was going to get much, much worse very, very quickly.

"What's up, sweetheart?" Ke'isha said at her side in a low, sweet voice. "What can we do for you?"

Hannah peered around Eric to see Jonathan holding court with the press, telling some story that was causing riotous laughter as he poured them all yet another glass of wine.

"Ke'isha," Hannah said as casually as she could, relaxing back against the chair, "without being too obvious, could you please grab a blanket or a coat or something else that's big with lots of coverage? Nothing from your designer line, please, because it's about to get ruined with amniotic fluid."

Ke'isha's sucked in a breath between her teeth and nodded. As she sauntered off, trying not to betray her urgency, Hannah took Eric's hand. "Eric, when Ke'isha comes back, I need you to get me out of here as quickly as possible. You have your car keys on you?"

Wordlessly, Eric tapped his right front jeans pocket.

"Good. I promise you I will replace your upholstery myself if necessary." She grimaced. "I already suspect I'm on the hook for this poor chair."

Returning with a large, brown cape in her arms, Ke'isha made a show of holding it up for Hannah, as if her customer were shopping specifically for heavy woolen outerwear in the fine spring weather. "This is on clearance. Is this what you had in mind, honey?"

"Perfect." Hannah took the cape from Ke'isha and draped it around the lower half of her body like a blanket. It reached from her belly to her ankles. "Ready, Eric?"

"Whenever you are, Hannah."

At her nod, Eric scooped her up in his arms and was out the door of the store before anyone inside had noticed their departure. Hannah felt the dam give way as Eric placed her in the back seat of his pickup truck, grateful he wasn't driving a Mercedes or Porsche. To Hannah's immense relief, Natty opened the door on the other side and slid in beside her in one smooth, graceful movement, dropping Hannah's handbag and her own fistful of keys between them.

"Where to, Hannah?" Eric asked as the engine roared into life. Natty reached around Hannah and buckled her in, arranging the seat belt as best she could around her girth.

"Mercy Hospital."

"You okay, Mom? Is there much pain?"

"None at all," she answered. "I'm apparently not in labor yet. But could you do me a favor, Natasha? Could you get my phone from the outside pocket of my bag and call Dr. A?"

Nodding, Natty poked around until she located the phone and dialed Dr. A's personal cell number. "It's going to voicemail," she said with a questioning look. Hannah took the phone with the hand that was not currently gripping the door handle and waited for the beep.

"Dr. A, it's Hannah. It's sometime after 4:00 on Monday afternoon. My water just broke, but I'm not having any contractions. We're en route to Mercy and should be there in about ten minutes. If I don't answer, please call Natasha's cell phone; she's listed as my emergency contact."

When they arrived at the hospital, Eric pulled around to the Emergency entrance and Natty dashed inside to get some help. Although Hannah was uncomfortably damp, she was otherwise oddly serene. She had a team; everything was under control.

In less than a minute, Natty returned, accompanied by a nurse pushing a wheelchair. Eric lifted Hannah out of the truck, removing the sodden cape as the nurse said, "I'll take it from here." As she was wheeled into Emergency, Hannah blew a kiss to Eric and said, "Thanks for being my knight in shining armor, Eric. Tell Ke'isha I'll call her when I can.

"And sorry about your upholstery!"

⌒

"YOU'RE NOT DILATED AT ALL YET," Dr. A said, rolling back from her spot at the foot of Hannah's hospital bed and removing her gloves. "You're not in labor. In other circumstances, I would send you home. But because of the unusual nature of your pregnancy, I'm going to keep you here and put the fetal monitor on to keep tabs on the baby, at least for a little while."

"How long will it take for me to go into labor?"

"It could be within twelve to twenty-four hours, but if it doesn't start on its own, we'll induce you." She stood up. "Try to get some rest, Hannah. You're going to need it for your labor."

Now that the moment was finally upon her, Hannah found that rest was the last thing on her mind. Though she was worried about what was coming next, she was still energized from her shower. At her request, Natty sat next to her on the bed and showed her photos from the party. "You took these on your tablet?" Hannah asked. She could see that Natty had a flair for composition. Another skill, like the origami, which Hannah had somehow overlooked. "They're very good."

"Thanks." Natty seemed pleased. Hannah chastised herself for not having realized for so long how much her daughter, not unlike herself, needed to hear these things said aloud and vowed in the future to be more outspoken about them.

"Hey, did Jonathan post anything from after we left? I'd love to see how everyone reacted to our disappearing act."

Natty laughed a little under her breath as she scrolled around on her tablet. "You can imagine that 'Kelsey and Company' weren't too pleased that the biggest part of the story took place when they weren't paying attention." She pulled up a video Ke'isha had taken after their departure. Although a few guests had apparently been witness to Eric's rescue mission—and Hannah could tell precisely which ones, including Kayla, by their conspiratorial smiles and rapidly texting thumbs—the party had continued for several more minutes without lagging until Jonathan shut off the music and announced, "May I have your attention, please?

"You might notice that our guest of honor is no longer in the room with us." Everyone swiveled their heads to look at Hannah's recently vacated chair. "That is because Hannah's water has broken, and she is even now on her way to the hospital!"

Gasps, applause, laughter, and the occasional whoop filled the store. Ke'isha's video zoomed in on the media people, who were hastily gathering their equipment and making urgent phone calls as they made for the door.

"If I could read lips," Hannah said, her voice mirthful, "I might guess that their comments would not be fit for general audiences." Natty laughed in appreciation.

"Call your bookies, ladies," Jonathan said, and the camera swung back to focus on him. "The countdown to the biggest birth of the year starts now." The noise level in the room increased appreciably as the video ended.

"Jonathan really knows how to play the crowd," Natty said admiringly. Hannah was warmed by the affection that was so obvious on Natty's face.

"He's very special."

"That he is."

"I know you're not asking for my approval, Natasha, but for what it's worth, I think he's wonderful."

Natty gave her a long look. "I only ever wanted your approval, Mom."

Hannah's eyes filled with tears. "You know, Natasha, I ..."

She was interrupted by a twinge from deep inside her, which traveled up to her face and expressed itself as a look of surprise.

"A contraction?" Natty asked.

"It would certainly seem so." The mild Braxton-Hicks cramping that had come and gone during her last two months of pregnancy had not prepared her for a real contraction—which was a bit disquieting.

"Oh! Should I get the nurse?" Natty asked, getting to her feet.

"No, no." Hannah shook her head. "This might last a very long time, Natasha. We're in for the duration."

Nurses periodically stopped by anyway to check the fetal monitor and, Hannah was sure, to be able to brag to friends later that they had taken the blood pressure of a certain pregnant local celebrity.

Hannah glanced at the time on her phone. "Are you hungry? You can go get yourself something to eat."

"Eh. Maybe I'll get a soda or something. You want anything?"

"Not now. I think I had enough at the party. Maybe I should work off that for a while."

"I don't know, Mom," she said with a smirk. "I imagine it won't be long till all you can have are ice chips."

"True enough."

With Natty out of the room, Hannah was left alone with her thoughts. This was not necessarily a good thing. At first, she simply watched the output on the fetal monitor with fascination, noting the changes that came along with a brief but more intense contraction. She couldn't believe that she was nearing the finish line in this marathon and yet the hard work, as Natty had succinctly pointed out, was just beginning.

Was she ready to be a mother again? To raise an infant for the first time? What had she been thinking, going through with this pregnancy and birth at her age? Even before she got pregnant, she had often stepped out of bed with aches and pains that possibly signaled the onset of arthritis. There was the more than occasional "senior moment" when she forgot what she was about to do, what she needed in a room, what she was retrieving from the refrigerator. And she was lost without her reading glasses. Hannah pictured herself at the playground, trying to pick up a chubby toddler, straining her back, calling for help. In her mind, she had aged rapidly, and her imagined self was closer to Dolores's age, and just as slow and weak. Without Ryan there to back her up, how would she manage?

Would she have unreasonable expectations of this child? Had she had unreasonable expectations of Natty? Had she been at least somewhat more affectionate and encouraging a mother than Dolores had been? Would she ever be able to tell?

Hannah's mind raced on: What unknown maladies would this late-in-life child be afflicted with, suffer with, because of her selfishness? How had Natty suffered because of her selfishness?

By the time Natty returned to the room, sipping from a can of Coke and carrying a Styrofoam container smelling unmistakably of grilled cheese, Hannah's two children had conflated: Natty's problems were the baby's problems, and vice versa.

Even the memory of the pregnant dog left on her doorstep—her big, doleful eyes; her fear and distress—came back to accuse her. She couldn't even take care of a poor, homeless dog. What kind of mother would she be?

Hannah turned to her daughter, distraught.

"Natty, what am I doing? I don't know what I'm doing!"

"You're having a baby, Mom," Natty responded calmly, drifting toward Hannah's side. She put the can down on the side table, grasped Hannah's hand, and very pointedly did *not* correct the use of her nickname.

"What do I know about having a baby? What do I know about being a mother? I've been a lousy mother!"

"Mom, that's not true. You did a great job. Look how well I turned out."

"That's not *because of* me, that's *in spite of* me. I screwed up at every opportunity. You've got it together now, Natty, but I'm so, so sorry."

"For what?"

Now Hannah was sobbing, gripped by panic and then by a contraction strong enough to rack her whole body.

"Oh, my God," she moaned when it had passed. "Now I understand why women scream during labor. I always swore I would be tougher than that, given the chance. I take it all back."

"We've had twelve weeks of preparation, Mom, and I think you're going to handle it pretty well."

"Are you sure? Because I swear I felt that one from my hair follicles down to my toenails." And this was still early labor, hours and hours of it stretching ahead of her before the serious contractions started. "I don't know how I'm going to do it."

"I'll be with you the whole time, Mom."

"No matter how long it takes?"

"No matter how long it takes."

"I'm so tired already, and I'm probably a mess."

"Well," Natty smiled, "I've seen you look better. But let me show you how I'll always imagine you." With that, Natty pulled the right shoulder of her sweater down and turned to show Hannah. It was the St. Hannah logo, about two inches in diameter, tattooed in full color on the smooth, white skin of Natty's shoulder. She must have had it for several weeks; it looked completely healed.

"I never thought I'd say these words, but that's the most beautiful tattoo I've ever seen."

"Glad you like it, Mom."

"Thank you for everything, Natasha. I'm sorry I ever doubted you."

Natty's smile in reply, the unalloyed happiness Hannah hadn't seen nearly often enough, was everything she had ever wanted.

Then Natty turned serious.

"You know, Mom, I never said it, but I'm grateful to you. Don't think I don't know what my life would have been like if I'd been left in Russia, in that orphanage. I've done my research; I've seen the pictures. You and Dad, you rescued me. Dad gave you most of the credit for that, by the way. We talked about it, years ago, before I really understood what it meant. He said you chose me; that you insisted it could only be me. And you gave me a great life. Jonathan reminds me of that when I forget. I have nothing to complain about, and in fact I want you to know that I ..."

The moment was broken by a commotion in the hallway. One of the nurses who had been in to see Hannah—her name was Trinika, and she was as beautiful and rounded as a statue of a fertility goddess—stepped into the labor room, looking thoroughly displeased.

"Excuse me, Mrs. Murrow," she said, her voice heavy with disgust, "but there is a *camera crew* in the hallway and they are insisting that they have the right to come into this room."

Hannah groaned. She didn't want the world to see her this way.

"Sorry, Mom. Jonathan held Kelsey and the crew off as long as he could. They were plenty pissed when we left the shower without letting them know. But they do have a point. I'm pretty sure the contract guarantees them access to labor and delivery."

"'*Except in cases of maternal or fetal distress*,'" Dr. A quoted calmly as she stepped into the room. Natty and Hannah gawped at her. "Your contract was part of the paperwork Dr. Felcher sent over to my office. I do believe the camera crew can be put off in 'cases of extreme maternal or fetal distress.' No need to be alarmed; the baby is fine. But I'm going to declare that the mother is in extreme distress." She smiled pleasantly at Hannah. "You are extremely distressed, are you not?"

"Oh, I am, I am!" No lie there.

"Well, then, Trinika, would you please inform the crew that the doctor has said that, in the interest of the well-being of the mother, there may not be any other observers during labor and delivery."

Trinika smiled on her way out the door. "With pleasure."

"Thank God for your Uncle Jason and his contract," Hannah said to Natty, relaxing back against the bed. "Remind me to send him a nice fruit basket."

"Nah, I've got a better idea: send him a cheesecake instead. Something gooey, really high in fat and sugar. That ought to drive Aunt Missy up the wall."

WITH THE FIRST STAGE of her labor progressing slowly and normally, Hannah was allowed out of bed. Although she would have liked to walk the hallways, she understood it was out of the question, especially now that the camera crew had been dismissed. There were too many eyes, too many cell phones. So Hannah and Natty worked through set after set of exercises—squats and butterflies and pelvic rocking—pausing when a contraction hit, resting when Hannah needed it.

There was time, plenty of time, in between contractions, to talk. Hannah wasn't feeling particularly garrulous, her energy dedicated to her preparations, her mouth dry. There was one thing, though, that she just had to know.

"Natasha?" she asked, wetting her lips with her tongue. She was pausing for breath before her next set of butterflies.

"Hm?"

"The keys. What's with the keys?"

"Which keys? Oh! You mean *my* keys?"

"Yes. Why so many?"

"Yeah, that. Well, remember Jacob Marley?"

Why was that name so familiar? Hannah struggled to concentrate. "Your boyfriend Jake? The snowboarder? Was that his name?"

Natty laughed. "No, Mom, not Jake," she said, her amusement still rumbling in her throat. "Jacob Marley. You know, from *A Christmas Carol*? Dickens?"

"Oh. Of course. Scrooge's partner. Right." How embarrassing.

"He wore the chains he'd forged in life," Natty paraphrased with a lofty accent. "It made an impression on me when we read it in tenth grade."

"You struggled a lot that year." Hannah had fought hard, both with Natty and for Natty, to make sure she didn't fall behind. "I'm glad you were able to take something meaningful from it."

"Oh, not right away. It wasn't until later, much later. Okay, so I started with the keys to our house: front door, side door. When I moved out, I got keys to the place I shared with Jake. Then I got keys for the apartment I took with Ian, plus the keys to the tattoo parlor. I never gave any of them back. My bad. I decided to keep them all to remind me of the mistakes I'd made. Carrying them around with me meant I couldn't forget. Like Marley's chains.

"But I've got Jonathan now, and I think I've finally gotten it right. I think it's time to lose the keys. I don't need them anymore."

That was a greater comfort to Hannah than any anesthesia could have been. At least, until the next contraction hit.

WHEN THE CONTRACTIONS STARTED coming closer together, Natty guided Hannah back to the bed and helped her lie down on her side. She then showed Hannah a photo of herself, sleeping. "This is how you're positioned at your most comfortable," Natty said, arranging the pillows to mimic that position. As embarrassed as Hannah was at the photo—her face mashed into the pillow, her mouth agape, her hair in every direction—she was grateful that Natty had paid so much attention to their childbirth training.

Sometime during the sixth hour, or so Natty told her later, Hannah looked up, bleary-eyed, as she was introduced to Dr. Benford, the anesthesiologist, a slightly built black man of perhaps Hannah's age with the hooded, dark eyes and tidy pencil mustache of a 1940s film star. "I know the nurse anesthetist explained your pain relief options earlier," Dr. Benford said. He waited for Hannah to respond.

Hannah looked at Natty, who nodded. Shrugging, Hannah supposed that to be true, though she no longer remembered.

Accepting that as an acknowledgment, Dr. Benford continued, "Some mothers prefer to have their babies without any anesthesia, and you might have been encouraged to decline it by your birthing class instructors. But I want you to know there's no shame in requesting pain relief, up to and including an epidural, if it's something you think will make your birthing experience more pleasant." Based on what he must have seen in Hannah's face, he added, "Or simply bearable."

"What do you want to do, Mom?" Natty asked.

Hannah thought about what she'd learned in her childbirth classes and what she'd endured thus far. She thought about what she wanted from this delivery, knowing it would be the only time she would ever have the opportunity to experience it. So she decided she would experience it. Agony and all.

"No thanks."

"Really?" Natty's brows shot up. "Mom, are you sure? You, um, look like you could use a little something to take the edge off."

Hannah laughed a little. "I know I look like crap. I feel like crap. But I'm sure. Not a thing."

"I'll stop back in again," Dr. Benford said with a knowing nod as he headed out the door, "just in case you change your mind."

"I'm proud of you, Mom."

"Really?" Hannah asked weakly.

"Really. You could take the easy way out, but you're allowing nature to take its course and doing what's best for the baby. That takes guts."

Hannah grinned. She was proud of herself, too. Having Natty's approval all but confirmed to her that she had made the right decision.

Abruptly, though, Hannah's peace was gone. Nausea rose up suddenly and her entire body started to shake, vibrating as if she had the flu. She found herself gripped by a self-doubt as debilitating as any contraction she'd had up till now.

"Oh, my God," she gulped. "I can't do this. I give up."

"I hate to break this to you, Mom, but there's no turning back now."

"What if everyone was right, and I was wrong, and a woman my age has no business having a baby?" Hannah gasped through the pain, grabbing Natty's arm. "What if I die?"

Natty winced.

"You're not going to die, Hannah," Dr. A said in her most reassuring voice. Natty took a soft towel to the sweat running from Hannah's face. "You're doing very well. You're at seven centimeters; you're going through transition. It won't be long now."

"And anyway, you can't die now, Mom," Natty said, her voice a little broken despite her attempt at levity, "not when we're finally starting to get along so well."

"Natty, Natty, if I die ..."

"What, Mom?" She seemed near tears now.

"Do *not* give your Aunt Missy the living room table."

The laughter that ensued provided a much-needed respite to the tension and pain of the imminent birth. It also made Hannah clear-headed enough to know she wanted a lasting record of the moment her child came into the world, and that she was uniquely positioned to do something about it.

"Natty, where is the camera crew now?"

The question took both Natty and Dr. A by surprise. "Don't tell me you've changed your mind?" Natty asked.

"I have. I want you to call them and tell them I'm no longer in distress. But tell them they can't use their lights; they'll just have to manage with what we've got."

"Are you sure about this, Hannah?" Dr. A said, frowning. Hannah knew how thoroughly she disapproved. "Birth is not a public act. Are you certain you want the world to see you *in extremis*?"

"I know it sounds crazy. But I'm not going to remember much of this, and I'll want to know exactly what I missed."

And that was that. Before long, the camera crew finally entered the room. They set up quickly and quietly, and Hannah tuned them out now as effectively as she had done over the past several months. Natty, too, ignored them as she fed Hannah ice chips and rubbed her back.

"You're doing great, Mom," she cooed. "You're amazing. You're putting all those younger women to shame." Hannah was glad the crew was there to capture Natty's affectionate praise so she would be able, during the tough times she knew would be ahead, to listen to it again and again and again.

It was some twelve hours into the labor when Dr. A finally declared, "You're fully dilated now, Hannah. You'll be able to push now when the urge comes on."

Pushing. Pushing came next.

"We're coming up on the finish line, Mom," Natty whispered urgently. "You're almost there!"

A drained and sweaty Hannah looked up at Natty and wheezed: "Forgive me, Natty? For not being the kind of mother you wanted?"

"Don't be stupid, Mom," Natty said. "You're exactly the kind of mother I *needed*. I love you, you know. I'm sorry that I didn't say it enough."

"All right, Hannah," Dr. A said. "Are you ready to meet your baby?"

"Grace," Hannah said, her voice hoarse. "Her name is Grace Frances."

Dr. A nodded. "A lovely name. Very appropriate."

"Frances for Grandpa," Natty added with a sad smile.

"Yes."

"It's time to push now, Hannah," Dr. A said. "Push!"

"Push, Mom!" Natty echoed.

And Hannah pushed.

ACKNOWLEDGMENTS

I have been incredibly lucky to have the support and encouragement of so many people, starting with my wonderful husband, Roy, who will never read a word of this book but will nevertheless declare that I am a wonderful writer whose work everyone should appreciate. I thank him for allowing me the time and space to pursue my dream. My beloved children, Daniel and Brynn, who likewise have no interest in this subject matter, have also cheered me on with all their love the entire way. My parents, Sandy and Bob Gardner, deserve special thanks for always allowing me to be my creative self, even when it meant changing majors in college, leaving a more lucrative career path to become ... *a writer?*

My friends have been just as important: the Cape Cod crew (Diane Giordano, Amy Goldsmith, Paula Goldstein, Jody Meth, April Rachmuth), who were among the first to read the manuscript; Maria Gribbin and Maureen Ellison, who provided invaluable input; Carol Mackey, who has been helping me toward this goal for years; Gillian Faust, who was always there with an ear and a shoulder; and especially Dr. Debra Blaine, who accompanied me on this journey. I'd also like to give a shout-out to the incredibly literate ladies of the Happy Bookers book club of southeastern Michigan, whose company always inspires me, and to my fellow Resisters from Indivisible, who have grown from brothers- and sisters-in-arms into great friends.

I'd like to express my appreciation to the hard-working ladies of Warren Publishing—Mindy Kuhn, Amy Ashby, and Jennifer Hurvitz—for being true partners in the process, and to my editor, Uma Hayes, for her guidance.

Thank you all; I owe you so much.

CPSIA information can be obtained
at www.ICGtesting.com
Printed in the USA
FSHW021303160819
61099FS